The Prairie (

Arthur Stringer

Alpha Editions

This edition published in 2024

ISBN 9789361478536

Design and Setting By

Alpha Editions

www.alphaedis.com

Email - info@alphaedis.com

Contents

Friday the Eighth of March

"But the thing I can't understand, Dinky-Dunk, is how you ever *could*."

"Could what?" my husband asked in an aerated tone of voice.

I had to gulp before I got it out.

"Could kiss a woman like that," I managed to explain.

Duncan Argyll McKail looked at me with a much cooler eye than I had expected. If he saw my shudder, he paid no attention to it.

"On much the same principle," he quietly announced, "that the Chinese eat birds' nests."

"Just what do you mean by that?" I demanded, resenting the fact that he could stand as silent as a December beehive before my morosely questioning eyes.

"I mean that, being married, you've run away with the idea that all birds' nests are made out of mud and straw, with possibly a garnish of horse hairs. But if you'd really examine these edible nests you'd find they were made of surprisingly appealing and succulent tendrils. They're quite appetizing, you may be sure, or they'd never be eaten!"

I stood turning this over, exactly as I've seen my Dinkie turn over an unexpectedly rancid nut.

"Aren't you, under the circumstances, being rather stupidly clever?" I finally asked.

"When I suppose you'd rather see me cleverly stupid?" he found the heart to suggest.

"But that woman, to me, always looked like a frog," I protested, doing my best to duplicate his pose of impersonality.

"Well, she doesn't make love like a frog," he retorted with his first betraying touch of anger. I turned to the window, to the end that my Eliza-Crossing-the-Ice look wouldn't be entirely at his mercy. A belated March blizzard was slapping at the panes and cuffing the house-corners. At the end of a long winter, I knew, tempers were apt to be short. But this was much more than a matter of barometers. The man I'd wanted to live with like a second "Suzanne de Sirmont" in Daudet's *Happiness* had not only cut me to the quick but was rubbing salt in the wound. He had said what he did with deliberate intent to hurt me, for it was only too obvious that he was tired of being on the defensive. And it did hurt. It couldn't help hurting. For the man, after all, was my husband. He was the husband to whom I'd given up the best part of my life, the two-legged basket into which I'd packed all my eggs of allegiance. And now he was scrambling that precious collection for a cheap omelette of amorous adventure. He was my husband, I kept reminding myself. But that didn't cover the entire case. No husband whose heart is right stands holding another woman's shoulder and tries to read her shoe-numbers through her ardently upturned eyes. It shows the wind is not blowing right in the home circle. It shows a rent in the dyke, a flaw in the blade, a breach in the fortress-wall of faith. For marriage, to the wife who is a mother as well, impresses me as rather like the spliced arrow of the Esquimos: it is cemented together with blood. It is a solemn matter. And for the sake of *mutter-schutz*, if for nothing else, it must be kept that way.

There was a time, I suppose, when the thought of such a thing would have taken my breath away, would have chilled me to the bone. But I'd been through my refining fires, in that respect, and you can't burn the prairie over twice in the same season. I tried to tell myself it was the setting, and not the essential fact, that seemed so odious. I did my best to believe it wasn't so much that Duncan Argyll McKail had stooped to make advances to this bandy-legged she-teacher whom I'd so charitably housed at Casa Grande since the beginning of the year—for I'd long since learned not to swallow the antique claim that of all terrestrial *carnivora* only man and the lion are truly monogamous—but more the fact it had been made such a back-stairs affair with no solitary redeeming touch of dignity.

Dinky-Dunk, I suppose, would have laughed it away, if I hadn't walked in on them with their arms about each other, and the bandy-legged one breathing her capitulating sighs into his ear. But there was desperation in the eyes of Miss Alsina Teeswater, and it was plain to see that if my husband had been merely playing with fire it had become a much more serious matter with the lady in the case. There was, in fact, something almost dignifying in that strickenly defiant face of hers. I was almost sorry for her when she turned and walked white-lipped out of the room. What I resented most, as I stood facing my husband, was his paraded casualness, his refusal to take a tragic situation tragically. His attitude seemed to imply that we were about to have a difference over a small thing—over a small thing with brown eyes. He could even stand inspecting me with a mildly amused glance, and I might have forgiven his mildness, I suppose, if it had been without amusement, and that amusement in some way at my expense. He even managed to laugh as I stood there staring at him. It was neither an honest nor a natural laugh. It merely gave me the feeling that he was trying to entrench himself behind a raw mound of mirth, that any shelter was welcome until the barrage was lifted.

"And what do you intend doing about it?" I asked, more quietly than I had imagined possible.

"What would you suggest?" he parried, as he began to feel in his pockets for his pipe.

And I still had a sense, as I saw the barricaded look come into his face, of entrenchments being frantically thrown up. I continued to stare at him as he found his pipe and proceeded to fill it. I even wrung a ghostly satisfaction out of the discovery that his fingers weren't so steady as he might have wished them to be.

"I suppose you're trying to make me feel like the Wicked Uncle edging away from the abandoned Babes in the Woods?" he finally demanded, as though exasperated by my silence. He was delving for matches by this time, and seemed disappointed that none was to be found in his pockets. I don't know why he should seem to recede from me, for he didn't move an inch from where he stood with that defensively mocking smile on his face. But abysmal gulfs of space seemed to blow in like sea-mists between him and me, desolating and lonely stretches of emptiness which could never again be spanned by the tiny bridges of hope. I felt alone, terribly alone, in a world over which the last fire had swept and the last rains had fallen. My throat tightened and my eyes smarted from the wave of self-pity which washed through my body. It angered me, ridiculously, to think that I was going to break down at such a time.

But the more I thought over it the more muddled I grew. There was something maddening in the memory that I was unable to act as my instincts prompted me to act, that I couldn't, like the outraged wife of screen and story, walk promptly out of the door and slam it epochally shut after me. But modern life never quite lives up to its fiction. And we are never quite free, we women who have given our hostages to fortune, to do as we wish. We have lives other than our own to think about.

"But it's all been so—so *dishonest!*" I cried out, stopping myself in the middle of a gesture which might have seemed like wringing my hands.

That, apparently, gave Dinky-Dunk something to get his teeth into. The neutral look went out of his eye, to be replaced by a fortifying stare of enmity.

"I don't know as it's any more dishonest than the long-distance brand of the same thing!"

I knew, at once, what he meant. He meant Peter. He meant poor old Peter Ketley, whose weekly letter, year in and year out, came as regular as clockwork to Casa Grande. Those letters came to my son Dinkie, though it couldn't be denied they carried many a cheering word and many a companionable message to Dinkie's mother. But it brought me up short, to think that my own husband would try to play cuttle-fish with a clean-hearted and a clean-handed man like Peter. The wave that went through my body, on this occasion, was one of rage. I tried to say something, but I couldn't. The lion of my anger had me down, by this time, with his paw on my breast. The power of speech was squeezed out of my carcass. I could only stare at my husband with a denuding and devastating stare of incredulity touched with disgust, of abhorrence skirting dangerously close along the margins of hate. And he stared back, with morose and watchful defiance on his face.

Heaven only knows how it would have ended, if that tableau hadn't gone smash, with a sudden offstage clatter and thump and cry which reminded me there were more people in the world than Chaddie McKail and her philandering old husband. For during that interregnum of parental preoccupation Dinkie and Poppsy had essayed to toboggan down the lower half of the front-stairs in an empty drawer commandeered from my bedroom dresser. Their descent, apparently, had been about as precipitate as that of their equally adventurous sire down the treads of my respect, for they had landed in a heap on the hardwood floor of the hall and I found Dinkie with an abraded shin-bone and Poppsy with a cut lip. My Poppsy was more frightened at the sight of blood than actually hurt by her fall, and Dinkie betrayed a not unnatural tendency to enlarge on his injuries in extenuation of his offense. But that suddenly imposed demand for first-aid took my mind out of the darker waters in which it had been wallowing, and by the time I had comforted my kiddies and completed my ministrations Dinky-Dunk had quietly escaped from the house and my accusatory stares by clapping on his hat and going out to the stables....

And that's the scene which keeps pacing back and forth between the bars of my brain like a jaguar in a circus-cage. That's the scene I've been living over, for the last few days, thinking of all the more brilliant things I might have said and the more expedient things I might have done. And that's the scene which has been working like yeast at the bottom of my sodden batter of contentment, making me feel that I'd swell up and burst, if all that crazy ferment couldn't find some relief in expression. So after three long years and more of silence I'm turning back to this, the journal of one irresponsible old Chaddie McKail, who wanted so much to be happy and who has in some way missed the pot of gold that they told her was to be found at the rainbow's end.

It seems incredible, as I look back, that more than three, long years should slip away without the penning of one line in this, the safety-valve of my soul. But the impulse to write rather slipped away from me. It wasn't that there was so little to record, for life is always life. But when it burns clearest it seems to have the trick of consuming its own smoke and leaving so very little ash. The crowded even tenor of existence goes on, with its tidal ups and downs, too listlessly busy to demand expression. Then the shock of tempest comes, and it's only after we're driven out of them that we realize we've been drifting so long in the doldrums of life. Then it comes home to us that there are the Dark Ages in the history of a woman exactly as there were the Dark Ages in the history of Europe. Life goes on in those Dark Ages, but it doesn't feel the call to articulate itself, to leave a record of its experiences. And that strikes me, as I sit here and think of it, as about the deepest tragedy that can overtake anything on this earth. Nothing, after all, is sadder than silence, the silence of dead civilizations and dead cities and dead souls. And nothing is more costly. For beauty itself, in actual life, passes away, but beauty lovingly recorded by mortal hands endures and goes down to our children. And I stop writing, at that word of "children," for miraculously, as I repeat it, I see it cut a window in the unlighted house of my heart. And that window is the bright little Gothic oriel which will always be golden and luminous with love and will always send the last shadow scurrying away from the mustiest corner of my tower of life. I have my Dinkie and my Poppsy, and nothing can take them away from me. It's on them that I pin my hope.

Sunday the Seventeenth

I've been thinking a great deal over what's happened this last week or so. And I've been trying to reorganize my life, the same as you put a house to rights after a funeral. But it wasn't a well-ordered funeral, in this case, and I was denied even the tempered satisfaction of the bereaved after the finality of a smoothly conducted burial. For nothing has been settled. It's merely that Time has been trying to encyst what it can not absorb. I felt, for a day or two, that I had nothing much to live for. I felt like a feather-weight who'd faced a knock-out. I saw Pride go to the mat, and take the count, and if I was dazed, for a while, I suppose it was mostly convalescence from shock. Then I tightened my belt, and reminded myself that it wasn't the first wallop Fate had given me, and remembered that in this life you have to adjust yourself to your environment or be eliminated from the game. And life, I suppose, has tamed me, as a man who once loved me said it would do. The older I get the more tolerant I try to be, and the more I know of this world the more I realize that Right is seldom all on one side and Wrong on the other. It's a matter of give and take, this problem of traveling in double-harness. I can even smile a little, as I remember that college day in my teens when Matilda-Anne and Katrina and Fanny-Rain-in-the-Face and myself solemnly discussed man and his make-up, over a three-pound box of Maillard's, and resolutely agreed that we would surrender our hearts to no suitor over twenty-six and marry no male who'd ever loved another woman—not, at least, unless the situation had become compensatingly romanticized by the death of any such lady preceding us in our loved one's favor. Little we knew of men and ourselves and the humiliations with which life breaks the spirit of arrogant youth! For even now, knowing what I know, I've been doing my best to cooper together a case for my unstable old Dinky-Dunk. I've been trying to keep the thought of poor dead Lady Alicia out of my head. I've been wondering if there's any truth in what Dinky-Dunk said, a few weeks ago, about a mere father being like the male of the warrior-spider whom the female of the species stands ready to dine upon, once she's assured of her progeny.

I suppose I *have* given most of my time and attention to my children. And it's as perilous, I suppose, to give your heart to a man and then take it even partly away again as it is to give a trellis to a rose-bush and then expect it to stand alone. My husband, too, has been restless and dissatisfied with prairie life during the last year or so, has been rocking in his own doldrums of inertia where the sight of even the humblest ship—and the Wandering Sail in this case always seemed to me as soft and shapeless as a boned squab-pigeon!—could promptly elicit an answering signal.

But I strike a snag there, for Alsina has not been so boneless as I anticipated. There was an unlooked-for intensity in her eyes and a mild sort of tragedy in her voice when she came and told me that she was going to another school in the Knee-Hill country and asked if I could have her taken in to Buckhorn the next morning. Some one, of course, had to go. There was one too many in this prairie home that must always remain so like an island dotting the lonely wastes of a lonely sea. And triangles, oddly enough, seem to flourish best in city squares. But much as I wanted to talk to Alsina, I was compelled to respect her reserve. I even told her that Dinkie would miss her a great deal. She replied, with a choke in her voice, that he was a wonderful child. That, of course, was music to the ears of his mother, and my respect for the tremulous Miss Teeswater went up at least ten degrees. But when she added, without meeting my eye, that she was really fond of the boy, I couldn't escape the impression that she was edging out on very thin ice. It was, I think, only the silent misery in her half-averted face which kept me from inquiring if she hadn't rather made it a family affair. But that, second thought promptly told me, would seem too much like striking the fallen. And we both seemed to feel, thereafter, that silence was best.

Practically nothing passed between us, in fact, until we reached the station. I could see that she was dreading the ordeal of saying good-by. That unnamed sixth sense peculiar to cab-drivers and waiters and married women told me that every moment on the bald little platform was being a torture to her. As the big engine came lumbering up to a standstill she gave me one quick and searching look. It was a look I shall never forget. For, in it was a question and something more than a question. An unworded appeal was there, and also an unworded protest. It got past my outposts of reason, in some way. It came to me in my bitterness like the smell of lilacs into a sick-room. I couldn't be cruel to that poor crushed outcast who had suffered quite as much from the whole ignoble affair as I had suffered. I suddenly held out my hand to her, and she took it, with that hungry questioning look still on her face.

"It's all right," I started to say. But her head suddenly went down between her hunched-up shoulders. Her body began to shake and tears gushed from her eyes. I had to help her to the car steps.

"It was all my fault," she said in a strangled voice, between her helpless little sobs.

It was brave of her, of course, and she meant it for the best. But I wish she hadn't said it. Instead of making everything easier for me, as she intended, she only made it harder. She left me disturbingly conscious of ghostly heroisms which transposed what I had tried to regard as essentially ignoble into some higher and purer key. And she made it harder for me to look at my husband, when I got home, with a calm and collected eye. I felt suspiciously like Lady Macbeth after the second murder. I felt that we were fellow-sharers of a guilty secret it would never do to drag too often into the light of every-day life.

But it will no more stay under cover, I find, than a dab-chick will stay under water. It bobs up in the most unexpected places, as it did last night, when Dinkie publicly proclaimed that he was going to marry his Mummy when he got big.

"It would be well, my son, not to repeat the mistakes of your father!" observed Dinky-Dunk. And having said it, he relighted his quarantining pipe and refused to meet my eye. But it didn't take a surgical operation to get what he meant into my head. It hurt, in more ways than one, for it struck me as suspiciously like a stone embodied in a snowball—and even our offspring recognized this as no fair manner of fighting.

"Then it impresses you as a mistake?" I demanded, seeing red, for the coyote in me, I'm afraid, will never entirely become house-dog.

"Isn't that the way you regard it?" he asked, inspecting me with a non-committal eye.

I had to bite my lip, to keep from flinging out at him the things that were huddled back in my heart. But it was no time for making big war medicine. So I got the lid on, and held it there.

"My dear Dinky-Dunk," I said with an effort at a gesture of weariness, "I've long since learned that life can't be made clean, like a cat's body, by the use of the tongue alone!"

Dinky-Dunk did not look at me. Instead, he turned to the boy who was watching that scene with a small frown of perplexity on his none too approving face.

"You go up to the nursery," commanded my husband, with more curtness than usual.

But before Dinkie went he slowly crossed the room and kissed me. He did so with a quiet resoluteness which was not without its tacit touch of challenge.

"You may feel that way about the use of the tongue," said my husband as soon as we were alone, "but I'm going to unload a few things I've been keeping under cover."

He waited for me to say something. But I preferred remaining silent.

"Of course," he floundered on, "I don't want to stop you martyrizing yourself in making a mountain out of a mole-hill. But I'm getting a trifle tired of this holier-than-thou attitude. And—"

"And?" I prompted, when he came to a stop and sat pushing up his brindled front-hair until it made me think of the Corean lion on the library mantel, the lion in pottery which we invariably spoke of as the Dog of Fo. My wintry smile at that resemblance seemed to exasperate him.

"What were you going to say?" I quietly inquired.

"Oh, hell!" he exclaimed, with quite unexpected vigor.

"I hope the children are out of hearing," I reminded him, solemn-eyed.

"Yes, the children!" he cried, catching at the word exactly as a drowning man catches at a lifebelt. "The children! That's just the root of the whole intolerable situation. This hasn't been a home for the last three or four years; it's been nothing but a nursery. And about all I've been is a retriever for a *crèche*, a clod-hopper to tiptoe about the sacred circle and see to it there's enough flannel to cover their backs and enough food to put into their stomachs. I'm an accident, of course, an intruder to be faced with fortitude and borne with patience."

"This sounds quite disturbing," I interrupted. "It almost leaves me suspicious that you are about to emulate the rabbit and devour your young."

Dinky-Dunk fixed me with an accusatory finger.

"And the fact that you can get humor out of it shows me just how far it has gone," he cried with a bitterness which quickly enough made me sober again. "And I could stand being deliberately shut out of your life, and shut out of their lives as far as you can manage it, but I can't see that it's doing either them or you any particular good."

"But I am responsible for the way in which those children grow up," I said, quite innocent of the *double entendre* which brought a dark flush to my husband's none too happy face.

"And I suppose I'm not to contaminate them?" he demanded.

"Haven't you done enough along that line?" I asked.

He swung about, at that, with something dangerously like hate on his face.

"Whose children are they?" he challenged.

"You are their father," I quietly acknowledged. It rather startled me to find Dinky-Dunk regarding himself as a fur coat and my offspring as moth-eggs which I had laid deep in the pelt of his life, where we were slowly but surely eating the glory out of that garment and leaving it as bald as a prairie dog's belly.

"Well, you give very little evidence of it!"

"You can't expect me to turn a cart-wheel, surely, every time I remember it?" was my none too gracious inquiry. Then I sat down. "But what is it you want me to do?" I asked, as I sat studying his face, and I felt sorriest for him because he felt sorry for himself.

"That's exactly the point," he averred. "There doesn't seem anything to do. But this can't go on forever."

"No," I acknowledged. "It seems too much like history repeating itself."

His head went down, at that, and it was quite a long time before he looked up at me again.

"I don't suppose you can see it from my side of the fence?" he asked with a disturbing new note of humility in his voice.

"Not when you force me to stay on the fence," I told him. He seemed to realize, as he sat there slowly moving his head up and down, that no further advance was to be made along that line. So he took a deep breath and sat up.

"Something will have to be done about getting a new teacher for that school," he said with an appositeness which was only too painfully apparent.

"I've already spoken to two of the trustees," I told him. "They're getting a teacher from the Peg. It's to be a man this time."

Instead of meeting my eye, he merely remarked: "That'll be better for the boy!"

"In what way?" I inquired.

"Because I don't think too much petticoat is good for any boy," responded my lord and master.

"Big or little!" I couldn't help amending, in spite of all my good intentions.

Dinky-Dunk ignored the thrust, though it plainly took an effort.

"There are times when even kindness can be a sort of cruelty," he patiently and somewhat platitudinously pursued.

"Then I wish somebody would ill-treat me along that line," I interjected. And this time he smiled, though it was only for a moment.

"Supposing we stick to the children," he suggested.

"Of course," I agreed. "And since you've brought the matter up I can't help telling you that I always felt that my love for my children is the one redeeming thing in my life."

"Thanks," said my husband, with a wince.

"Please don't misunderstand me. I'm merely trying to say that a mother's love for her children has to be one of the strongest and holiest things in this hard old world of ours. And it seems only natural to me that a woman should consider her children first, and plan for them, and make sacrifices for them, and fight for them if she has to."

"It's so natural, in fact," remarked Dinky-Dunk, "that it has been observed in even the Bengal tigress."

"It is my turn to thank you," I acknowledged, after giving his statement a moment or two of thought.

"But we're getting away from the point again," proclaimed my husband. "I've been trying to tell you that children are like rabbits: It's only fit and proper they should be cared for, but they can't thrive, and they can't even live, if they're handled too much."

"I haven't observed any alarming absence of health in my children," I found the courage to say. But a tightness gathered about my heart, for I could sniff what was coming.

"They may be all right, as far as that goes," persisted their lordly parent. "But what I say is, too much cuddling and mollycoddling isn't good for that boy of yours, or anybody else's boy." And he proceeded to explain that my Dinkie was an ordinary, every-day, normal child and should be accepted and treated as such or we'd have a temperamental little bounder on our hands.

I knew that my boy wasn't abnormal. But I knew, on the other hand, that he was an exceptionally impressionable and sensitive child. And I couldn't be sorry for that, for if there's anything I abhor in this world it's torpor. And whatever he may have been, nothing could shake me in my firm conviction that a child's own mother is the best person to watch over his growth and shape his character.

"But what is all this leading up to?" I asked, steeling myself for the unwelcome.

"Simply to what I've already told you on several occasions," was my husband's answer. "That it's about time this boy of ours was bundled off to a boarding-school."

I sat back, trying to picture my home and my life without Dinkie. But it was unbearable. It was unthinkable.

"I shall never agree to that," I quietly retorted.

"Why?" asked my husband, with a note of triumph which I resented.

"For one thing, because he is still a child, because he is too young," I contended, knowing that I could never agree with Dinky-Dunk in his thoroughly English ideas of education even while I remembered how he had once said that the greatness of England depended on her public-schools, such as Harrow and Eton and Rugby and Winchester, and that she had been the best colonizer in the world because her boys had been taken young and taught not to overvalue home ties, had been made manlier by getting off with their own kind instead of remaining hitched to an apron-string.

"And you prefer keeping him stuck out here on the prairie?" demanded Dinky-Dunk.

"The prairie has been good enough for his parents, this last seven or eight years," I contended.

"It hasn't been good enough for me," my husband cried out with quite unlooked-for passion. "And I've about had my fill of it!"

"Where would you prefer going?" I asked, trying to speak as quietly as I could.

"That's something I'm going to find out as soon as the chance comes," he retorted with a slow and embittered emphasis which didn't add any to my peace of mind.

"Then why cross our bridges," I suggested, "until we come to them?"

"But you're not looking for bridges," he challenged. "You don't want to see anything beyond living like Doukhobours out here on the edge of Nowhere and remembering that you've got your precious offspring here under your wing and wondering how many bushels of Number-One-Hard it will take to buy your Dinkie a riding pinto!"

"Aren't you rather tired to-night?" I asked with all the patience I could command.

"Yes, and I'm talking about the thing that makes me tired. For you know as well as I do that you've made that boy of yours a sort of anesthetic. You put him on like a nose-cap, and forget the world. He's about all you remember to think about. Why, when you look at the clock, nowadays, it isn't ten minutes to twelve. It's always Dinkie minutes to Dink. When you read a book you're only reading about what your Dinkie might have done or what your Dinkie is some day to write. When you picture the Prime Minister it's merely your Dinkie grown big, laying down the law to a House of Parliament made up of other Dinkies, rows and rows of 'em. When the sun shines you're wondering whether it's warm enough for your Dinkie to walk in, and when the snow begins to melt you're wondering whether it's soft enough for the beloved Dinkie to mold into snowballs. When you see a girl you at once get busy speculating over whether or not she'll ever be beautiful enough for your Dinkie, and when one of the Crowned Heads of Europe announces the alliance of its youngest princess you fall to pondering if Dinkie wouldn't have made her a better husband. And when the flowers come out in your window-box you wonder if they're fair enough to bloom beside your Dinkie. I don't suppose I ever made a haystack that you didn't wonder whether it wasn't going to be a grand place for Dinkie to slide down. And when Dinkie draws a goggle-eyed man on his scribbler you see Michael Angelo totter and Titian turn in his grave. And when Dinkie writes a composition of thirty crooked lines on the landing of Hengist you feel that fate did Hume a mean trick in letting him pass away before inspecting that final word in historical record. And heaven's just a row of Dinkies with little gold harps tucked under their wings. And you think you're breathing air, but all you're breathing is Dinkies, millions and millions of etherealized Dinkies. And when you read about the famine in China you inevitably and adroitly hitch the death of seven thousand Chinks in Yangchow on to the interests of your immortal offspring. And I suppose Rome really came into being for the one ultimate end that an immortal young Dinkie might possess his full degree of Dinkiness and the glory that was Greece must have been merely the tom-toms tuning up for the finished dance of our Dinkie's grandeur. Day and night, it's Dinkie, just Dinkie!"

I waited until he was through. I waited, heavy of heart, until his foolish fires of revolt had burned themselves out. And it didn't seem to add to his satisfaction to find that I could inspect him with a quiet and slightly commiserative eye.

"You are accusing me," I finally told him, "of something I'm proud of. And I'm afraid I'll always be guilty of caring for my own son."

He turned on me with a sort of heavy triumph.

"Well, it's something that you'll jolly well pay the piper for, some day," he announced.

"What do you mean by that?" I demanded.

"I mean that nothing much is ever gained by letting the maternal instinct run over. And that's exactly what you're doing. You're trying to tie Dinkie to your side, when you can no more tie him up than you can tie up a sunbeam. You could keep him close enough to you, of course, when he was small. But he's bound to grow away from you as he gets bigger, just as I grew away from my mother and you once grew away from yours. It's a natural law, and there's no use crocking your knees on it. The boy's got his own life to live, and you can't live it for him. It won't be long, now, before you begin to notice those quiet withdrawals, those slippings-back into his own shell of self-interest. And unless you realize what it means, it's going to hurt. And unless you reckon on that in the way you order your life you're not only going to be a very lonely old lady but you're going to bump into a big hole where you thought the going was smoothest!"

I sat thinking this over, with a ton of lead where my heart should have been.

"I've already bumped into a big hole where I thought the going was smoothest," I finally observed.

My husband looked at me and then looked away again.

"I was hoping we could fill that up and forget it," he ventured in a valorously timid tone which made it hard, for reasons I couldn't quite fathom, to keep my throat from tightening. But I sat there, shaking my head from side to side.

"I've got to love something," I found myself protesting. "And the children seem all that is left."

"How about me?" asked my husband, with his acidulated and slightly one-sided smile.

"You've changed, Dinky-Dunk," was all I could say.

"But some day," he contended, "you may wake up to the fact that I'm still a human being."

"I've wakened up to the fact that you're a different sort of human being than I had thought."

"Oh, we're all very much alike, once you get our number," asserted my husband.

"You mean men are," I amended.

"I mean that if men can't get a little warmth and color and sympathy in the home-circle they're going to edge about until they find a substitute for it, no matter how shoddy it may be," contended Dinky-Dunk.

"But isn't that a hard and bitter way of writing life down to one's own level?" I asked, trying to swallow the choke that wouldn't stay down in my throat.

"Well, I can't see that we get much ahead by trying to sentimentalize the situation," he said, with a gesture that seemed one of frustration.

We sat staring at each other, and again I had the feeling of abysmal gulfs of space intervening between us.

"Is that all you can say about it?" I asked, with a foolish little gulp I couldn't control.

"Isn't it enough?" demanded Dinky-Dunk. And I knew that nothing was to be gained, that night, by the foolish and futile clash of words.

Tuesday the Twenty-Third

I've been doing a good deal of thinking over what Dinky-Dunk said. I have been trying to see things from his standpoint. By a sort of mental ju-jutsu I've even been trying to justify what I can't quite understand in him. But it's no use. There's one bald, hard fact I can't escape, no matter how I dig my old ostrich-beak of instinct under the sands of self-deception. There's one cold-blooded truth that will have to be faced. *My husband is no longer in love with me.* Whatever else may have happened, I have lost my heart-hold on Duncan Argyll McKail. I am still his wife, in the eyes of the law, and the mother of his children. We still live together, and, from force of habit, if from nothing else, go through the familiar old rites of daily communion. He sits across the table from me when I eat, and talks casually enough of the trivially momentous problems of the minute, or he reads in his slippers before the fire while I do my sewing within a spool-toss of him. But a row of invisible assegais stand leveled between his heart and mine. A slow glacier of green-iced indifference shoulders in between us; and gone forever is the wild-flower aroma of youth, the singing spirit of April, the mysterious light that touched our world with wonder. He is merely a man, drawing on to middle age, and I am a woman, no longer young. Gone now are the spring floods that once swept us together. Gone now is the flame of adoration that burned clean our altar of daily intercourse and left us blind to the weaknesses we were too happy to remember. For there was a time when we loved each other. I know that as well as Duncan does. But it died away, that ghostly flame. It went out like a neglected fire. And blowing on dead ashes can never revive the old-time glow.

"So they were married and lived happy ever afterward!" That is the familiar ending to the fairy-tales I read over and over again to my Dinkie and Poppsy. But they are fairy-tales. For who lives happy ever afterward? First love chloroforms us, for a time, and we try to hug to our bosoms the illusion that Heaven itself is only a sort of endless honeymoon presided over by Lohengrin marches. But the anesthetic wears away and we find that life isn't a bed of roses but a rough field that rewards us as we till it, with here and there the cornflower of happiness laughing unexpectedly up at us out of our sober acres of sober wheat. And often enough we don't know happiness when we see it. We assuredly find it least where we look for it most. I can't even understand why we're equipped with such a hunger for it. But I find myself trending more and more to that cynic philosophy which defines happiness as the absence of pain. The absence of pain—that is a lot to ask for, in this life!

I wonder if Dinky-Dunk is right in his implication that I am getting hard? There are times, I know, when I grate on him, when he would probably give anything to get away from me. Yet here we are, linked together like two convicts. And I don't believe I'm as hard as my husband accuses me of being. However macadamized they may have made life for me, there's at least one soft spot in my heart, one garden under the walls of granite. And that's the spot which my two children fill, which my children keep green, which my children keep holy. It's them I think of, when I think of the future—when I should at least be thinking a little of my grammar and remembering that the verb "to be" takes the nominative, just as discontented husbands seem to take the initiative! That's why I can't quite find the courage to ask for freedom. I have seen enough of life to know what the smash-up of a family means to its toddlers. And I want my children to have a chance. They can't have that chance without at least two things. One is the guardianship of home life, and the other is that curse of modern times known as money. We haven't prospered as we had hoped to, but heaven knows I've kept an eagle eye on that savings-account of mine, in that absurdly new and resplendent red-brick bank in Buckhorn. Patiently I've fed it with my butter and egg money, joyfully I've seen it grow with my meager Nitrate dividends, and grimly I've made it bigger with every loose dollar I could lay my hands on. There's no heroism in my going without things I may have thought I needed, just as there can be little nobility in my sticking to a husband who no longer loves me. For it's not Chaddie McKail who counts now, but her chicks. And I'll have to look for my reward through them, for I'm like Romanes' rat now, too big to get into the bottle of cream, but wary enough to know I can dine from a tail still small enough for insertion. I'm merely a submerged prairie-hen with the best part of her life behind her.

But it bothers me, what Duncan says about my always thinking of little Dinkie first. And I'm afraid I do, though it seems neither right nor fair. I suppose it's because he was my first-born—and having come first in my life he must come first in my thoughts. I was made to love somebody—and my husband doesn't seem to want me to love him. So he has driven me to centering my thoughts on the child. I've got to have something to warm up to. And any love I may lavish on this prairie-chick of mine, who has to face life with the lack of so many things, will not only be a help to the boy, but will be a help to me, the part of Me that I'm sometimes so terribly afraid of.

Yet I can't help wondering if Duncan has any excuses for claiming that it's personal selfishness which prompts me to keep my boy close to my side. And am I harming him, without knowing it, in keeping him here under my wing? Schools are all right, in a way, but surely a good mother can do as much in the molding of a boy's mind as a boarding-school with a file of

Ph.D.'s on its staff. But am I a good mother? And should I trust myself, in a matter like this, to my own feelings? Men, in so many things, are better judges than women. Yet it has just occurred to me that all men do not think alike. I've been sitting back and wondering what kindly old Peter would say about it. And I've decided to write Peter and ask what he advises. He'll tell the truth, I know, for Peter is as honest as the day is long....

I've just been up to make sure the children were properly covered in bed. And it disturbed me a little to find that without even thinking about it I went to Dinkie first. It seemed like accidental corroboration of all that Duncan has been saying. But I stood studying him as he lay there asleep. It frightened me a little, to find him so big. If it's true, as Duncan threatens, that time will tend to turn him away from me, it's something that I'm going to fight tooth and nail. And I've seen no sign of it, as yet. With every month and every year that's added to his age he grows more companionable, more able to bridge the chasm between two human souls. We have more interests in common, more things to talk about. And day by day Dinkie is reaching up to my clumsily mature way of looking at life. He can come to me with his problems, knowing I'll always give him a hearing, just as he used to come to me with his baby cuts and bruises, knowing they would be duly kissed and cared for. Yet some day, I have just remembered, he may have problems that can't be brought to me. But that day, please God, I shall defer as long as possible. Already we have our own little secrets and private compacts and understandings. I don't want my boy to be a mollycoddle. But I want him to have his chance in the world. I want him to be somebody. I can't reconcile myself to the thought of him growing up to wear moose-mittens and shoe-packs and stretching barb-wire in blue-jeans and riding a tractor across a prairie back-township. I refuse to picture him getting bent and gray wringing a livelihood out of an over-cropped ranch fourteen miles away from a post-office and a world away from the things that make life most worth living. If he were an ordinary boy, I might be led to think differently. But my Dinkie is not an ordinary boy. There's a spark of the unusual, of the exceptional, in that laddie. And I intend to fan that spark, whatever the cost may be, until it breaks out into genius.

Sunday the Twenty-Eighth

I've had scant time for introspection during the last five days, for Struthers has been in bed with lumbago, and the weight of the housework reverted to me. But Whinstane Sandy brought his precious bottle of Universal Ointment in from the bunk-house, and while that fiery mixture warmed her lame back, the thought of its origin probably warmed her lonely heart. I have suddenly wakened up to the fact that Struthers is getting on a bit. She is still the same efficient and self-obliterating mainstay of the kitchen that she ever was, but she grows more "sot" in her ways, more averse to any change in her daily routine, and more despairing of ever finally and completely capturing that canny old Scotsman whom we still so affectionately designate as Whinnie, in short for Whinstane Sandy. Whinnie, I'm afraid, still nurses the fixed idea that everything in petticoats and as yet unwedded is after him. And it is only by walking with the utmost circumspection that he escapes their wiles and by maintaining an unbroken front withstands their unseemly advances.

The new school-teacher has arrived, and is to live with us here at Casa Grande. I have my reasons for this. In the first place, it will be a help to Dinkie in his studies. In the second place, it means that the teacher can pack my boy back and forth to school, in bad weather, and next month when Poppsy joins the ranks of the learners, can keep a more personal eye on that little tot's movements. And in the third place the mere presence of another male at Casa Grande seems to dilute the acids of home life.

Gershom Binks is the name of this new teacher, and I have just learned that in the original Hebrew "Gershom" not inappropriately means "a stranger there." He is a sophomore (a most excellent word, that, when you come to inquire into its etymology!) from the University of Minnesota and is compelled to teach the young idea, for a time, to accumulate sufficient funds to complete his course, which he wants to do at Ann Arbor. And Gershom is a very tall and very thin and very short-sighted young man, with an Adam's apple that works up and down with a two-inch plunge over the edge of his collar when he talks—which he does somewhat extensively. He wears glasses with big bulging lenses, glasses which tend to hide a pair of timid and brown-October-aleish eyes with real kindliness in them. He looks ill-nourished, but I can detect nothing radically wrong with his appetite. It's merely that, like Cassius, he thinks too much. And I'm going to fatten that boy up a bit, before the year is out, or know the reason why. He may be a trifle self-conscious and awkward, but he's also amazingly clean of both body and mind, and it will be no hardship, I know, to have him under our roof. And for all his devotion to Science, he reads his Bible every night—which is more than Chaddie McKail does! He rather took the wind out of my sails by demanding, the first morning at breakfast, if I knew that one half-ounce of the web of the spider—the arachnid of the order *Araneida*, he explained—if stretched out in a straight line would reach from the city of Chicago to the city of Paris. I told him that this was a most wonderful and a most interesting piece of information and hoped that some day we could verify it by actual test. Yet when I inquired whether he meant merely the environs of the city of Paris, or the very heart of the city such as the Place de l'Opéra, he studied me with the meditative eye with which Huxley must have once studied beetles.

Dinky-Dunk, I notice, is as restive as a bull-moose in black-fly season. He's doing his work on the land, as about every ranch-owner has to, whether he's happily married or not, but he's doing it without any undue impression of its epical importance. I heard him observe, yesterday, that if he could only get his hands on enough ready money he'd like to swing into land business in a live center like Calgary. He has a friend there, apparently, who has just made a clean-up in city real estate and bought his wife a Detroit Electric and built a home for himself that cost forty thousand dollars. I reminded Dinky-Dunk, when he had finished, that we really must have a new straining-mesh in the milk-separator. He merely looked at me with a sour and morose eye as he got up and went out to his team.

Surely these men-folks are a dissatisfied lot! Gershom to-night complained that his own name of "Gershom Binks" impressed him as about the ugliest name that was ever hitched on to a scholar and a gentlemen. And later on, after I'd opened my piano and tried to console myself with a tu'penny draught of Grieg, he inspected the instrument and informed me that it was really evolved from the six-stringed harps of the fourth Egyptian dynasty, which in the fifth dynasty was made with a greatly enlarged base, thus giving the rudimentary beginning of a soundboard.

I am learning a lot from Gershom! And so are my kiddies, for that matter. I begin, in fact, to feel like royalty with a private tutor, for every night now Dinkie and Poppsy and Gershom sit about the living-room table and drink of the founts of wisdom. But we have a teacher here who loves to teach. And he is infinitely patient and kind with my little toddlers. Dinkie already asks him questions without number, while Poppsy gratefully but decorously vamps him with her infantine gazes. Then Gershom—Heaven bless his scholastic old high-browed solemnity—has just assured me that Dinkie betrays many evidences of an exceptionally bright mind.

Friday the Second

My husband yesterday accused me of getting moss-backed. He had been harping on the city string again and asked me if I intended to live and die a withered beauty on a back-trail ranch.

That "withered beauty" hurt, though I did my best to ignore it, for the time at least. And Dinky-Dunk went on to say that it struck him as one of life's little ironies that *I* should want to stick to the sort of life we were leading, remembering what I'd come from.

"Dinky-Dunk," I told him, "it's terribly hard to explain exactly how I feel about it all. I suppose I could never make you see it as I see it. But it's a feeling like loyalty, loyalty to the land that's given us what we have. And it's also a feeling of disliking to see one old rule repeating itself: what has once been a crusade becoming merely a business. To turn and leave our land now, it seems to me, would make us too much like those soulless soil-robbers you used to rail at, like those squatters who've merely squeezed out what they could and have gone on, like those land-miners who take all they can get and stand ready to put nothing back. Why, if we were all like that, we'd have no country here. We'd be a wilderness, a Barren Grounds that went from the Border up to the Circle. But there's something bigger than that about it all. I love the prairie. Just why it is, I don't know. It's too fundamental to be fashioned into words, and I never realized how deep it was until I went back to the city that time. One can just say it, and let it go at that: *I love the prairie.* It isn't merely its bigness, just as it isn't altogether its freedom and its openness. Perhaps it's because it keeps its spirit of the adventurous. I love it the same as my children love *The Arabian Nights* and *The Swiss Family Robinson.* I thought it was mostly cant, once, that cry about being next to nature, but the more I know about nature the more I feel with Pope that naught but man is vile, to speak as impersonally, my dear Diddums, as the occasion will permit. I'm afraid I'm like that chickadee that flew into the bunk-house and Whinnie caught and put in a box-cage for Dinkie. I nearly die at the thought of being cooped up. I want clean air and open space about me."

"I never dreamed you'd been Indianized to that extent," murmured my husband.

"Being Indianized," I proceeded, "seems to carry the inference of also being barbarized. But it isn't quite that, Dinky-Dunk, for there's something almost spiritually satisfying about this prairie life if you've only got the eyes to see it. I think that's because the prairie always seems so majestically beautiful to me. I can see your lip curl again, but I know I'm right. When I throw open my windows of a morning and see that placid old never-ending plain under its great wash of light something lifts up in my breast, like a bird, and no matter how a mere man has been doing his best to make me miserable that something stands up on the tip of my heart and does its darnedest to sing. It impresses me as life on such a sane and gigantic scale that I want to be an actual part of it, that I positively ache to have a share in its immensities. It seems so fruitful and prodigal and generous and patient. It's so open-handed in the way it produces and gives and returns our love. And there's a completeness about it that makes me feel it can't possibly be wrong."

"The Eskimo, I suppose, feels very much the same in his little igloo of ice with a pot of whale-blubber at his elbow," observed my husband.

"You're a brute, my dear Diddums, and more casually cruel than a Baffin-land cannibal," I retorted. "But we'll let it pass. For I'm talking about something that's too fundamental to be upset by a bitter tongue. There was a time, I know, when I used to fret about the finer things I thought I was losing out of life, about the little hand-made fripperies people have been forced to conjure up and carpenter together to console them for having to live in human beehives made of steel and concrete. But I'm beginning to find out that joy isn't a matter of geography and companionship isn't a matter of over-crowded subways. And the strap-hangers and the train-catchers and the first-nighters can have what they've got. I don't seem to envy them the way I used to. I don't need a Louvre when I've got the Northern Lights to look at. And I can get along without an Æolian Hall when I've got a little music in my own heart—for it's only what you've got there, after all, that really counts in this world!"

"All of which means," concluded my husband, "that you are most unmistakably growing old!"

"You have already," I retorted, "referred to me as a withered beauty."

Dinky-Dunk studied me long and intently. I even felt myself turning pink under that prolonged stare of appraisal.

"You are still easy to look at," he over-slangily and over-generously admitted. "But I do regret that you aren't a little easier to live with!"

I could force a little laugh, at that, but I couldn't quite keep a tremor out of my voice when I spoke again.

"I'm sorry you see only my bad side, Dinky-Dunk. But it's kindness that seems to bring everything that is best out of us women. We're terribly like sliced pineapple in that respect: give us just a sprinkling of sugar, and out come all the juices!"

It was Dinky-Dunk's color that deepened a little as he turned and knocked out his pipe.

"That's a Chaddie McKail argument," he merely observed as he stood up. "And a Chaddie McKail argument impresses me as suspiciously like Swiss cheese: it doesn't seem to be genuine unless you can find plenty of holes in it."

I did my best to smile at his humor.

"But this isn't an argument," I quietly corrected. "I'd look at it more in the nature of an ultimatum."

That brought him up short, as I had intended it to do. He stood worrying over it as Bobs and Scotty worry over a bone.

"I'm afraid," he finally intoned, "I've been repeatedly doing you the great injustice of underestimating your intelligence!"

"That," I told him, "is a point where I find silence imposed upon me."

He didn't speak until he got to the door.

"Well, I'm glad we've cleared the air a bit anyway," he said with a grim look about his Holbein Astronomer old mouth as he went out.

But we haven't cleared the air. And it disturbs me more than I can say to find that I have reservations from my husband. It bewilders me to see that I can't be perfectly candid with him. But there are certain deeper feelings that I can no longer uncover in his presence. Something holds me back from explaining to him that this fixed dread of mine for all cities is largely based on my loss of little Pee-Wee. For if I hadn't gone to New York that time, to Josie Langdon's wedding, I might never have lost my boy. They did the best they could, I suppose, before their telegrams brought me back, but they didn't seem to understand the danger. And little did I dream, before the Donnelly butler handed me that first startling message just as we were climbing into the motor to go down to the Rochambeau to meet Chinkie and Tavvy, that within a week I was to sit and watch the cruelest thing that can happen in this world. I was to see a small child die. I was to watch my own Pee-Wee pass quietly away.

I have often wondered, since, why I never shed a tear during all those terrible three days. I couldn't, in some way, though the nurse herself was crying, and poor old Whinnie and Struthers were sobbing together next to the window, and dour old Dinky-Dunk, on the other side of the bed, was racking his shoulders with smothered sobs as he held the little white hand in his and the warmth went forever out of the little fingers where his foolish big hand was trying to hold back the life that couldn't be kept there. The old are ready to die, or can make themselves ready. They have run their race and had their turn at living. But it seems cruel hard to see a little tot, with eagerness still in his heart, taken away, taken away with the wonder of things still in his eyes. It stuns you. It makes you rebel. It leaves a scar that Time itself can never completely heal.

Yet through it all I can still hear the voice of valorous old Whinnie as he patted my shoulder and smiled with the brine still in the seams of his furrowed old face. "We'll thole through, lassie; we'll thole through!" he said over and over again. Yes; we'll thole through. And this is only the uncovering of old wounds. And one must keep one's heart and one's house in order, for with us we still have the living.

But Dinky-Dunk can't completely understand, I'm afraid, this morbid hankering of mine to keep my family about me, to have the two chicks that are left to me close under my wing. And never once, since Pee-Wee went, have I actually punished either of my children. It may be wrong, but I can't help it. I don't want memories of violence to be left corroding and rankling in my mind. And I'd hate to see any child of mine cringe, like an ill-treated dog, at every lift of the hand. There are better ways of controlling them, I begin to feel, than through fear. Their father, I know, will never agree with me on this matter. He will always insist on mastery, open and undisputed mastery, in his own house. He is the head of this Clan McKail, the sovereign of this little circle. For we can say what we will about democracy, but when a child is born unto a man that man unconsciously puts on the purple. He becomes the ruler and sits on the throne of authority. He even seeks to cloak his weaknesses and his mistakes in that threadbare old fabrication about the divine right of kings. But I can see that he is often wrong, and even my Dinkie can see that he is not always right in his decrees. More and more often, of late, I've observed the boy studying his father, studying him with an impersonal and critical eye. And this habit of silent appraisal is plainly something which Duncan resents, and resents keenly. He's beginning to have a feeling, I'm afraid, that he can't quite get *at* the boy. And there's a youthful shyness growing up in Dinkie which seems to leave him ashamed of any display of emotion before his father. I can see that it even begins to exasperate Duncan a little, to be shut out behind those incontestable walls of reserve. It's merely, I'm sure, that the child is so terribly afraid of ridicule. He already nurses a hankering to be regarded as one of the grown-ups and imagines there's something rather babyish in any undue show of feeling. Yet he is hungry for affection. And he aches, I know, for the approbation of his male parent, for the approval of a full-grown man whom he can regard as one of his own kind. He even imitates his father in the way in which he stands in front of the fire, with his heels well apart. And he gives me chills up the spine by pulling short on one bridle-rein and making Buntie, his mustang-pony, pirouette just as the wicked-tempered Briquette sometimes pirouettes when his father is in the saddle. Yet Dinky-Dunk's nerves are a bit ragged and there are times when he's not always just with the boy, though it's not for me to confute what the instinctive genius of childhood has already made reasonably clear to Dinkie's discerning young eye. But I can not, of course, encourage insubordination. All I can do is to ignore the unwelcome and try to crowd it aside with happier things. I want my boy to love me, as I love him. And I think he does. I *know* he does. That knowledge is an azure and bottomless lake into which I can toss my blackest pebbles of fear, my flintiest doubts of the future.

Sunday the Fourth

I wish I could get by the scruff of the neck that sophomoric old philosopher who once said nothing survives being thought of. For I've been learning, this last two or three days, just how wide of the mark he shot. And it's all arisen out of Dinky-Dunk's bland intimation that I am "a withered beauty." Those words have held like a fish-hook in the gills of my memory. If they'd come from somebody else they mightn't have meant so much. But from one's own husband—Wow!—they go in like a harpoon. And they have given me a great deal to think about. There are times, I find, when I can accept that intimation of slipping into the sere and yellow leaf without revolt. Then the next moment it fills me with a sort of desperation. I refuse to go up on the shelf. I see red and storm against age. I refuse to bow to the inevitable. My spirit recoils at the thought of decay. For when you're fading you're surely decaying, and when you're decaying you're approaching the end. So stop, Father Time, stop, or I'll get out of the car!

But we can't get out of the car. That's the tragic part of it. We have to go on, whether we like it or not. We have to buck up, and grin and bear it, and make the best of a bad bargain. And Heaven knows I've never wanted to be one of the Glooms! I've no hankering to sit with the Sob Sisters and pump brine over the past. I'm light-hearted enough if they'll only give me a chance. I've always believed in getting what we could out of life and looking on the sunny side of things. And the disturbing part of it is, I don't *feel* withered—not by a jugful! There are mornings when I can go about my homely old duties singing like a prairie Tetrazzini. There are days when I could do a hand-spring, if for nothing more than to shock my solemn old Dinky-Dunk out of his dourness. There are times when we go skimming along the trail with the crystal-cool evening air in our faces and the sun dipping down toward the rim of the world when I want to thank Somebody I can't see for Something-or-other I can't define. *Dum vivimus vivamus.*

But it seems hard to realize that I'm a sedate and elderly lady already on the shady side of thirty. A woman over thirty years old—and I can remember the days of my intolerant youth when I regarded the woman of thirty as an antiquated creature who should be piously preparing herself for the next world. And it doesn't take thirty long to slip into forty. And then forty merges into fifty—and there you are, a nice old lady with nervous indigestion and knitting-needles and a tendency to breathe audibly after ascending the front-stairs. No wonder, last night, it drove me to taking a volume of George Moore down from the shelf and reading his chapter on "The Woman of Thirty." But I found small consolation in that over-uxorious essay, feeling as I did that I knew life quite as well as any amorous studio-rat who ever made copy out of his mottled past. So I was driven, in the end, to studying myself long and intently in the broken-hinged mirrors of my dressing-table. And I didn't find much there to fortify my quailing spirit. I was getting on a bit. I was curling up a little around the edges. There was no denying that fact. For I could see a little fan-light of lines at the outer corner of each eye. And down what Dinky-Dunk once called the honeyed corners of my mouth went another pair of lines which clearly came from too much laughing. But most unmistakably of all there was a line coming under my chin, a small but tell-tale line, announcing the fact that I wasn't losing any in weight, and standing, I suppose, one of the foot-hills which precede the Rocky-Mountain dewlaps of old age. It wouldn't be long, I could see, before I'd have to start watching my diet, and looking for a white hair or two, and probably give up horseback riding. And then settle down into an ingle-nook old dowager with a hassock under *my* feet and a creak in my knees and a fixed conviction that young folks never acted up in *my* youth as they act up nowadays.

I tried to laugh it away, but my heart went down like a dredge-dipper. Whereupon I set my jaw, which didn't make me look any younger. But I didn't much care, for the mirror had already done its worst.

"Not muchee!" I said as I sat there making faces at myself. "You're still one of the living. The bloom may be off in a place or two, but you're sound to the core, and serviceable for many a year. So *sursum corda! 'Rung ho! Hira Singh!*' as Chinkie taught us to shout in the old polo days. And that means, Go in and win, Chaddie McKail, and die with your boots on if you have to."

I was still intent on that study of my robust-looking but slightly weather-beaten map when Dinky-Dunk walked in and caught me in the middle of my Narcissus act.

"'All is vanity saith the Preacher,'" he began. But he stopped short when I swung about at him. For I hadn't, after all, been able to carpenter together even a whale-boat of consolation out of my wrecked schooner of hope.

"Oh, Kakaibod," I wailed, "I'm a pie-faced old has-been, and nobody will ever love me again!"

He only laughed, on his way out, and announced that I seemed to be getting my share of loving, as things went. But he didn't take back what he said about me being withered. And the first thing I shall do to-morrow, when Gershom comes down to breakfast, will be to ask him how old Cleopatra was when she brought Antony to his knees and how antiquated Ninon D'Enclos was when she lost her power over that semi-civilized creature known as Man. Gershom will know, for Gershom knows everything.

Wednesday the Seventh

Gershom has been studying some of my carbon-prints. He can't for the life of him understand why I consider Dewing's *Old-fashioned Gown* so beautiful, or why I should love Childe Hassam's *Church at Old Lyme* or see anything remarkable about Metcalf's *May Night*. But I cherish them as one cherishes photographs of lost friends.

A couple of the Horatio Walker's, he acknowledged, seemed to mean something to him. But Gershom's still in the era when he demands a story in the picture and could approach Monet and Degas only by way of Meissonier and Bouguereau. And a print, after all, is only a print. He's slightly ashamed to admire beauty as mere beauty, contending that at the core of all such things there should be a moral. So we pow-wowed for an hour and more over the threadbare old theme and the most I could get out of Gershom was that the lady in *The Old-fashioned Gown* reminded him of me, only I was more vital. But all that talk about landscape and composition and line and tone made me momentarily homesick for a glimpse of Old Lyme again, before I go to my reward.

But the mood didn't last. And I no longer regret what's lost. I don't know what mysterious Divide it is I have crossed over, but it seems to be peace I want now instead of experience. I'm no longer envious of the East and all it holds. I'm no longer fretting for wider circles of life. The lights may be shining bright on many a board-walk, at this moment, but it means little to this ranch-lady. What I want now is a better working-plan for that which has already been placed before me. Often and often, in the old days, when I realized how far away from the world this lonely little island of Casa Grande and its inhabitants stood, I used to nurse a ghostly envy for the busier tideways of life from which we were banished. I used to feel that grandeur was in some way escaping me. I could picture what was taking place in some of those golden-gray old cities I had known: The Gardens of the Luxembourg when the horse-chestnuts were coming out in bloom, and the Château de Madrid in the Bois at the luncheon hour, or the Pre Catalan on a Sunday with heavenly sole in lemon and melted butter and a still more heavenly waltz as you sat eating *fraises des bois* smothered in thick *crême d'Isigny*. Or the Piazzi di Spagna on Easter Sunday with the murmur of Rome in your ears and the cars and carriages flashing through the green-gold shadows of the Pincio. Or Hyde Park in May, with the sun sifting through the brave old trees and flashing on the helmets of the Life Guards as the King goes by in a scarlet uniform with the blue Order of the Garter on his breast, or Park Lane on a glorious light-and-shadow afternoon in

June and a dip into the familiar old Americanized clangor at the Cecil; or Chinkie's place in Devonshire about a month earlier, sitting out on the terrace wrapped in steamer-rugs and waiting for the moon to come up and the first nightingale to sing. Of Fifth Avenue shining almost bone-white in the clear December sunlight and the salted nuts and orange-blossom cocktails at Sherry's, or the Plaza tea-room at about five o'clock in the afternoon with the smell of Turkish tobacco and golden pekoe and hot-house violets and Houbigant's *Quelque-fleurs* all tangled up together. Or the City of Wild Parsley in March with a wave of wild flowers breaking over the ruins of Selinunte and the tumbling pillars of the Temple of Olympian Zeus lying time-mellowed in the clear Sicilian sunlight!

They were all lovely enough, and still are, I suppose, but it's a loveliness in some way involved with youth. So the memory of those far-off gaieties, which, after all, were so largely physical, no longer touch me with unrest. They're wine that's drunk and water that's run under the bridge. Younger lips can drink of that cup, which was sweet enough in its time. Let the newer girls dance their legs off under the French crystals of the Ritz, and powder their noses over the Fountain of the Sunken Boat, and eat the numbered duck so reverentially doled out at La Tour d'Argent and puff their cigarettes behind the beds of begonias and marguerites at the Château Madrid. They too will get tired of it, and step aside for others. For the petal falls from the blossom and the blossom plumps out into fruit. And all those golden girls, when their day is over, must slip away from those gardens of laughter. When they don't, they only make themselves ridiculous. For there's nothing sadder than an antique lady of other days decking herself out in the furbelows of a lost youth. And I've got Dinky-Dunk's overalls to patch and my bread to set, so I can't think much more about it to-night. But after I've done my chores, and before I go up to bed, I'm going to read *Rabbi Ben Ezra* right through to the end. I'll do it in front of the fire, with my feet up and with three Ontario Northern Spy apples on a plate beside me, to be munched as Audrey herself might have munched them, oblivious of any Touchstone and his reproving eyes.

I have stopped to ponder, however, how much of this morbid dread of mine for big cities is due to that short and altogether unsatisfactory visit to New York, to that sense of coming back a stranger and finding old friends gone and those who were left with such entirely new interests.

I was out of it, completely and dishearteningly out of it. And my clothes were all wrong. My hats were wrong; my shoes were wrong; and every rag I had on me was in some way wrong. I was a tourist from the provinces. And I wasn't up-to-date with either what was on me or was *in* me. I didn't even know the new subway routes or the telephone rules or the proper places to go for tea. The Metropolitan looked cramped and shoddy and *Tristan* seemed shoddily sung to me. There was no thrill to it. And even *The Jewels of the Madonna* impressed me as a bit garish and off color, with the Apache Dance of the last act almost an affront to God and man. I even asked myself, when I found that I had lost the trick of laughing at bridal-suite farces, if it was the possession of children that had changed me. For when you're with children you must in some way match their snowy innocence with a kindred coloring of innocence, very much as the hare and the weasel and the ptarmigan turn white to match the whiteness of our northern winter. Yet I was able to wring pure joy out of Rachmaninoff's playing at Carnegie Hall, with a great man making music for music's sake. I loved the beauty and balance and splendid sanity of that playing, without keyboard fire-works and dazzle and glare. But Rachmaninoff was the exception. Even Central Park seemed smaller than of old, and I couldn't remember which drives Dinky-Dunk and I had taken in the historic old hansom-cab after our equally historic marriage by ricochet. Fifth Avenue itself was different, the caterpillar of trade having crawled a little farther up the stalk of fashion, for the shops, I found, went right up to the Park, and the old W. K. house where we once danced our long-forgotten Dresden China Quadrille, in imitation of the equally forgotten Eighty-Three event, confronted me as a beehive of business offices. I couldn't quite get used to the new names and the new faces and the new shops and the side-street theaters and the thought of really nice girls going to a prize-fight in Madison Square Garden, and the eternal and never-ending talk about drinks, about where and how to get them, and how to mix them, and how much Angostura to put into 'em, and the musty ale that used to be had at Losekam's in Washington, and the *Beaux Arts* cocktails that used to come with a dash of absinthe, and the shipment of pinch-neck Scotch which somebody smuggled in on his cruiser-yacht from the east end of Cuba, and so-forth and so-forth until I began to feel that the only important thing in the world was the possession and dispensation of alcohol. And out of it I got the headache without getting the fun. I had the same dull sense of being cheated which came to me in my flapper days when I fell asleep with a mouthful of contraband gum and woke up in the morning with my jaw-muscles tired—I'd been facing all the exertion without getting any of the satisfaction.

The one bright spot to me, in that lost city of my childhood, was the part of Madison Avenue which used to be known as Murray Hill, the right-of-way along the west sidewalk of which I once commandeered for an afternoon's coasting. I could see again, as I glanced down the familiar slope, the puffy figure of old Major Elmes, who in those days was always pawing somebody, since he seemed to believe with Novalis that he touched heaven when he placed his hand on a human body. I could see myself sky-hooting down that icy slope on my coaster, approaching the old Major from the rear and peremptorily piping out: "One side, please!" For I was young then, and I expected all life to make way for me. But the old Major betrayed no intention of altering his solemnly determined course at any such juvenile suggestion, with the result that he sat down on me bodily, and for the next two blocks approached his club in Madison Square in a manner and at a speed which he had in no wise anticipated. But, *Eheu*, how long ago it all seemed!

Saturday the Tenth

Peter has written back in answer to my question as to the expediency of sending my boy off to a boarding-school. He put all he had to say in two lines. They were:

"I had a mother like Dinkie's, I'd stick to her until the stars were dust."

That was very nice of Peter, of course, but I don't imagine he had any idea of the peck of trouble he was going to stir up at Casa Grande. For Dinky-Dunk picked up the sheet of paper on which that light-hearted message had been written and perused the two lines, perused them with a savagery which rather disturbed me. He read them for the second time, and then he put them down. His eye, as he confronted me, was a glacial one.

"It's too bad we can't run this show without the interference of outsiders," he announced as he stalked out of the room.

I've been thinking the thing over, and trying to get my husband's view-point. But I can't quite succeed. There has always been a touch of the satyric in Dinky-Dunk's attitude toward Peter's weekly letter to my boy. He has even intimated that they were written in a new kind of Morse, the inference being that they were intended to carry messages in cipher to eyes other than Dinkie's. But Peter is much too honest a man for any such resort to subterfuge. And Dinky-Dunk has always viewed with a hostile eye the magazines and books and toys which big-hearted Peter has showered out on us. Peter always was ridiculously open-handed. And he always loved my Dinkie. And it's only natural that our thoughts should turn back to where our love has been left. Peter, I know, gets quite as much fun out of those elaborately playful letters to Dinkie as Dinkie does himself. And it's left the boy more anxious to learn, to the end that he may pen a more respectable reply to them.

Some of Peter's gifts, it is true, have been embarrassingly ornate, but Peter, who has been given so much, must have remembered how little has come to my kiddies. It was my intention, for a while, to talk this over with Dinky-Dunk, to try to make him see it in a more reasonable light. But I have now given up that intention. There's a phantasmal something that holds me back....

I dreamt last night that my little Dinkie was a grown youth in a Greek academy, wearing a toga and sitting on a marble bench overlooking a sea of lovely sapphire. There both Peter and Percy, also arrayed in togas, held solemn discourse with my offspring and finally agreed that once they were through with him he would be the Wonder of the Age....

Dinky-Dunk asked me point-blank to-day if I'd consider the sale of Casa Grande, provided he got the right price for the ranch. I felt, for a moment, as though the bottom had been knocked out of my world. But it showed me the direction in which my husband's thoughts have been running of late. And I just as pointedly retorted that I'd never consent to the sale of Casa Grande. It's not merely because it's our one and only home. It's more because of the little knoll where the four Manitoba maples have been set and the row of prairie-roses have been planted along the little iron fence, the little iron fence which twice a year I paint a virginal white, with my own hands. For that's where my Pee-Wee sleeps, and that lonely little grave must never pass out of my care, to be forgotten and neglected and tarnished with time. It's not a place of sorrow now, but more an altar, duly tended, the flower-covered bed of my Pee-Wee, of my poor little Pee-Wee who was so brimming with life and love. He used to make me think of a humming-bird in a garden—and now all I have left of him is my small chest of toys and trinkets and baby-clothes. God, I know, will be good to that lonely little newcomer in His world of the statelier dead, in His gallery of whispering ghosts. Oh, be good to him, God! Be good to him, or You shall be no God of mine! I can't think of him as dead, as going out like a candle, as melting into nothingness as the little bones under their six feet of earth molder away. But my laddie is gone. And I must not be morbid. As Peter once said, misery loves company, but the company is apt to seek more convivial quarters. Yet something has gone out of my life, and that something drives me back to my Dinkie and my Poppsy with a sort of fierceness in my hunger to love them, to make the most of them.

Gershom, who has been giving Poppsy a daily lesson at home, has just inquired why she shouldn't be sent to school along with Dinkie. And her father has agreed. It gave me the wretched feeling, for a moment or two, that they were conspiring to take my last baby away from me. But I have to bow to the fact that I no longer possess one, since Poppsy announced her preference, the other day, for a doll "with real livings in it." She begins to show as fixed an aversion to baby-talk as that entertained by old Doctor Johnson himself, and no longer yearns to "do yidin on the team-tars," as she used to express it. The word "birthday" is still "birfday" with her, and "water" is still "wagger," but she now religiously eschews all such reiterative diminutives as "roundy-poundy" and "Poppsy-Woppsy" and "beddy-bed." She has even learned, after much effort, to convert her earlier "keam of feet" into the more legitimate and mature "cream of wheat." And now that she has a better mastery of the sibilants the charm has rather gone out of the claim, which I so laboriously taught her, that "Daddy is all feet," meaning, of course, that he was altogether sweet—which he gave small sign of being when he first caught the point of my patient schooling. She is not so quick-tongued as her brother Dinkie, but she has a natural fastidiousness which makes her long for alignment with the proprieties. She is, in fact, a conformist, a sedate and dignified little lady who will never be greatly given to the spilling of beans and the upsetting of apple-carts. She is, in many ways, amazingly like her pater. She will, I know, be a nice girl when she grows up, without very much of that irresponsibility which seems to have been the bugbear of her maternal parent. I'm even beginning to believe there's something in the old tradition about ancestral traits so often skipping a generation. At any rate, that crazy-hearted old Irish grandmother of mine passed on to me a muckle o' her wildness, the mad County Clare girl who swore at the vicar and rode to hounds and could take a seven-barred gate without turning a hair and was apt to be always in love or in debt or in hot water. She died too young to be tamed, I'm told, for say what you will, life tames us all in the end. Even Lady Hamilton took to wearing red-flannel petticoats before she died, and Buffalo Bill faded down into plain Mr. William Cody, and the abducted Helen of Troy gave many a day up to her needlework, we are told, and doubtlessly had trouble with both her teeth and her waist measurement.

Dinky-Dunk is proud of his Poppsy and has announced that it's about time we tucked the "Poppsy" away with her baby-clothes and resorted to the use of the proper and official "Pauline Augusta." So Pauline we shall try to have it, after this. There are several things, I think, which draw Dinky-Dunk and his Poppsy—I mean his Pauline—together. One is her likeness to himself. Another is her tractability, though I hate to hitch so big a word on to so small a lady. And still another is the fact that she is a girl. There's a subliminal play of sex-attraction about it, I suppose, just as there probably is between Dinkie and me. And there's something very admirable in Pauline Augusta's staid adoration of her dad. She plays up to him, I can see, without quite knowing she's doing it. She's hungry for his approval, and happiest, always, in his presence. Then, too, she makes him forget, for the time at least, his disappointment in a soul-mate who hasn't quite measured up to expectations! And I devoutly thank the Master of Life and Love that my solemn old Dinky-Dunk can thus care for his one and only daughter. It softens him, and keeps the sordid worries of the moment from vitrifying his heart. It puts a rainbow in his sky of every-day work, and gives him something to plan and plot and live for. And he needs it. We all do. It's our human and natural hunger for companionship. And as he observed not long ago, if that hunger can't be satisfied at home, we wander off and snatch what we can on the wing. Some day when they're rich, I overheard Dinky-Dunk announcing the other night, Pauline Augusta and her Dad are going to make the Grand Tour of Europe. And there, undoubtedly, do their best to pick up a Prince of the Royal Blood and have a château in Lombardy and a villa on the Riviera and a standing invitation to all the Embassy Balls!

Well, not if I know it. None of that penny-a-liner moonshine for my daughter. And as she grows older, I feel sure, I'll have more influence over her. She'll begin to realize that the battle of life hasn't scarred up for nothing this wary-eyed old mater who's beginning to know a hawk from a henshaw. I've learned a thing or two in my day, and one or two of them are going to be passed on to my offspring.

Thursday the Fifteenth

Struthers and I have been house-cleaning, for this is the middle of May, and our reluctant old northern spring seems to be here for good. It has been backward, this year, but the last of the mud has gone, and I hope to have my first setting of chicks out in a couple of days. Dinkie wants to start riding Buntie to school, but his pater says otherwise. Gershom goes off every morning, with Calamity Kate hitched to the old buckboard, with my two kiddies packed in next to him and provender enough for himself and the kiddies and Calamity Kate under the seat. The house seems very empty when they are away. But some time about five, every afternoon, I see them loping back along the trail. Then comes the welcoming bark of old Bobs, and a raid on the cooky-jar, and traces of bread-and-jelly on two hungry little faces, and the familiar old tumult about the reanimated rooms of Casa Grande. Then Poppsy—I beg her ladyship's pardon, for I mean, of course, Pauline Augusta—has to duly inspect her dolls to assure herself that they are both well-behaved and spotless as to apparel, for Pauline Augusta is a stickler as to decorum and cleanliness; and Dinkie falls to working on his air-ship, which he is this time making quite independent of Whinnie, whose last creation along that line betrayed a disheartening disability for flight. But even this second effort, I'm afraid, is doomed to failure, for more than once I've seen Dinkie back away and stand regarding his incompetent flier with a look of frustration on his face. He is always working over machinery—for he loves anything with wheels—and I'm pretty well persuaded that the twentieth-century mania of us grown-ups for picking ourselves to pieces is nothing more than a development of this childish hunger to get the cover off things and see the works go round. Dinkie makes wagons and carts and water-wheels, but some common fatality of incompetence overtakes them all and they are cast aside for enterprises more novel and more promising. He announces, now, that he intends to be an engineer. And that recalls the time when I was convinced in my own soul that he was destined for a life of art, since he was forever asking me to draw him "a li'l' man," and later on fell to drawing them himself. He would do his best to inscribe a circle and then emboss it with perfectly upright hair, as though the person in question had just been perusing the most stirring of penny-dreadfuls. Then he would put in two dots of eyes, and one abbreviated and vertical line for the nose, and another elongated and horizontal line for the mouth, and arms with extended and extremely elocutionary fingers, to say nothing of extremely attenuated legs which invariably toed-out, to make more discernible the silhouette of the ponderously booted feet. I have several dozen of these "li'l' men" carefully treasured in an old cigar-box. But he soon lost interest in these purely anthropocentric creations and broadened out into the delineation of boats and cars and wheel-barrows and rocking-chairs and tea-pots, lying along the floor on his stomach for an hour at a time, his tongue moving sympathetically with every movement of his pencil. He held the latter clutched close to the point by his stubby little fingers.

I had to call a halt on all such artistry, however, for he startled me, one day, by suddenly going crosseyed. It came, of course, from working with his nose too close to the paper. I imagined, with a sinking heart, that it was an affliction which was to stay with him for the rest of his natural life. But a night's sleep did much to restore the over-taxed eye-muscles and before the end of a week they had entirely righted themselves.

To-morrow Dinkie will probably want to be an aeronaut, and the next day a cowboy, and the next an Indian scout, for I notice that his enthusiasms promptly conform to the stimuli with which he chances to be confronted. Last Sunday he asked me to read Macaulay's *Horatius* to him. I could see, after doing so, that it was going to his head exactly as a second Clover-Club cocktail goes to the head of a sub-deb. On Tuesday, when I went out about sun-down to get him to help me gather the eggs, I found that he had made a sword by nailing a bit of stick across a slat from the hen-house, and also observed that he had possessed himself of my boiler-top. So I held back, slightly puzzled. But later on, hearing much shouting and clouting and banging of tin, I quietly investigated and found Dinkie in the corral-gate, holding it against all comers. So earnest was he about it, so rapt was he in that solemn business of warfare, that I decided to slip away without letting him see me. He was sixteen long centuries away from Casa Grande, at that moment. He was afar off on the banks of the Tiber, defending the Imperial City against Lars Porsena and his footmen. All Rome was at his back, cheering him on, and every time his hen-coop slat thumped that shredded old poplar gate-post some proud son of Tuscany bit the dust.

Sunday the Twenty-Fifth

Duncan, it's plain to see, is still in the doldrums. He is uncommunicative and moody and goes about his work with a listlessness which is more and more disturbing to me. He surprised his wife the other day by addressing her as "Lady Selkirk," for the simple reason, he later explained, that I propose to be monarch of all I survey, with none to dispute my domain. And a little later he further intimated that I was like a miser with a pot of gold, satisfied to live anywhere so long as my precious family-life could go clinking through my fingers.

That was last Sunday—a perfect prairie day—when I sat out on the end of the wagon-box, watching Poppsy and Dinkie. I sat in the warm sunlight, in a sort of trance, staring at those two children as they went about their solemn business of play. They impressed me as two husky and happy-bodied little beings and I remembered that whatever prairie-life had cost me, it had not cost me the health of my family. My two bairns had been free of those illnesses and infections which come to the city child, and I was glad enough to remember it. But I was unconscious of Dinky-Dunk's cynic eye on me as I sat there brooding over my chicks. When he spoke to me, in fact, I was thinking how odd it was that Josie Langdon, on the very day before her marriage, should have carried me down to the lower end of Fifth Avenue and led me into the schoolroom of the Church of the Ascension, and asked me to study Sorolla's *Triste Herencia* which hangs there.

I can still see that wonderful canvas where the foreshore of Valencia, usually so vivacious with running figures and the brightest of sunlight on dancing sails, had been made the wine-dark sea of the pagan questioner with the weight of immemorial human woe to shadow it. Josie had been asking me about marriage and children, for even she was knowing her more solemn moments in the midst of all that feverishly organized merriment. But I was surprised, when she slipped a hand through my arm, to see a tear run down her nose. So I looked up again at Sorolla's picture of the naked little cripples snatching at their moment's joy along the water's edge, at his huddled group of maimed and cast-off orphans trying to be happy without quite knowing how. I can still see the stunted little bodies, naked in sunlight that seemed revealing without being invigorating, clustered about the guardian figure of the tall old priest in black, the somberly benignant old figure that towered above the little wrecks on crutches and faced, as majestic as Millet's *Sower*, as austere and unmoved as Fate itself, a dark sea overhung by a dark sky. Sorolla was great in that picture, to my way of thinking. He was great in the manner in which he attunes nature to a human mood, in which he gives you the sunlight muffled, in some way, like the sunlight during a partial eclipse, and keys turbulence down to quietude, like the soft pedal that falls on a noisy street when a hearse goes by.

Josie felt it, and I felt it, that wordless thinning down of radiance, that mysterious holding back of warmth, until it seemed to strike a chill into the bones. It was the darker wing of Destiny hovering over man's head, deepening at the same time that it shadows the receding sky-line, so that even the memory of it, a thousand miles away, could drain the jocund blitheness out of the open prairie and give an air of pathos and solitude to my own children playing about my feet. Sorolla, I remembered, had little ones of his own. He *knew*. Life had taught him, and in teaching, had enriched his art. For the artist, after all, is the man who cuts up the loaf of his own heart, and butters it with beauty, and at tuppence a slice hands it to the hungry children of the world.

So when Dinky-Dunk laughed at me, for going into a trance over my own children, I merely smiled condoningly back at him. I felt vaguely sorry for him. He wasn't getting out of them what I was getting. He was being cheated, in some way, out of the very harvest for which he had sowed and waited. And if he had come to me, in that mood of relapse, if he had come to me with the slightest trace of humility, with the slightest touch of entreaty, on his face, I'd have hugged his salt-and-peppery old head to my bosom and begged to start all over again with a clean slate....

Gershom and I get along much better than I had expected. There's nothing wrong with the boy except his ineradicable temptation to impart to you his gratuitous tidbits of information. I can't object, of course, to Gershom having a college education: what I object to is his trying to give me one. I don't mind his wisdom, but I do hate to see him tear the whole tree of knowledge up by the roots and floor one with it. He has just informed me that there are estimated to be 30,000,000,000,000 red blood corpuscles in this body of mine, and I made him blink by solemnly challenging him to prove it. Quite frequently and quite sternly, too, he essays to correct my English. He reproved me for saying: "Go to it, Gershom!" And he declared I was in error in saying "The goose hangs high," as that was merely a vulgar corruption for "The goose whangs high," the "whanging" being the call of the wild geese high in the air when the weather is settled and fair. We live and learn!

But I can't help liking this pedagogic old Gershom who takes himself and me and all the rest of the world so seriously. I like him because he shares in my love for Dinkie and stands beside Peter himself in the fondly foolish belief that Dinkie has somewhere the hidden germ of greatness in him. Not that my boy is one of those precocious little bounders who are so precious in the eyes of their parents and so odious to the eyes of the rest of the world. He is a large-boned boy, almost a rugged-looking boy, and it is only I, knowing him as I do, who can fathom the sensibilities housed in that husky young body. There is a misty broodiness in his eyes which leaves them indescribably lovely to me as I watch him in his moments of raptness. But that look doesn't last long, for Dinkie can be rough in play and at times rough in speech, and deep under the crust of character I imagine I see traces of his Scottish father in him. I watch with an eagle eye for any outcroppings of that Caledonian-granite strain in his make-up. I inspect him as Chinkie used to inspect his fruit-trees for San José scale, for if there is any promise of hardness or cruelty there I want it killed in the bud.

But I don't worry as I used to, on that score. He may be rough-built, but moods cluster thick about him, like butterflies on a shelf of broken rock. And he is both pliable and responsive. I can shake him, when in the humor, by the mere telling of a story. I can control his color, I can excite him and exalt him, and bring him to the verge of tears, if I care to, by the mere tone of my voice as I read him one of his favorite tales out of one of Peter's books. But I shrink, in a way, from toying with those feelings. It seems brutal, cruel, merciless. For he is, after all, a delicate instrument, to be treated with delicacy. The soul of him must be kept packed away, like a violin, in its case of reserve well-padded with discretion. Two things I see in him: tenseness and beauty. And these are things which are lost, with rough handling. He shrinks away from brutality. Always, when he came to the picture of Samson pulling down the pillars of the temple, in Whinstane Sandy's big old illustrated Bible, he used to cover with one small hand a certain child on the temple steps as though to protect to the last that innocent one from the falling columns and cornices.

But I'm worried, at times, about Dinky-Dunk's attitude toward the boy. There are ways in which he demands too much from the child. His father is often unnecessarily rough in his play with him, seeming to take a morose delight in goading him to the breaking point and then lamenting his lack of grit, edging him on to the point of exasperation and then heaping scorn on him for his weakness. More than once I've seen his father actually hurt him, although the child was too proud to admit it. Dinky-Dunk, I think, really wants his boy to be a bigger figure in the world than his dad. Milord's a middle-aged man now and knows his limitations. He has realized just how high the supremest high-water mark of his life will stand. And being human, he must nurse his human regrets over his failures in life. So now he wishes to see his thwarted powers come to fuller fruit in his offspring. I'm afraid he'd even run the risk of sacrificing the boy's happiness for the sake of knowing Dinkie's wagon was to be hitched to the star of success. For I know my husband well enough to realize that he has always hankered after worldly success, that his god, if he had any, has always been the god of Power. I, too, want to see my son a success. But I want him to be happy first. I want to see him get some of the things I've been cheated out of, that I've cheated myself out of. That's the only way now I can get even with life. I can't live my own days over again. But I can catch at the trick of living them over again in my Dinkie.

Thursday the Twenty-Ninth

We have arrived at an armistice, Dinky-Dunk and I. It was forced on us, for things couldn't have gone on in the old intolerable manner. Dinky-Dunk, I fancy, began to realize that he hadn't been quite fair, and started making oblique but transparent enough efforts at appeasement. When he sat down close beside me, and I moved away, he said in a spirit of exaggerated self-accusation: "I'm afraid I've got a peach-stain on my reputation!" I retorted, at that, that she had never impressed me as much of a peach. Whereupon he merely laughed, as though it were a joke out of a Midnight Revue. Then he clipped a luridly illustrated advertisement of a nerve-medicine out of his newspaper and pinned it on my bedroom door, after I had ignored his tentative knock thereon the night before. The picture showed an anemic and woebegone couple haggling and shaking their fists at each other, while a large caption announced that "Thousands of Married Folks Lead a Cat and Dog Life—Are Cross, Crabbed and Grumpy!"—all of which could be obviated if they used Oxygated Iron.

What made it funny, of course, was the ridiculousness of the drawing. Then Dinky-Dunk, right before the blushing Gershom, accused me of being a love-piker. I could sniff which way the wind was blowing, but I sat tight. Then, to cap the climax, my husband announced that he had something for me which was surely going to melt my mean old prairie heart. And late that afternoon he came trundling up to Casa Grande with nothing more nor less than an old prairie-schooner.

It startled me, when I first caught sight of it. But its acquisition was not so miraculous as it might have seemed. Dinky-Dunk, who is a born dickerer, has been trading some of his ranch-stock for town-lots on the outskirts of Buckhorn. On the back of one of these lots stood a tumble-down wooden building, and hidden away in this building was the prairie-schooner. Something about it had caught his fancy, so he had insisted that it be included in the deal. And home he brought it, with Tithonus and Tumble-Weed yoked to its antique tongue and his own Stetsoned figure high on the driving seat. They had told Dinky-Dunk it wasn't a really-truly authentic prairie-schooner, since practically all of the trekking north of the Fiftieth Parallel has been done by means of the Red River cart. But Dinky-Dunk, after looking more carefully over the heavy-timbered running-gear and the cumbersome iron-work, and discovering even the sturdy hooks under its belly from which the pails and pots of earlier travelers must have hung, concluded that it was one of the genuine old-timers, one of the "Murphies" once driven by a "bull-whacker" and drawn by "wheelers" and "pointers."

Where it originally came from, Heaven only knows. But it had been used, five years before, for a centenary procession in the provincial capital and had emerged into the open again last summer for a town-booming *Rodeo* twenty miles down the steel from Buckhorn. It looked like the dinosaur skeleton in the Museum of Natural History, with every vestige of its tarpaulin top gone. But Whinnie has already sewed together a canvas covering for its weather-beaten old roof-ribs, and has put clean wheat-straw in its box-bottom, so that it makes a kingly place for my two kiddies to play. I even spotted Dinkie, enthroned high on the big driving-seat, with a broken binder-whip in his hand, imagining he was one of the original Forty-Niners pioneering along the unknown frontiers of an unknown land. I could see him duck at imaginary arrows and frenziedly defend his family from imaginary Sioux with an imaginary musket. And I stood beside it this morning, dreaming of the adventures it must have lumbered through, of the freight it must have carried and the hopes it must have ferried as it once crawled westward along the floor of the world, from water-hole to lonely water-hole. I've been wondering if certain perforations in its side-boards can be bullet-holes and if certain dents and abrasions in its timbers mean the hostile arrows of skulking Apaches when women and children crouched low behind the ramparts of this tiny wooden fortress. I can't help picturing what those women and children had to endure, and how trivial, after all, are our puny hardships compared with theirs.

And I don't intend to dwell on those hardships. I'm holding out the hand of compromise to my fellow-trekker. Existence is only a prairie-schooner, and we have to accommodate ourselves to it. And I thank Heaven now that I can see things more clearly and accept them more quietly. That's a lesson Time teaches us. And Father Time, after all, has to hand us something to make up for so mercilessly permitting us to grow old. It leaves us more tolerant. We're not allowed to demand more life, but we can at least ask for more light. So I intend to be cool-headedly rational about it all. I'm going to keep Reason on her throne. I'm going to be a bitter-ender, in at least one thing: I'm going to stick to my Dinky-Dunk to the last ditch. I'm going to patch up the old top and forget the old scars. For we're in the same schooner, and we must make the most of it. And if I have to eat my pot of honey on the grave of all our older hopes, I'm at least going to dig away at that pot until its bottom is scraped clean. I'm going to remain the neck-or-nothing woman I once prided myself on being. I'm even going to overlook Dinky-Dunk's casual cruelty in announcing, when I half-jokingly inquired why he preferred other women to his own Better-Half, that no horse eats hay after being turned out to fresh grass. I'm going on, I repeat, no matter what happens. I'm going on to the desperate end, like my own Dinkie with the chocolate-cake when I warned him he'd burst if he dared to eat another piece and he responded: "Then pass the cake, Mummy—and everybody stand back!"

Tuesday the Fourth

Sursum corda is the word—so here goes! I am determined to be blithe and keep the salt of humor sprinkled thick across the butter-crock of concession. Dinky-Dunk watches me with a guarded and wary eye and Pauline Augusta does not always approve of me. Yesterday, when I got on Briquette and made that fire-eater jump the two rain-barrels put end to end Dinky-Dunk told me I was too old to be taking a chance like that. So I promptly and deliberately turned a somersault on the prairie-sod, just to show him I wasn't the old lady he was trying to make me out. Gershom, who'd just got back with the children and was unhitching Calamity Kate, retreated with his eyebrows up, toward the stable. And on the youthful face of Pauline Augusta I saw nothing but pained incredulity touched with reproof, for Poppsy is not a believer in the indecorous. She has herself staidly intimated that she'd prefer the rest of the family to address her as "Pauline Augusta" instead of "Poppsy" which still so unwittingly creeps into our talk. So hereafter we must be more careful. For Pauline Augusta can already sew a fine seam and array her seven dolls with a preciseness and neatness which is to be highly commended.

On Saturday, when we motored into Buckhorn for supplies, I escorted Pauline Augusta to Hunk Granby, the town barber, to have her hair cut Dutch. Her lip quivered and she gave every indication of an outbreak, for she was mortally afraid of that strange man and his still stranger clipping-machine. But I spotted a concert-guitar on a bench at the back of Hunk's emporium and as it was the noon-hour and there was no audience, I rendered a jazz *obbligato* to the snip of the scissors.

"Say, Birdie, you'll sure have me buck and wing dancin' if you keep that up!" remarked the man of the shears. I merely smiled and gave him *Texas Tommy, cum gusto*, whereupon he acknowledged he was having difficulty in making his feet behave. We became quite a companionable little family, in fact, as the bobbing process went on, and when Dinky-Dunk called for us as he'd promised he was patently scandalized to find his superannuated old soul-mate sight-reading *When Katy Couldn't Katy Wouldn't*—it was a new one to me—in the second ragged plush shaving-chair of a none too clean barber-shop festooned with lithographs which would have made old Anthony Comstock turn in his grave. But you have to be feathered to the toes like a ptarmigan in this northern country so that rough ways and rough winds can't strike a chill into you. The barber, in fact, refused to take any money for Dutching my small daughter's hair, proclaiming that the music was more than worth it. But my husband, with a dangerous light in his eye, insisted on leaving four bits on the edge of the shelf loaded down with bottled beautifiers, and escorted us out to the muddy old devil-wagon where Dinkie sat awaiting us.

"Dinky-Dunk," I said with a perfectly straight face as we climbed in, "what is it gives me such a mysterious influence over men?"

Instead of answering me, he merely ground his gears as though they had been his own teeth. So I repeated my question.

"Why don't you ask that school-teacher of yours?" he demanded.

"But what," I inquired, "has Gershom got to do with it?"

He turned and inspected me with such a pointed stare that we nearly ran into a Bain wagon full of bagged grain.

"You don't suppose I can't see that that beanpole's fallen in love with you?" he rudely and raucously challenged.

"Why, I feel exactly like a mother to that poor boy," I innocently protested.

"Mother nothing!" snorted my lord and master. "Any fool could see he's going mushy on you!"

I pretended to be less surprised than I really was, but it gave me considerable to think over. My husband was wrong, in a way, but no woman feels bad at the thought that somebody is fond of her. It's nice to know there's a heart or two at which one can still warm one's outstretched hands. The short-cut to ruin, with a man, is the knowledge that women are fond of him. But let a woman know that she is not unloved and she walks the streets of Heaven, to say nothing of nearly breaking her neck to make herself worthy of those transporting affections.

But I soon had other things to think of, that afternoon, for Dinkie and I had a little secret shopping to do. And in the midst of it I caught the familiar tawny look which occasionally comes into my man-child's eyes. It's the look of dreaming, the look of brooding wildness where some unknown Celtic great-great-grandfather of a great-great-grandfather stirs in his moorland grave like a collie-dog in his afternoon sleep. And it all arose out of nothing more than a blind beggar sitting on an upturned nail-keg at the edge of the sidewalk and rather miraculously playing a mouth-organ and a guitar at one and the same time. The guitar was a dog-eared old instrument that had most decidedly seen better days, stained and bruised and greasy-looking along the shank. The mouth-organ was held in position by two wires that went about the beggar's neck, to leave his hands free for strumming on the larger instrument. The music he made was simple enough, rudimentary old waltz-tunes and plaintive old airs that I hadn't heard for years. But I could see it go straight to the head of my boy. His intent young face took on the fierce emptiness of a Barres lion overlooking some time-worn desert. He forgot me, and he forgot the shopping that had kept him awake about half the night, and he forgot Buckhorn and the fact that he was a small boy on the streets of a bald little prairie town. He was thousands of years and thousands of miles away from me. He was a king's son in Babylon, commanding the court-musicians to make sweet discourse for him. He was Saul harkening to David. He was a dreamy-eyed Pict listening to music wafted at dusk from a Roman camp about which helmeted sentries paced. He was a medieval prince, falsely imprisoned, leaning from dark and lonely towers to catch the strains of some wandering troubadour from his native Southlands. He was a Magyar chieftain listening to the mountain-side music of valleyed goat-herders with a touch of madness to it. It engulfed him and entranced him and awoke ancestral tom-toms in his blood. And I waited beside him until the afternoon sunlight grew thinner and paler and my legs grew tired, for I knew that his hungry little soul was being fed. His eye met mine, when it was all over, but he had nothing to say. I could see, however, that he had been stirred to the depths,—and by a tin mouth-organ and a greasy-sided guitar!

To-night I found Dinkie poring over the pictures in my Knight edition of Shakespeare. He seemed especially impressed, as I stopped and looked over his shoulder, by a steel engraving of Gérôme's *Death of Cæsar*, where the murdered emperor lies stretched out on the floor of the Forum, now all but empty, with the last of the Senators crowding out through the door. Two of the senatorial chairs are overturned, and Cæsar's throne lies face-down on the dais steps. So Dinkie began asking questions about a drama which he could not quite comprehend. But they were as nothing to the questions he asked when he turned to another of the Gérôme pictures, this one being the familiar old *Cleopatra and Cæsar*. He wanted to know why the lady hadn't more clothes on, and why the big black man was hiding down behind her, and what Cæsar was writing a letter for, and why he was looking at the lady the way he did. So, glancing about to make sure that Dinky-Dunk was within ear-shot, I did my best to explain the situation to little Dinkie.

"Cæsar, my son, was a man who set out in the world to be a great conqueror. But when he got quite bald, as you may see by the picture, and had reached middle age, he forgot about being a great conqueror. He even forgot about being so comfortably middle-aged and that it was not easy for a man of his years to tumble gracefully into love, for those romantic impulses, my son, are associated more with irresponsible youth and are apt to be called by rather an ugly name when they occur in advanced years. But Cæsar fell in love with the lady you see in the picture, whose name was Cleopatra and who was one of the greatest man-eaters that ever came out of Egypt. She had a weakness for big strong men, and although certain authorities have claimed that she was a small and hairy person with a very uncertain temper, she undoubtedly set a very good table and made her gentlemen friends very comfortable, for Cæsar stayed feasting and forgetting himself for nearly a year with her. It must have been very pleasant, for Cæsar loved power, and intended to be one of the big men of his time. But the lady also loved power, and was undoubtedly glad to see that she could make Cæsar forget about going home, though it was too bad that he forgot, for always, even after he had lived to write about all the great things he had done in the world, people remembered more about his rather absurd infatuation for the lady than about all the battles he had won and all the prizes he had captured. And the lady, of course—"

But I was interrupted at this point. And it was by Dinky-Dunk.

"Oh, hell!" he said as he flung down his paper and strode out into the other room. And those exits, I remembered, were getting to be a bit of a habit with my harried old Diddums.

Sunday the Fifth

The Day of Rest seems to be the only day left to me now for my writing. There are no idlers in the neighborhood of Casa Grande. The days are becoming incredibly long, but they still seem over-short for all there is to do. The men are much too busy on the land to give material thought to any thing so womanish as a kitchen-garden. So I have my own garden to see to. And sometimes I work there until I'm almost ready to drop. On a couple of nights, recently, when it came watering-time, even these endless evenings had slipped into such darkness that I could scarcely see the plants I was so laboriously irrigating by hand. It wasn't until the water turned the soil black that the growing green stood pallidly out against the mothering dark earth.... But it is delightful work. I really love it. And I love to see things growing. After the bringing up of a family, the bringing up of a garden surely comes next.

Yet too much work, I find, can make tempers a trifle short. I spoke rather sharply to Dinky-Dunk yesterday regarding the folly of leaving firearms about the house where children can reach them. And he was equally snappy as he flung his ugly old Colt in its ugly old holster up over the top corner of our book-cabinet. So, to get even with him, when Dinkie came in with some sort of wide-petaled field-flower and asked if I didn't want my fortune told, I announced I rather fancied it was pretty well told already.... Scotty, by the way, now follows Dinkie to school and waits outside and comes loping home with him again. And my two bairns have a new and highly poetic occupation. It is that of patiently garnering youthful potato-bugs and squashing the accumulated harvest between two bricks.

Sunday the Twelfth

I have been examining Gershom with a more interested eye. And when he changed color, under that inspection, I apologized for making him blush. And as that only added to his embarrassment, I artlessly asked him what a blush really was. That, of course, was throwing the rabbit straight back into the brier-patch, as far as Gershom was concerned. For he promptly and meticulously informed me that a blush was a miniature epilepsy, a vasomotor impulse leading to the dilation or constriction of the facial blood-vessels, some psychologists even claiming the blush to be a vestigial survival of the prehistoric flight-effort of the heart, coming from the era of marriage by capture, when to be openly admired meant imminent danger.

"That isn't a bit pretty," I told Gershom. "It's as horrid as what my husband said about handshaking originating in man's desire to be dead sure his gentleman friend didn't have a knife up his sleeve, for use before the greeting was over. It would have been so much nicer, Gershom, if you could have told me that the first blush was born on the same day as the first kiss."

"Kissing," that youth solemnly informed me, "was quite unknown to primitive man. It evolved, in fact, out of the entirely self-protective practice of smelling, to determine the health of a prospective mate, though this in turn evolved into the ceremonial habit of the rubbing together of noses, which is still the form of affectionate salutation largely prevalent among the natives of the South Sea Islands."

"What a perfectly horrible origin for such a heavenly pastime," I just as solemnly announced to Gershom, who studied me with a stern and guarded eye, and having partaken of his eleventh flap-jack, escaped to the stable and the matutinal task of harnessing Calamity Kate.

Sunday the Second

Summer is here, in earnest, and the last few days have been hot and windless. School is over, for the next eight weeks, and I shall have my kiddies close beside me. Gershom, after a ten-day trip down to Minneapolis for books and clothes, is going to come back to Casa Grande and help Dinky-Dunk on the land, as long as the holidays last. He thinks it will build him up a bit. He is also solemnly anxious to study music. He feels it would round out his accomplishments, which, he acknowledged, have threatened to become overwhelmingly scientific. So I'm to give Gershom music lessons in exchange for his tutoring Dinkie. They will be rather awful, I'm afraid, for Gershom has about as much music in his honest old soul as Calamity Kate. I may not teach him much. But all the time, I know, I will be learning a great deal from Gershom. He informed me, last night, that he had carefully computed that the Bible mentioned nineteen different precious stones, one hundred and four trees or plants, six metals, thirty-five animals, thirty-nine birds, six fishes, twenty insects, and eleven reptiles.

As I've already said, summer is here. But it doesn't seem to mean as much to me as it used to, for my interests have been taken away from the land and more and more walled up about my family. Dinky-Dunk's grain, however, has come along satisfactorily, and there is every promise of a good crop. Yet this entirely fails to elate my husband. Every small mischance is a sort of music-cue nowadays to start him singing about the monotony of prairie-life. Ranching, he protests, isn't the easy game it used to be, now that cattle can't be fattened on the open range and now that wheat itself is so much lower in price. One has to work for one's money, and watch every dollar. And my Diddums keeps railing about the government doing so little for the farmer and driving the men off the land into the cities. He has fallen into the habit of protesting he can see nothing much in life as a back-township hay-tosser and that all the big chances are now in the big centers. I had been hoping that this was a new form of spring-fever which would eventually work its way out of his system. But I can see now that the matter is something more mental than physical. He hasn't lost his strength, but he has lost his driving power. He is healthy enough, Heaven knows. Indeed, he impresses me as being a bit too much that way, for he has quite lost his old-time lean and hungry look and betrays a tendency to take on a ventral contour unmistakably aldermanic. He may be heavy, but he is hard-muscled and brown as an old meerschaum. There is a canker, however, somewhere about the core of his heart. And I can see him more clearly than I used to. He is a strong man, but he is a strong man without earnestness. And being such, I vaguely apprehend in him some splendid failure. For the wings that soar to success in this world are plumed with faith and feathered with conviction.

It did not surprise me this morning when Dinky-Dunk announced that he felt a trifle stale and suggested that the family take a holiday on Tuesday and trek out to Dead-Horse Lake for the day. We're to hitch Tumble-Weed and Tithonus to the old prairie-schooner—for we'll be taking side-trails where no car could venture—and pike off for a whole blessed day of care-free picnicking. So to-morrow Struthers and I will be solemnly busy in the kitchen concocting suitable dishes to be taken along in the old grub-box, and when that is over we'll patch together something in the form of bathing-suits, for there'll be a chance for a dip in the slough-water, and our kiddies have arrived at an age imposing fit and proper apparel on their sadly pagan but chastened parents.

Wednesday the Fifth

We have had our day at Dead-Horse Lake, but it wasn't the happy event I had anticipated. Worldly happiness, I begin to feel, usually dies a-borning: it makes me think of wistaria-bloom, for invariably one end is withering away before the other end is even in flower. At any rate, we were off early, the weather was perfect, and the sky was an inverted tureen of lazulite blue. Dinkie drove the team part of the way, his dad smoked beside him up on the big driving-seat, and I raised my voice in song until Pauline Augusta fell asleep and had to be bedded down in the wagon-straw and covered with a blanket.

Dead-Horse Lake is really a slough, dolorously named because a near-by rancher once lost eight horses therein, the foolish animals wandering out on ice that was too thin to hold them up.

We were hungry by the time we had hobbled out our teams and gathered wood and made a fire. And after dinner Dinky-Dunk fell asleep and the children and I tried to weave a willow basket, which wasn't a success. Poppsy, in fact, cut her finger with her pater's pocket-knife and because of this physical disability declined to don her bathing-suit when we made ready for the water.

The slough-water was enticingly warm, under the hot July sun, and we ventured in at the west end where a firmer lip of sand and alkali gave us footing. And I enjoyed the swim, although Dinky-Dunk made fun of my improvised bathing-suit. It seemed like old times, to bask lazily in the sun and float about on my back with my fingers linked under my head. My lord and master even acknowledged that my figure wasn't so bad as he had expected, in a lady of my years. I splashed him for that, and he dove for my ankles, and nearly drowned me before I could get away.

It was all light-hearted enough, until Dinky-Dunk happened to notice that Dinkie wasn't enjoying the water as an able-bodied youngster ought. The child, in fact, was afraid of it—which was only natural, remembering what a land-bird he had been all his life. His father, apparently, decided to carry him out and give him a swimming-lesson.

I was on shore by this time, trying to sun out my sodden mop of hair, which I had fondly imagined I could keep dry. I heard Dinkie's cry as his father captured him, and I called out to Dinky-Dunk, through my combed out tresses, to have a heart.

Dinky-Dunk called back that the Indian way, after all, was the only way to teach a youngster. I didn't give much thought to the matter until the two of them were out in deeper water and I heard Dinkie's scream of stark terror. It came home to me then that the Indian method in such things was to toss the child into deep water and leave him there to struggle for his life.

Dinky-Dunk, I suppose, hadn't intended to do quite that. But the boy was naturally terrified at being carried out beyond his depth, and when I looked up I could see his bony little body struggling to free itself. That timidity, I take it, angered the boy's father. And he intended to cure it. He was doing his best, in fact, to fling the clutching and clawing little body away from him when I heard those repeated short screams of horror and promptly took a hand in the matter. Something snapped in my skull, and I saw red. I hated my husband for what he was doing. I hated him for the mere thought that he could do it. And I hated him for calling out that this was what people got by mollycoddling their children.

But that didn't stop me. I made for Dinky-Dunk like a hundred-weight of wildcats. I went through the water like a hell-diver, and without quite knowing what I was doing I got hold of him and tried to garrote him. I don't remember what I said, but I have a hazy idea it was not the most ladylike of language. He stared at me, as I tore Dinkie away from him, stared at me with a hard and slightly incredulous eye. For I'm afraid I was ready to fight with my teeth and nails, if need be, and I suppose my expression wasn't altogether angelic. We were both shaking, at any rate, when we got back to dry land. Dinky-Dunk stood staring at us, for a silent moment or two, with a look of black disgust on his wet face. I'm even afraid it was something more than disgust. Then he strode away and proceeded to dress on the other side of the prairie-schooner, without so much as a second look at us. And then he went off for the horses, absenting himself a quite unnecessary length of time. But I took advantage of that to have a talk with Dinkie.

"Dinkie," I said, "you and I are going to walk out into that water, and this time you're not going to be afraid!"

I could see his eye searching mine, although he did not speak.

I put one hand on the wet tangle of his hair.

"Will you come?" I asked him.

He took a deep breath. Then he looked at the slough-water. Then he looked back into my eyes.

"Yes," he said, though I noticed his lips were not so red as usual.

So side by side and hand in hand the two of us walked out into Dead-Horse Lake. His eyes questioned me, once, as the water came up about his armpits. But he shut his teeth tight and made no effort to draw back. I could see the involuntary spasms of his chest as that terrifying flood closed in about his little body, yet he was ready enough to show me he wasn't a coward. And when I saw that he had met and faced his ordeal I turned him about and led him quietly back to land. We were both prouder and happier for what had just happened. We didn't even need to talk about it, for each knew that the other understood. What still disturbs me, though, is something not in my boy's make-up, but in my own. During the long and silent drive home I noticed a mark on my husband's neck. And I was the termagant who must have put it there, though I have no memory of doing so. But from it I realize that I haven't the control over myself every civilized and self-respecting woman should have. I begin to see that I can't altogether trust myself where my female-of-the-species affections are involved. I'm no better, I'm afraid, than the Bengal tigress which Dinky-Dunk once intimated I was, the Bengal tigress who will battle so unreasoningly for her offspring. It may be natural in mothers, whether they wear fur or feathers or lisle-thread stockings—but it worries me. I was an engine running wild. And when you run wild you are apt to run into catastrophe.

Friday the Seventh

Dinky-Dunk is on his dignity. He has put a fence around himself to keep me at a distance, the same as he puts a fence around his haystacks to keep off the cattle. We are coolly polite to each other, but that is as far as it goes. There is something radically wrong with this home, as a home, but I seem helpless to put the matter right. It's about all I have left, in this life of mine, but I'm in some way failing in my duty as a house-wife. "Home" is a beautiful word, and home-life should be beautiful. Any sacrifice and any concession a woman is willing to make to keep that home, and to keep ugliness out of it, ought to be well considered by the judge of her final destinies. I'm ready to do my part, but I don't know where to begin. I'm depressed by a teasing sense of frustration, not quite tangible enough to fight, like cobwebs across your face. It's not easy to carry around the milk of human kindness after they've pretty well kicked the bottom out of your can!

Torrid and tiring are these almost endless summer days. But it's what the grain needs, and who am I to look this gift-horse of heat in the face. Yet there are two things, I must confess, in which the prairie is sadly lacking. One is trees; and the other is shade, the cool green sun-filtering shade of woodlands where birds can sing and mossy little brooks can babble. I've been longing all day for just an hour up in an English cherry tree, with the pectoral smell of the leaves against my face and the chance of eating at least half my own weight of fresh fruit. But even in the matter of its treelessness, I'm told, the prairie is reforming. There are men living who remember when there were no trees west of Brandon, except in the coulées and the river-bottoms. Now that fire no longer runs wild, however, the trees are creeping in, mile by mile and season by season. Already the eastern line of natural bush country reaches to about ten miles from Regina two hundred miles west. Oxbow and Estevan, Dinky-Dunk once told me, had no trees whatever when first settled, though much of that country now has a comfortable array of bluffs. And forestry, of course, is giving nature a friendly push along, in the matter. In the meantime, we have to accommodate ourselves to the conditions that prevail, just as the birds of the air must do. Here the haughty crow of the east is compelled to nest in the low willows of the coulée and raise its young within hand-reach of mother earth. Like our women, it can enjoy very little privacy of family life. The only thing that saves us and the crows, I suppose, is that the men-folks of this country are too preoccupied with their own ends to go around bird-nesting. They are too busy to break up homes, either in willow-tops or women's hearts.... I ought to be satisfied. But I've been dogged, this last day or two, by a longing to be scudding in a single-sticker off Orienta Point again or to motor-cruise once more along the Sound in a smother of spray.

Thursday the Thirteenth

Dinky-Dunk has been called to Calgary on business. It sounds simple enough, in these Unpretentious Annals of an Unloved Worm, but I can't help feeling that it marks a trivially significant divide in the trend of things. It depresses me more than I can explain. My depression, I imagine, comes mostly from the manner in which Duncan went. He was matter-of-fact enough about it all, but I can't get rid of the impression that he went with a feeling very much like relief. His manner, at any rate, was not one to invite cross-examination, and he insisted, to the end, on regarding his departure as an every-day incident in the life of a preoccupied rancher. So I caught my cue from him, and was as quiet about it all as he could have wished. But under the crust was the volcano....

The trouble with the tragedies of real life is that they are never clear-cut. It takes art to weave a selvage about them or fit them into a frame. But in reality they're as ragged and nebulous as wind-clouds. The days drag on into weeks, and the weeks into months, and life on the surface seems to be running on, the same as before. There's the same superficial play of all the superficial old forces, but in the depths are dangers and uglinesses and sullen bombs of emotional TNT we daren't even touch!

Heigho! I nearly forgot my *sursum-corda* rôle. And didn't old Doctor Johnson say that peevishness was the vice of narrow minds? So here's where we tighten up the belt a bit. But we humans, who come into the world alone, and go out of it alone, are always hungering for companionship which we can't quite find. Our souls are islands, with a coral-reef of reserve built up about them. Last night, when I was patching some of Gershom's undies for him, I wickedly worked an arrow-pierced heart, in red yarn, on one leg of his B.V.D.'s. This morning, I noticed, his eye evaded mine and there was marked constraint in his manner. I even begin to detect unmistakable signs of nervousness in him when we happen to be alone together. And during his last music lesson there was a *vibrata* of emotion in his voice which made me think of an April frog in a slough-end.

Even my little Dinkie, day before yesterday, asked me if I'd mind not bathing him any more. He explained that he thought he could manage very nicely by himself now. It seemed trivial enough, and yet, in a way, it was momentous. I am to be denied the luxury of tubbing my own child. I, who always loved even the smell of that earthy and soil-grubbing young body, who could love it when it wasn't any too clean and could glory in its musky and animal-like odors as well as the satin-shine of the light on its well-soaped little ribs, must now stand aside before the reservations of sex. It makes me feel that I've reached still another divide on the continent of motherhood.

This afternoon, when I wandered into the study, I observed Dinkie stooping over a Chesterfield pillow with his right hand upraised in a perplexingly dramatic manner. He turned scarlet when he saw me standing there watching him. But the question in my eyes did not escape him.

"I was pr'tendin' to be King Arthur when he found out Guinevere was in love with Launcelot," he rather lamely explained as he walked away to the window and stood staring out over the prairie. But for the life of me I can't understand what should have turned his thoughts into that particular channel of romance. Those are matters with which the young and the innocent should have nothing to do. They are matters, in fact, which it behooves even the old and the wary to eschew.

Sunday the Sixteenth

It seems strange, in such golden summer weather, that every man and woman and child on this sunbathed footstool of God shouldn't be sanely and supremely happy.... My husband, I am glad to say, is once more back in his home. And I have been realizing, the last few days, that home is an empty and foolish place without its man about. It's a ship without a captain, a clan without a chief. Yet I found it both depressing and humbling to be brought once more face to face with that particular fact.

Dinky-Dunk, on the other hand, has come back with both an odd sense of elation and an odd sense of estrangement. He has taken on a vague something which I find it impossible to define. He is blither and at the same time he is more solemnly abstracted. And he protests that his journey was a success.

"I'm going to ride two horses, from now on," he announced to me this morning. "I've got my chance and I'm going to grab it. I've swapped my Buckhorn lots for some inside Calgary stuff and I'm lumping everything that's left of my Coast deal for a third-interest in those Barcona coal-fields. There's a quarter of a million waiting there for the people with money enough to swing it. And I'm going to edge in while it's still open."

"But is it possible to ride two horses?" I asked, waywardly depressed by all this new-found optimism.

"It's *got* to be possible, until we find out which horse is the better traveler," announced Dinky-Dunk. Then he added, without caring to meet my eye: "And I can't say I see much promise of action out of this particular end of the team."

I must have flamed red, at that speech, for I thought at the moment he was referring to me. It was only after I'd turned the thing over in my mind, as I helped Struthers put together our new butter-worker, that I saw he really referred to Casa Grande. But my husband knows I will never part with this ranch. He will never be so foolish as to ask me to do that. Yet one thing is plain. His heart is no longer here. He will stick to this prairie farm of ours only for what he can get out of it.

Dinkie warmed the cockles of my heart by telling me this afternoon when we were out salting the horses that he never wanted to go away from Casa Grande and his mummy. The child, I imagine, had overheard some of this morning's talk. He put his arm around my knees and hugged me tight. And I could see the tawny look come into his hazel eyes speckled with brown.

My Dinkie is a prairie child. His soul is not a cramped little soul, but has depth and wideness and undiscerned mysteries.

Sunday the Thirtieth

Two weeks have slipped by. Two weeks have gone, and left no record of their going. But a prairie home is a terribly busy one, at times, and it's idleness that leads to the ink-pot. I'm still trying to make the best of a none too promising situation, and I'll thole through, as Whinstane Sandy puts it. After breakfast this morning, in fact, when Pauline Augusta was swept by one of those little gales of lonesomeness to which children and women are so mysteriously subjected, she climbed up into my lap and I rocked her on my shoulder as I might have rocked a baby. Dinky-Dunk wandered in and inspected that performance with a slightly satiric eye. So, resenting his expression, I promptly began to sing:

"Bye-bye, Baby Bunting,
Daddy's gone a-hunting,
To gather up a pile of tin
To wrap the Baby Bunting in!"

Dinky-Dunk, when the significance of this lilted flippancy of mine had sunk home, regarded me with a narrowed and none too friendly eye.

"Feeling a bit larkier than usual this morning, aren't you?" he inquired with what was merely a pretense at carelessness.

It was merely a pretense, I know, because we'd been over the old ground the night before, and the excursion hadn't added greatly to the happiness of either of us. Duncan, in fact, had rather horrified me by actually asking if I thought there was a chance of his borrowing eleven thousand dollars from Peter Ketley.

"We can't all trade on that man's generosity!" I cried, without giving much thought to the manner in which I was expressing myself.

"Oh, *that's* the way you feel about it!" retorted my husband. And I could see his face harden into Scotch granite. I could also see the look of perplexity in my small son's eyes as he stood studying his father.

"Is there anything abnormal in my feeling the way I do?" I parried, resenting the beetling brow of the Dour Man.

"Not if you regard him as your personal and particular fairy god-father," retorted my husband.

"I've no more reason for regarding him as that," I said as calmly as I could, "than I have for regarding him as a professional money-lender."

Duncan must have seen from my face that it would be dangerous to go much further. So he merely shrugged a flippant shoulder.

"They tell me he's got more money than he knows what to do with," he said with a heavy jocularity which couldn't quite rise.

"Then lightening his burdens is a form of charity we can scarcely afford to indulge in," I none too graciously remarked. And I saw my husband's face harden again.

"Well, I've got to have ready money and I've got to have it before the year's out," was his retort. He told me, when the air had cleared a little, that he'd have to open an office in Calgary as soon as harvesting was over. There was already too much at stake to take chances. Then he asked me if there were any circumstances under which I'd be willing to sell Casa Grande. And I told him, quite promptly and quite definitely, that there was none.

"Then how about the old Harris Ranch?" he finally inquired.

"But why should we sell that?" I asked. Alabama Ranch, I knew, was in my name, and I had always regarded it as a sort of nest-egg for the children. It was something put by for a rainy day, something to fall back on, if ill-luck ever overtook us again.

"Because I can double and treble every dollar we get out of it, inside of a year," averred Dinky-Dunk.

"But how am I to know that?" I contended, hating to seem hard and selfish and narrow in the teeth of an ambitious man's enterprise.

"You'd have to take my word for it," retorted my husband.

"But we've more than ourselves to consider," I contended, knowing he'd merely scoff at that harping on the old string of the children.

"That's why I intend to get out of this rut!" he cried with unexpected bitterness. And a few minutes later he made the suggestion that he'd deed Casa Grande entirely over to me if I'd consent to the sale of Alabama Ranch and give him a chance to swing the bigger plans he intended to swing.

The suggestion rather took my breath away. My rustic soul, I suppose, is stupidly averse to change. But I realize that when you travel in double-harness you can't forever pull back on your team-mate. So I've asked Dinky-Dunk to give me a few days to think the thing over.

Wednesday the Second

Casa Grande has had an invasion of visitors. It was precious old Percy and his Olga who blew in on us, after being swallowed up by the Big Silence for almost four long years. They came without warning, which is the free and easy way of the westerner, appearing in a mud-splattered and dust-covered Ford that had carried them blithely over two hundred and thirty miles of prairie trails. And with them they brought a quartet of rampageous young buckaroos who promptly turned our sedate homestead into a rodeo.

Percy himself is browner and stouter and more rubicund than I might have expected, with just a sprinkling of gray under his lopsided Stetson to announce that Time hasn't been standing still for any of us. But one would never have taken him for an ex-lunger. And there is a wholesomeness about the man, for all his quietness, which draws one to him. Olga herself still again impressed me as a Zorn etching come to life, as a Norse myth in petticoats, with the same old largeness of limb and the same old suggestion of sky-line vastnesses about her. She still looks as though the Lord had made her when the world was young and the women of Homer did their spinning in the sunlight. Some earlier touch of morning freshness is gone from her, it's true, for you can't move about with four little toddlers in your wake and still suggest the budding vine. But that morning freshness has been supplanted by a full and mellow noonday contentedness which is not without its placid appeal. To her husband, at any rate, she seems mysteriously perfect. He can still sit and stare at her with a startlingly uxorious eye. And she, in turn, bathes him in that pale lunar stare of meditative approval which says plainer than words just how much her "man" means to her.

Percy and his family stayed overnight with us and hit the trail again yesterday morning. An old friend of Percy's from Brasenose has taken a parish some forty odd miles south of Buckhorn—a parish, by the way, which ought to shake a little of the Oxford dreaminess out of his system— and Olga and her husband are "packing" their newly-arrived Toddler Number Four down to the new curate to have him christened.

We were all a bit shy and constrained, during our first hour together but this soon wore away. It wasn't long before Olga's offspring and mine were fraternizing together, over-running the bathroom tub and emptying our water-tank, and making a concerted attack on one of Dinky-Dunk's self-binders, which would have been dismantled in short order, if Percy hadn't gone out to investigate the cause of the sudden quiet.

"My boy loves everything with wheels," explained the proud Olga, in extenuation of her Junior's oil-blackened fingers.

That brought me up short, for I was on the point of making the same statement about my Dinkie. After thinking it over, in fact, I realized that *every* normal boy loves everything with wheels. And it began to dawn on me that there was nothing so extraordinary, after all, in my son's fondness for machinery. I began to see that he was merely one of a very wide-spread clan, when, an hour later, the entire excited six united in playing Indian about the haystacks, and kept it up until even the docile Pauline Augusta was driven to revolt against so persistently being the Pale-face captive. She announced that she was tired of being scalped. So, for variety's sake, the boys turned to riding and roping and hog-tying one another like the true little westerners they were, and many an imaginary brand was planted on many a bleating set of ribs.

But now they are gone, and I've been thinking a great deal about Olga. I fancy I have even been envying her a little. She's of that annealing softness which can rivet and hold a family together. I've even been trying to solace myself with the claim that she's a trifle ox-like in her make-up. But that is not being just to Olga. She makes a perfect wife. She is as tranquil-minded as summer moonlight on a convent-roof. She is as soft-spoken as a wind-harp swinging in an abbey door. She surrenders to the will of her husband and neither frets nor questions nor walks with discontent. I suppose she has a will of her own, packed somewhere away in that benignant big body of hers, but she never obtrudes it. She placidly awaits her time, as the bosom of the prairie awaits its harvesting. And I've been wondering if that really isn't the best type of woman for married life, the autumnally contented and pensively quiet woman who can remain unruffled by man and his meanderings.

I wasn't built according to that plan, and I suppose I've had to pay for it. I've just about concluded, in fact, that I would have been a hard nut for any man to crack. I've never been conspicuous for my efforts at self-obliteration. I've a temper that's as brittle as a squirrel bone. I'm too febrile and flightly, too chameleon-mooded and critical. The modern wife should be always a conservative. She should hold back her husband's impulses of nervous expenditure, conserving his tranquil-mindedness about the same as cotton-waste in a journal-box conserves oil. Heaven knows I started with theories enough—but I must be a good deal like old Schramm, that teacher of Heine's who was so busy inditing a study of Universal Peace that his boys had all the chance they could wish for pummeling one another. But I've been thinking, Reuben. And I'm going to see if I can't save what's left of the ship. I'm no Renaissance cherub on a cloudlet, but I'm going to knuckle down and see if I can't jibe along a little better with my old Dinky-

Dunk. I've decided to back off and give him his chance. If he's set on selling Alabama Ranch, on the terms he's mentioned, I'm not going to object. He's determined to make money, to advance. And I don't want to see him accusing me of lying down in the shafts!... What is more, I'm going out in the fields, when the push is on, to help stook the wheat. That may wear me down and make me a little more like Olga.

Thursday the Tenth

It's difficult to be a woman, as the over-sensitive Jean Christophe once remarked. Men are without those confounding emotions which women seem to be both cursed with and blessed with. When I announced to Dinky-Dunk my willingness to part with Alabama Ranch, he took it quite as a matter of course. He betrayed no tendency to praise me for my sacrifices, for my willingness to surrender to strangers the land which had once been our home, the acres on which we'd once been happy and heavy-hearted. He merely remarked that under the circumstances it seemed the most sensible thing to do. There's a one-horse lawyer in Buckhorn who has been asking about the Harris Ranch and Dinky-Dunk says he suspects this inquiring one has a client up his sleeve.

What I had looked forward to as a talk which might possibly beat down a few of the barriers of reserve between us proved a bit of a disappointment. My husband refused to accept me as a heroine. And on his way out, as ill-luck would have it, he stopped to observe Pauline Augusta struggling over a letter to her "Uncle Peter." It was a maiden effort along that line and she was dictating her messages to Dinkie, who, in turn, was laboriously and carefully inscribing them on my writing-pad, with a nose and a sympathetically working tongue not more than ten inches away from the paper. Pauline Augusta, in fact, had just proclaimed to her amanuensis that "we had a geese for dinner to-day" when her father stopped to size up the situation.

"To whom are you describing the home circle?" questioned Pauline Augusta's parent, with an intonation that didn't escape me.

"It's a letter to Uncle Peter," explained Dinkie's little sister. And I could see Duncan's face harden.

"It's funny my whole family should fall for that damned Quaker!" were the words he flung over his shoulder at me as he walked out of the room.

Tuesday the Fifth

School has started again. And it's a solemn business, this matter of planting wisdom in little prairie heads. Dinky-Dunk, who has been up to his ears in haying and is now watching his grain with a nervous eye, remarked that our offspring would be once more mingling with Mennonites and Swedes and Galicians and Ukrainians. I resented that speech, though I said nothing in reply to it. But I decided to investigate Gershom's school.

So yesterday afternoon I drove over in the car. I had a blow-out on the way, a blow-out which I had to patch up with my own hands, so I arrived too late to inspect Gershom conducting his classes. It was almost four, in fact, before I got there, so I pulled up beside the school-gate and sat waiting for the children to come out. And as I sat there in the car-seat, under a sky of unimaginable blue, with the prairie wind whipping my face, I couldn't help studying that bald little temple of learning which stood out so clear-cut in the sharp northern sunlight. It was a plain little frame building set in one corner of a rancher's half-section, an acre of land marked off by a wire fence where the two trails crossed, the two long trails that melted away in the interminable distance. It seemed a lonely little house of scholarship, with its playground worn so bare that even two months of idleness had given scant harborage for the seeds that wind and bird must have brought there. But as I stared at it it seemed to take on a dignity all its own, the dignity of a fixed and far-off purpose. It was the nest of a nation's greatness. It was the outpost of civilization. It was the advance-guard of pioneering man, driving the wilderness deeper and deeper into the North. It was life preparing wistfully for the future.

From it I heard a sudden shrill chorus of voices and the clatter of feet, and I knew that the day's work was over. I saw the children emerge, like bees out of a beehive, and loneliness no longer reigned over that bald yard in the betraying northern sunlight. Yet they were not riotous, those children confronting the wine-like air of the open. They were more subdued than I had looked for, since I could only too easily remember one of my earlier calls for Dinkie at noon, when I found the entire class turned out and riding a rancher's pig, a heavy brood-sow that had in some luckless moment wandered into the school-yard and had been chased and raced until it was too weary to resent a young barbarian mounting its broad back and riding thereon, to the shouts of the other boys and the shrill cries of the girls. But now, from my car-seat, I could see Gershom surrounded by a multi-colored group of little figures, as he stopped to fix a strap-buckle on the school-bag of one of his pupils. And as he stood there in the slanting afternoon sunlight surrounded by his charges he suddenly made me think of the tall old priest in Sorolla's *Triste Herencia* surrounded by his waifs. I caught the echo of something benignant and Lincoln-like from that raw-boned figure in the big-lensed eye-glasses and the clothes that didn't quite fit him. And my respect for Gershom went up like a Chinook-fanned thermometer. He took those children of his seriously. He liked them. He was trying to give them the best that was in him. And that solemn purpose saved him, redeemed him, ennobled his baldness just as it ennobled the baldness of the four-square little frame building behind him. I don't know why it was, but for some reason or other that picture of the northern prairie and the gaunt school-teacher surrounded by his pupils in the thinning afternoon sunlight became memorable to me. It photographed itself on my mind, not sharply, but softened with a fringing prism of feeling, like a picture taken with what camera-men call a "soft-focus." It touched my heart, in some way, and threatened to bring a choke up into my foolish old throat.

It was Pauline Augusta who saw me first. She came toward the car with her strapped school-books and her lunch-box in her hand and a prim little smile on her slightly freckled face. She impressed me as a startlingly shabby figure, in the old sealskin coat which I had made over for her, worn clean to the hide along the front, for even those early autumn days found a chill in the air when the sun began to get low. She had just climbed in beside me when I caught sight of Dinkie. I saw him come down the school-steps, stuffing something into the pocket of his reefer-jacket as he came. He looked startlingly tall, for a boy of his years. He seemed deep in thought. There was, indeed, an air of remoteness about him which for a moment rather startled me, an air of belonging, not to me, but to the world into which he was peering with such ardent young eyes. Then he caught sight of me, and at the same moment his face both lightened and brightened. He came toward the car quietly, none the less, and with that slightly sidewise twist of the body which overtakes him in his occasional moments of embarrassment, for it was plain that he stood averse to any undue display of emotion before his playmates. He merely said, "Hello, Mummy" and smiled awkwardly. But after he had climbed up into the car and wormed down between Pauline Augusta and me, and after I had tucked the old bear-robe about them and called out to Gershom that I'd carry my kiddies home, I could feel Dinkie's arm push shyly in behind my back and work its way as far around my waist as it was able to reach. He didn't speak. But his solemn little face gazed up at me, with its habitual hungry look, and I could see the hazel specks in the brown iris of the upturned eye as the arm tightened its hold on me. It made me ridiculously happy. For I knew that my boy loved me. And I love him. I love him so much that it brings a tapering spear-head of pain into my heart, and at the very moment I'm so happy I feel a tear just under the surface.

Sunday the Tenth

I have been reading Peter's latest letter to Dinkie, reading it for the second time. It is not so frolicsome as many of its fellows, but it impresses me as typical of its sender.

"I've to-day told fourteen cents' worth of postage-stamps to carry out to you, dear Dinkie, a copy of my own *Tales from Homer*, which may be muddy with a few big words but which the next year or two will surely see tramped down into easier going. You may not like it now, but later on, I know, you will like it better. For it tells of heroes and battles and travels which only a boy can really understand. It tells of the wanderings and adventures of strong and simple-hearted men, men who are as scarce, nowadays, as the shining helmets they used to wear. It tells of women superb and simple and lovely as goddesses, such as your own prairie might give birth to, such as your own mother must always seem to us. It tells of flashing temples and cities of marble overlooking singing seas of sapphire, of stately ships venturing over dark waters and landing on unknown islands, of siege and sword-fights and caves and giants and sea-goddesses and magic songs, and all that sunnier and simpler life which the world, as a prosaic old grown-up, has left behind....

"But I'm wrong in this, perhaps, for out in the land where you live there is still largeness and the gold-green ache of wonder beyond every sky-line. And I can't help envying you, Dinkie, for being a part of that world which is so much more heroic than mine. I live where a very shabby line of horse-cars used to run; and you live where the buffaloes used to run. I hear the rattle of the ash-cans in the morning; and you hear the song of the wind playing on the harp of summer. I pay five hundred dollars a year to wander about a smoky club no bigger than your corral; you wander about a Big Outdoors that rambles off up to the Arctic Circle itself. And you open a window at night and see the Aurora Borealis in all its beauty; and I open mine and observe an electric roof-sign announcing that Somebody's Tonic will take away my tired feeling. You put up your blind and see God's footstool bright with dew and dizzy with distance; I put up mine and overlook a wall of brick and mortar with one window wherein a fat man shaves himself. And you can go out in the morning and pick yellow crowfoot and range lilies; and all we can pick about this place of ours are milk-bottles and morning-papers packed full of murder and theft and tax-notices!"

Much of that letter, I know, was over Dinkie's head. But it carried a message or two to Dinkie's mother which in some way threw her heart into high. It was different from the letter that came the week before, the one arriving two days ahead of Kingsley's *Water Babies* with six lines of Hagedorn inscribed on its fly-leaf:

"And here you are to live, and help us live.
Bend close and listen, bird with folded wings.
Here is life's secret: Keep the upward glance;
Remember   Aries   is   your   relative,
The Moon's your uncle, and those twinkling things
Your sisters and your cousins and your aunts!"

This letter seemed like the Peter Ketley we knew best, the sad-eyed Peter with the feather of courage in his cap, the Peter who could caper and make you forget that his heart had ever been heavy. For he wrote:

"This time, Dinkie-Boy, I'm going to tell you about the sea. For the water-tank, as I remember it, is the biggest sea you have at Casa Grande—unless you count the mud when winter breaks up! And your prairie, with its long waves of green, is, I suppose, really a sea that has gone to sleep. But I mean the truly honest-to-goodness sea which has tides and baby-whales and steamers and cramps and sea-serpents in it. You saw it once at Santa Monica, I know, though you may have been too small to remember. But yesterday, I motored to a place called Atlantic City where they sell picture post-cards and push you in a wheeled chair and let you sit on the sand and watch the Water Babies, whom the policemen send to jail if they so much as walk along the beach without their stockings on. These Water Babies were not in a bottle—like the ones you'll read about in the book—but I think there was a bottle or two in some of them, from the way they acted. But one of them was in a pickle, for Father Neptune caught her in his under-tow—which you must not mix up with his under-toe, something with which only the mermaids are familiar—and a life-guard had to swim out and bring her in. And a few minutes after that I saw a real beach-comber. I had read about them in the South Sea Islands, but had never seen one before. This one sat under a striped parasol, with a mirror between her knees, and combed and combed her hair until it was quite dry again. I was disappointed in her knees, because I was hoping, at first, she wouldn't have any, but would be a mermaid who had come up on the sand to sun herself and would have a long and tapering tail covered with scales like a tarpon's. But all she had was beach-shoes tied with silk ribbons, and I preferred watching the water. For when I watch the ocean I always feel like Mr.

Hood and wish I was at least three small boys, so that I could pull off my three pairs of shoes and stockings and go paddling up to my six bare knees and let the rollers slap against my three startled little tummies and have thirty toes to step on the squids and star-fish with. And when I went back to the board-walk and watched all the gulls (I don't think I ever saw so many of 'em in one place at once) I couldn't help thinking it was too bad the Pilgrim Fathers didn't wait for three centuries and land at a bright and lively place like this, since it would have made them so much jollier and fizzier. They'd probably have turned the *Mayflower* into a diving-float and we'd never have had any Blue Laws to break and that curious thing known as The New England Conscience to keep us from being as happy as we feel we ought to be."

Sunday the Twenty-Fourth

Harvest is on us, and Casa Grande hums like a beehive. There are three extra "hands" to feed, and Whinnie is going about with a moody eye because Struthers is directing more attention than necessary toward one of the smooth-spoken cutthroats now nesting in our bunk-house. His name is Cuba Sebeck and in times of peace he professes to be a horse-wrangler. Struthers, intent on showing Whinnie that he is not the only man in her world, is placidly but patiently showering the lanky Cuba with a barrage of her fluffiest pastries. She has also given her hair an extra strong wash of sage-tea, which is Struthers' pet and particular way of putting on war-paint. Whinnie, I notice, shuts himself up after supper with that copy of Burns' poems we gave him last Christmas, morosely exiling himself from all the laughing and gaming and pow-wowing which takes place in the long cool twilights, just outside the bunk-house. Cuba undertook to serenade the dour one by donning certain portions of Struthers' apparel and playing my old banjo under his window. Whinnie quietly retaliated by emptying his bath-water on the musician's head—and the language was indescribable. I have been forced to speak to Dinky-Dunk, in fact, about the men's profanity before my children. It is something I will not endure. My husband, on the other hand, refuses to take the matter very seriously. But I have been keeping a close eye over my kiddies—and woe betide the horse-wrangler who uses unseemly language within their hearing. So far they seem to have gone through it unscathed, about the same as a child can go through the indecorous moments of *The Arabian Nights*, which stands profoundly wicked to only Arabs and old gentlemen.

Wednesday the Twenty-Eighth

Summer is slipping away. The days are shortening and there have been light frosts at night, but not enough to hurt Dinky-Dunk's late oats, which he has been watching with a worried eye. There is a saber-blade edge to the evening air now and we have been having some glorious displays of Northern Lights. I can't help feeling that these Merry Dancers of the Pole, as some one has called them, make up for what the prairie may lack in diversity. Dusk by dusk they drown our world in color, they smother our skies in glory. They are terrifying, sometimes, to the tenderfoot, giving him the feeling that his world is on fire. Poor old Struthers, during an especially active display, invariably gets out her Bible. Used to them as I am, I find they can still touch me with awe. They make me lonesome. They seem like the search-lights of God, showing up my human littlenesses of soul. They are Armadas of floating glory reminding me there are seas I can never traverse. And the farther north one goes, of course, the more magnificent the displays.

Last night we watched the auroral bands gather and grow in a cold green sky, straight to the north of us, and then waver and deepen until they reached the very zenith, where they hung, swaying curtains of fire. No wonder the redskins call that wild pageantry of color the ghost-dance of their gods. Even as we watched them, opal and gold and rose and orange and green, we could see them come wheeling down on our little world like an army of angels with incandescent swords. It made one imagine that the very heavens were aflame, going up in quivering veils of white and red and green. And when it was over I listened to a long argument about the Aurora Borealis, or the Aurora Polaris, as Gershom insisted it should be called.

Dinky-Dunk contended that one could *hear* these Northern Lights overhead, on a clear night. He described the sound as sometimes a faint crackling, like that of a comb drawn through your hair, and sometimes as a soft rustling noise, like the rustling of a silk petticoat heard through a closed door, coming closer and closer as the display wavered farther and farther toward the south.

Gershom was disposed to dispute this, so our old Klondiker, Whinstane Sandy, was called in to give evidence. He did so promptly and positively, saying he'd heard the Lights many a night in the Far North. Gershom is still unconvinced, but intends to look up his authorities on the matter. He attributes them to sun-spots and asserts it's a well-known fact they often put the telephone and telegraph wires out of commission. He has proposed that we sit up and study them some night, through his telescope, which he is disinterring from the bottom of his trunk....

My lord and master is going about with a less clouded eye, for he has succeeded in selling the Harris Ranch, and selling it for thirty-five hundred dollars more than he had expected. It is to go, eventually, to some tenderfoot out of the East, to some tenderfoot who can have very little definite knowledge of land-values in this jumping-off place on the edge of the world. But may that tenderfoot, whoever he is, be happy in his new home! Dinky-Dunk is now forever figuring up what he will get for his grain. He's preoccupied with his plans for branching out in the business world. His heart is no longer in his work here. I sometimes feel that we're all merely accidents in his life. And that feeling leaves me with a heart so heavy that I have to keep busy, or I'd fall to luxuriating in that self-pity which is good for neither man nor beast.

Yet Dinky-Dunk is not all hardness. He surprises me, now and then, by disturbing little gestures of boyishness. He announced to me the other night that the only way to get any use out of a worn-out husband was to revamp him, with the accent on the vamp. I understood what he meant, and I think I actually changed color a trifle. But I know of nothing more desolating than trying to make love to a man either against his will or against your own will. It would be a terrible thing to have him tell you there was no longer any kick in your kisses. So I remain on my dignity. I am companionable, and nothing more. When we were saying good-by, the last time he went off to the city, and he looked up at my perfunctory and quite meaningless peck on his cheek, I felt myself blushing before his quiet and half-quizzical stare. Then he laughed a little as he turned away and pulled on his gauntlets. "The sweeter the champagne, I suppose, the colder it should be served!" he rather cryptically remarked as he climbed into the waiting car. And yesterday he let his soul emerge from its tent of reticence when he climbed up on the wagon-box to stare out over his sea of all but ripened wheat. "Come, money!" he said, with his arms stretched out before him. Now, that was a trick which he had caught from my little Dinkie. I don't know how or where the boy first picked up the habit, but when he particularly wants something he stands solemnly out in the open, with his two little arms outstretched, as though he were supplicating Heaven itself, and says "Come, jack-knife!" or "Come, jelly-roll!" or "Come, rain!" according to his particular desires of the particular moment. I think he really caught it from an illustration in *The Arabian Nights*, from the picture of Cassim grandiloquently proclaiming "Open Sesame!" He is an imaginative little beggar. "Mummy," he said to me the other night, "see all the moonlight that's been spilled on the grass!" But children are made that way. Even my sage little Poppsy, when a marigold-leaf fell in the bowl of our solitary gold-fish, cried out to me: "See, Mummy, our fish has had a baby!" Sex is still an enigma to her, as much an enigma as it was away last spring when, not being quite sure whether her new kitten was a little boy-cat or a little girl-cat, she sagaciously christened it "Willie-Alice." And a few weeks later, when the unmistakable appearance of tail-feathers finally persuaded even her optimistic young heart that the two chicks which had been bequeathed to her were dishearteningly masculine in their tendencies, she officially re-christened the apostate "Elaine" and "Rowena," and thereafter solemnly accepted them as "Archie" and "Albert." And while speaking of this mysteriously ramifying factor of sex, I am compelled to acknowledge that I encountered a rather disturbing little back-flare of Freudian hell-fire only a couple of evenings ago. It took my thoughts galloping back to the time in our post-nuptial era when Dinky-Dunk went Berserker and chased me around the haystacks with my hair flying. I'd taken Dinkie upon my lap, and, without quite knowing it, sat stroking his frowsy young head. My thoughts, in fact, were a thousand miles away. Then, still without giving much attention to what I was doing, I squeezed that warm little body up close against my own. I was astounded, the next moment, to see my small offspring turn on me with all the lusty fierceness of the cave man. He got his arms about me and buried his face in my neck and kissed me as no gentleman, big or little, should ever kiss a lady. His small body was shaken with a subliminal and quite unexpected gust of feeling, just as I've seen a June-time garden shaken by an unexpected gust of wind. It passed away, of course, about as quickly as it came—but with it went a scattering of the white petals of childhood unconcern.

I don't suppose my poor little Dinkie has yet awakened to the fact that his body is a worn river-bed down which must race the freshets of far-off racial instincts. But the thing disturbed me more than I'd be willing to admit. There are murky corridors in the house of life. They stand there, and they must be faced. There are rooms where the air must be kept stirring, corners into which the clear sanity of sunlight must be thrown. Dinkie, since he has stepped into his first experience in the keeping of rabbits, has been asking me a number of rather disconcerting questions. His father, I notice, has the habit of half-diffidently referring the boy to me, just as I nursed the earlier habit of referring him to his father. But some time soon Dinkie and I will have to have a serious talk about this thing called Life, this Life which is so much more uncompromisingly brutal than the child-mind can conceive....

By the way, there's a lot of nonsense talked about motherhood softening women. It may soften them in some ways, but there are many others in which it hardens them. It draws their power of love together into a fixed point, just as the lens of a burning-glass concentrates the vague warmth of the sun into one small and fiercely illuminated area. It is a form of selfishness, I suppose, but it is a selfishness nature imposes upon us. And it is sanctified by the end it serves. At every turn, now, I find that I am thinking of my children. I seem to have my eyes set steadily on something far, far ahead. I'm not quite certain just what this something is. It's a sort of secret between me and the Master of Life. But the memory of it makes my days more endurable. It allows me to face the future without a quaver of regret. I am a woman, and I am no longer young. But it gives me courage to laugh in the teeth of Time.

And to laugh, to laugh whatever happens—that is the great thing! It isn't age I dread. But I'd hate to lose that lightness with which those blessed ones we call the young can move through the world, that self-renewing freshness which converts every daybreak into a dewy new world and mints every sunrise into a brand new life ... I asked Gershom to-day if he could possibly tell me how many Parker House rolls a square mile of wheat running forty bushels to the acre would make. And he surprised me by inquiring how many quarts of buttermilk it would take to shingle a cow. Gershom is widening out a bit....

Dinkie, I notice, has just compiled a list of horses. I read from his carefully ruled half-page:

"Draght horses; carriage horses; riding horses; racing horses; ponyies; percheron from france; Belgain from Beljium; shire clyesdale and saffold punch from great Britain; french coach and German coach; contucky saddle horses; through-breads; Shetland ponies; mushstand ponies; pacers and pintoes." Thus recordeth my Toddler.

Sunday the Ninth

I have had Dinkie in bed for the last five days, with a bruised foot. Duncan shortened the stirrups and put the boy on Briquette, who had just proved a handful for even an old horse-wrangler like Cuba Sebeck. Briquette bucked and threw the boy. And Dinkie, in the mix-up, got a hoof-pound on the ankle. No bones were broken, luckily, but the foot was very sore and swollen for a few days. No word about the episode has passed between Duncan and me. But I'm glad, all things considered, that I was not a witness of the accident. The clouds are already quite heavy enough over Casa Grande.

Dinkie and his mater, however, have been drawn much closer together during the last few days. I've talked to him, and read to him, and without either of us being altogether conscious of it there has been an opening of a closed door or two. Dinkie loves to be read to. The new world of the imagination is just opening up to him. And I envy the rapture of the child in books, rapture not yet spoiled by the intellectual conceit of the grown-up.

But I'm not the only reader about this ranch. I'm afraid the copy of Burns which Santa Claus brought to Whinstane Sandy last Christmas is not adding to his matrimonial tendencies as love-plaints of that nature should. At noon, as soon as dinner is over, he sits on the back step, poring over his beloved Tammas. And at night, now that the evenings are chillier, he retreats to the bunk-house stove, where he smokes and reads aloud. His own mother, he tells me, used to say many of those pieces to him when he was a wee laddie. He both outraged and angered poor Struthers, last Sunday, by reading *Tam O'Shanter* aloud to her. That autumnal vestal proclaimed that it was anything but suitable literature for an old philanderer who still saw fit to live alone. It showed, she averred, a shocking lack of respect for women-folk and should be taken over by the police.

Struthers even begins to suspect that this much-thumbed volume of Burns lies at the root of Whinnie's accumulating misanthropy. She has asked me if I thought a volume of Mrs. Hemans would be of service in leading the deluded old misogynist back to the light. The matter has become a more urgent one since Cuba Sebeck suffered a severe bilious attack and a consequent sea-change in his affections. But I'm afraid our Whinnie is too old a bird to be trapped by printer's ink. I notice, in fact, that Struthers is once more spending her evenings in knitting winter socks. And I have a shadow of a suspicion that they are for the obdurate one.

My Dinkie, by the way, has written his first poem, or, rather, his first two poems. The first one he slipped folded into my sewing-basket and I found it when I was looking for new buttons for Pauline Augusta's red sweater. It reads:

No more we smel the sweet clover,
Floting on the breeze all over.
But now we hear the wild geese calling;
And lissen, tis the grey owl yowling.

The second one, however, was a more ambitious effort. He worked over it, propped up in bed, for an hour or two. Then, having looked upon his work and having seen that it was good, he blushingly passed it over to me. So I went to the window and read it.

O   blue-bird,   happy   robbin—
Who teached those birds to stick theirselves together?
Who teached them how to put their tails on?
Who teached them how to hold tight on the tree tops?
Who gived them all the fetthers on their brest?
 Who gived them all the eggs with little birdies in them?
Who teached them how to make the shells so blue?
Who teached them how to com home in the dark?
Twas God. Twas God. He teached him!

I read it over slowly, with a crazy fluttering of the heart which I could never explain. They were so trivial, those little halting lines, and yet so momentous to me! It was life seeking expression, life groping so mysteriously toward music. It was man emerging out of the dusk of time. It was Rodin's *Penseur*, not in grim and stately bronze, but in a soft-eyed and white-bodied child, groping his stumbling way toward the border-land of consciousness, staring out on a new world and finding it wonderful. It was my Little Stumbler, my Precious Piece-of-Life, walking with his arm first linked through the arm of Mystery. It was my Dinkie looking over the rampart of the home-nest and breaking lark-like into song.

I went back to the bed and sat down on the edge of it, and took my man-child in my arms.

"It's wonderful, Dinkie," I said, trying to hide the tears I was so ashamed of. "It's so wonderful, my boy, that I'm going to keep it with me, always, as long as I live. And some day, when you are a great man, and all the world is at your feet, I'm going to bring it to you and show it to you. For I know now that you are going to be a great man, and that your old mother is going to live to be so proud of you it'll make her heart ache with joy!"

He hugged me close, in a little back-wash of rapture, and then settled down on his pillows.

"I could do better ones than that," he finally said, with a glowing eye.

"Yes," I agreed. "They'll be better and better. And that'll make your old Mummsy prouder and prouder!"

He lay silent for several minutes. Then he looked at the square of paper which I held folded in my hand.

"I'd like to send it to Uncle Peter," he rather startled me by saying.

Saturday the Twenty-Ninth

Once more I'm a grass widow. My Duncan is awa'. He scooted for Calgary as soon as his threshing-work was finished up. But that tumult is over and once more I've a chance to sit down and commune with my soul. Everything here is over-running with wheat. Our bins are bursting. The lord of the realm is secretly delighted, but he has said little about it. He has a narrow course to steer. He is grateful for the money that this wheat will bring in to him, yet he can see it would never do to harp too loudly on the productiveness of our land—on *my* land, I ought to say, for Casa Grande has now been formally deeded to me. I find no sense of triumph, however, in that transfer. I am depressed, in fact, at the very thought of it. It seems to carry a vague air of the valedictory. But I refuse to be intimidated by the future.

Gershom and I, indeed, have been indulging in the study of astronomy. The air was crystal clear last night, so that solemn youth suggested that we take out the old telescope and study the stars. Which we did. And which was much more wonderful than I had imagined. But Gershom had no reflector, so after getting a neck-ache trying to inspect the heavens while on our feet we took the old buffalo-robe and a couple of rugs out to a straw-pile that had been hauled in to protect our winter perennials. There we indecorously reposed on our backs and went stargazing in comfort. And Gershom even forgot that painful bashfulness of his when he fell to talking about the planets. He slipped out of his shell and spoke with genuine feeling.

He suggested that we begin with the Big Dipper, which I could locate easily enough well up in the northern sky. That, Gershom told me, was sometimes called the Great Bear, though it was only a part of the real *Ursa Major* of the astronomers. Then he showed me Benetnasch at the end of the Dipper's handle, and Mizar at the bend in the handle, then Alioth, and then Megrez, which joins the handle to the bowl. Then he showed me Phaed and Merak, which mark the bottom of the bowl, and then Dubhe at the bowl's outer rim.

I tried hard, but I was very stupid about getting the names right. Then Gershom asked me to look up at Mizar, and see if I could make out a small star quite close to it. I did so, without much trouble, and Gershom thereupon condescended to admit that I had exceptionally good eyes. For that star, he explained, was Alcor, and Alcor was Arabic for "the proof," and for centuries and centuries the ability to see that star had been accepted as the proof of good vision.

Then Gershom went on to the other constellations, and talked of suns of the first and second magnitude, and pointed out Sirius, in whose honor great temples had once been built in Egypt, and Arcturus, the same old Arcturus that a Hebrew poet by the name of Job had sung about, and Vega and Capella and Rigel, which he said sent out eight thousand times more light than our sun, and is at least thirty-four thousand times as big.

But it only made me dizzy and staggered my mind. I couldn't comprehend the distances he was talking about. I just couldn't make it, any more than a bronco that had been used to jumping a six-barred gate could vault over a windmill tower. And I had to tell Gershom that it didn't do a bit of good informing me that Sirius was comparatively close to us, as it stood only nine light-years away. I remembered how he had explained that light travels one hundred and eighty-six thousand miles a second, and that there are thirty million seconds in a year, so that a light-year is about five and a half million million of miles. But when he started to tell me that some of the so-called photographic stars are thirty-two thousand light-years away from us my imagination just curled up and died. It didn't mean anything to me. It couldn't. I tried in vain to project my puny little soul through all that space. At first it was rather bewildering. Then it grew into something touched with grandeur. Then it took on an aspect of awfulness. And from that it grew into a sort of ghastliness, until the machinery of the mind choked and balked and stopped working altogether, like an overloaded motor. I had to reach out in the cold air and catch hold of Gershom's arm. I felt a hunger to cling to something warm and human.

"We call this world of ours a pretty big world," Gershom was saying. "But look at Betelgeuse up there, which Michelson has been able to measure. He has, at least, succeeded in measuring the angle at the eye that Betelgeuse subtends, so that after estimating its parallax as given by a heliometer, it's merely a matter of trigonometry to work out the size of the star. And he estimated Betelgeuse to be two hundred and sixty million miles in diameter. That means it would take twenty-seven million of our suns to equal it in bulk. So that this big world of ours, which takes so many weeks to crawl about on the fastest ships and the fastest trains, is really a mote of dust, something smaller than the smallest pin-prick, compared to that far-away sun up there on the shoulder of Orion!"

"Stop!" I cried. "You're positively giving me a chill up my spine. You're making me feel so lonesome, Gershom, that you're giving me goose-flesh. You're not leaving me anything to get hold of. You haven't even left me anything to stand on. I'm only a little speck of Nothing on a nit of a world in a puny little universe which is only a little freckle on the face of some greater universe which is only a lost child in a city of bigger constellations which in turn have still lonelier suns to swing about, until I go on and on, and wonder with a gasp what is beyond the end of space. But I can't go on thinking about it. I simply can't. It upsets me, the same as an earthquake would, when you look about for something solid and find that even your solid old earth is going back on you!"

"On the contrary," said Gershom as he put down his telescope, "I know nothing more conducive to serenity than the study of astronomy. It has a tendency to teach you, in the first place, just how insignificant you are in the general scheme of things. The naked eye, in clear air like this, can see over eight thousand stars. The larger telescopes reveal a hundred million stars, and the photographic dry-plate has shown that there are several thousands of millions which can be definitely recorded. So that you and I are not altogether the whole works. And to remember that, when we are feeling a bit important, is good for our Ego!"

I didn't answer him, for I was busy just then studying the Milky Way. And I couldn't help feeling that it must have been on a night like this that a certain young shepherd watching his flocks on the uplands of Canaan sat studying the infinite stairways of star-dust that "sloped through darkness up to God" and was moved to say: "When I consider the heavens, the work of Thy fingers, the moon and the stars which Thou hast ordained, what is man that Thou art mindful of him, or the son of man that Thou visitest him?"

"Yes, Gershom, it's horribly humiliating," I said as I squinted up at those serene heavens. "They last forever. And we come and go out, and nobody knows why!"

"Pardon me," corrected the literal-minded Gershom. "They do not last forever. They come and go out, just as we do. Only they take longer. Consider the Dipper up there, for instance. A hundred thousand years from now that Dipper will be perceptibly altered, for we know the lateral movement of Dubhe and Benetnasch will give the outer line of the bowl a greater flare and make the crook of the handle a trifle sharper. Even a thousand years would show change enough for instruments to detect. And a million years will probably show the group pretty well broken up. But the one regrettable feature, of course, is that we will not be here to see it."

"Where will we be?" I asked Gershom.

"I don't know," he finally admitted, after an unexpectedly long silence.

"But will it all go on, forever and forever and forever?"

"To do so is not in the nature of things," was Gershom's quiet-toned reply. "It is the destiny of our own earth, of course, which most interests us. And however we look at it, that destiny is a gloomy one. Its heat may fail. Stupart, in fact, has established that its temperature is going down one and a half degrees every thousand years. Or its volcanic elevating forces may give out, so that the land will subside and the water wash over it from pole to pole. Or a comet may wipe up its atmosphere, the same as one sponge-sweep wipes up moisture from a slate. Or the sun itself may cool, so that the last of our race will stand huddled together in a solarium somewhere on the Equator. Or as our sun rushes toward Lyra, it may bump into a derelict sun, just as a ship bumps into a wreck. If that derelict were as big as our sun, astronomers would see it at least fifteen years before the collision. For five or six years it would even be visible to the naked eye, so that the race, or what remained of the race, would have plenty of time to think things over and put its house in order. Then, of course, we'd go up like a singed feather. And there'd be no more breakfasts to worry over, and no more wheat to thresh, and no more school fires to start in the morning, and no more children to make think you know more than you really do, and not even any more hearts to ache. There would be just Emptiness, just voiceless and never-ending Nothingness!"

Gershom stopped speaking and sat staring up at Orion. Then he turned and looked at me.

"What's the matter?" he asked, for he must have felt my shiver under the robe.

"Nothing," I said in a thin and pallid voice. "Only I think I'll go back to the house. And I'm going to make a pot of good hot cocoa!" ... And that's mostly what life is: making little pots of cocoa to keep our bodies warm in the midst of a never-ending chilliness!

Tuesday the Eighth

My husband is home again. He came back with the first blizzard of the winter and had a hard time getting through to Casa Grande. This gives him all the excuses he could desire for railing at prairie life. I told him, after patiently listening to him cussing about everything in sight, that it was plain to see that he belonged to the land of the beaver. He promptly requested to know what I meant by that.

"Doesn't the beaver regard it as necessary to dam his home before he considers it fit to live in?" I retorted. But Duncan, in that estranging new mood of his, didn't relax a line. He even announced, a little later on, that a quick-silver wit might be all right if it could be kept from running over. And it was my turn to ask if he had any particular reference to allusions.

"Well, for one thing," he told me, "there's this tiresome habit of hitching nicknames on to everything in sight."

I asked him what names he objected to.

"To begin right at home," he retorted, "I regard 'Dinkie' as an especially silly name for a big hulk of a boy. I think it's about time that youngster was called by his proper name."

I'd never thought about it, to tell the truth. His real name, I remembered, was Elmer Duncan McKail. That endearing diminutive of "Dinkie" had stuck to him from his baby days, and in my fond and foolish eyes, of course, had always seemed to fit him. But even Gershom had spoken to me on the matter, months before, asking me if I preferred the boy to be known as "Dinkie" to his school mates. And I'd told Gershom that I didn't believe we could get rid of the "Dinkie" if we wanted to. His father, I knew, had once objected to "Duncan," as he had no liking to be dubbed "Old Duncan" while his offspring would answer to "Young Duncan." And "Duncan," as a name, had never greatly appealed to me. But it is plain now that I have been remiss in the matter. So hereafter we'll have to make an effort to have our little Dinkie known as Elmer. It's like bringing a new child into the family circle, a new child we're not quite acquainted with. But these things, I suppose, have to be faced. So hereafter my laddie shall officially be known as "Elmer," Elmer Duncan McKail. And I have started the ball rolling by duly inscribing in his new books "Elmer D. McKail" and requesting Gershom to address his pupil as "Elmer."

I've been wondering, in the meantime, if Duncan is going to insist on a revision of all our ranch names, the names so tangled up with love and good-natured laughter and memories of the past. Take our horses alone: Tumble-weed and timeless Tithonus, Buntie and Briquette, Laughing-gas and Coco the Third, Mudski and Tarzanette. I'd hate now to lose those names. They are the register of our friendly love for our animals.

It begins to creep through this thick head of mine that my husband no longer nurses any real love for either these animals or prairie life. And if that is the case, he will never get anything out of prairie living. It will be useless for him even to try. So I may as well do what I can to reconcile myself to the inevitable. I am not without my moments of revolt. But in those moods when I feel a bit uppish I remember about my recent venture into astronomy. What's the use of worrying, anyway? There was one ice age, and there is going to be another ice age. I tell myself that my troubles are pretty trivial, after all, since I'm only one of many millions on this earth and since this earth is only one of many millions of other earths which will swing about their suns billions and billions of years after I and my children and my children's children are withered into dust.

It rather takes my breath away, at times, and I shy away from it the same as Pauline Augusta shies away from the sight of blood. It reminds me of Chaddie's New York lady with whom the Bishop ventured to discuss ultimate destinies. "Yes, I suppose I shall enter into eternal bliss," responded this fair lady, "but would you mind not discussing such disagreeable subjects at tea-time?"

Speaking of disagreeable subjects, we seem to have a new little trouble-maker here at Casa Grande. It's in the form of a brindle pup called Minty, which Dinkie—I mean, of course, which Elmer, acquired in exchange for a jack-knife and what was left of his *Swiss Family Robinson*. But Minty has not been well treated by the world, and was brought home with a broken leg. So Whinnie and I made splints out of an old cigar-box cover, and padded the fracture with cotton wool and bound it up with tape. Minty, in the moderated spirits of invalidism, was a meek and well behaved pup during the first few days after his arrival, sleeping quietly at the foot of Elmer's bed and stumping around after his new master like a war veteran awaiting his discharge. But now that Minty's leg is getting better and he finds himself in a world that flows with warm milk and much petting, he betrays a tendency to use any odd article of wearing apparel as a teething-ring. He has completely ruined one of my bedroom slippers and done Mexican-drawn-work on the ends of the two living-room window-curtains. But what is much more ominous, Minty yesterday got hold of Dinky-Dunk's Stetson and made one side of its rim look as though it had been put through a meat-chopper. So my lord and master has been making inquiries about Minty and Minty's right of possession. And the order has gone forth that hereafter no canines are to sleep in this house. It impresses me as a trifle unreasonable, all things considered, and Elmer, with a rather unsteady underlip, has asked me if Minty must be taken away from him. But I have no intention of countermanding Duncan's order. The crust over the volcano is quite thin enough, as it is. And whatever happens, I am resolved to be a meek and dutiful wife. But I've had a talk with Whinnie and he's going to fix up a comfortable box behind the stove in the bunk-house, and there the exiled Minty will soon learn to repose in peace. It's marvelous, though, how that little three-legged animal loves my Dinkie, loves my Elmer, I should say. He licks my laddie's shoes and yelps with joy at the smell of his pillow ... Poor little abundant-hearted mite, overflowing with love! But life, I suppose, will see to it that he is brought to reason. We must learn not to be too happy on this earth. And we must learn that love isn't always given all it asks for.

Thursday the Seventeenth

The crust over the volcano has shown itself to be even thinner than I imagined. The lava-shell gave way, under our very feet, and I've had a glimpse of the molten fury that can flow about us without our knowing it. And like so many of life's tragic moments, it began out of something that is almost ridiculous in its triviality.

Night before last, when Struthers was rather late in setting her bread, she heard Minty scratching and whimpering at the back door, and without giving much thought to what she was doing, let him into the house. Minty, of course, went scampering up to Dinkie's bed, where he slept secretly and joyously until morning. And all might have been well, even at this, had not Minty's return to his kingdom gone to his head. To find some fitting way of expressing his joy must have taxed that brindle pup's ingenuity, for, before any of us were up, he descended to the living-room, where he delightedly and diligently proceeded to remove the upholstery from the old Chesterfield. By the time I came on the scene, at any rate, there was nothing but a grisly skeleton of the Chesterfield left. Now, that particular piece of furniture had known hard use, and there were places where the mohair had been worn through, and I'd even discussed the expediency of having the thing done over. But I knew that Minty's efforts to hasten this movement would not meet with approval. So I discreetly decided to have Whinnie and Struthers remove the tell-tale skeleton to the bunk-house. Before that transfer could be effected, however, the Dour Man invaded the living-room and stood with a cold and accusatory eye inspecting that monument of destructiveness.

"Where's Elmer?" he demanded, with a grim look which started by heart pounding.

"Elmer's dressing," I said as quietly as I could. "Do you want him?"

"I do," announced my husband, whiter in the face than I had seen him for many a day.

"What for?" I asked.

"I think you know what for," he said, meeting my eye.

"I'm not sure that I do," I found the courage to retort. "But I'd prefer being certain."

Duncan, instead of answering me, went to the foot of the stairs and called his son. Then he strode out of the room and out of the house. Struthers, in the meantime, circumspectly took possession of Minty, who was still indecorously shaking a bit of mohair between his jocund young teeth. She and Minty vanished from the scene. A moment later, however, Duncan walked back into the room. He had a riding-quirt in his hand.

"Where's that boy?" he demanded.

I went out to the foot of the stairs, where I met Elmer coming down, buttoning his waist as he came. For just a moment his eye met mine. It was a questioning eye, but not a cowardly one. I had intended to speak to him, but my voice, for some reason, didn't respond to my will. So I merely took the boy's hand and led him into the living-room. There his father stood confronting him.

"Did that pup sleep on your bed last night?" demanded the man with the quirt.

"Yes," said the child, after a moment of silence.

"Did you hear me say that no dog was to sleep in this house?" demanded the child's father.

"Yes," said Elmer, with his own face as white as his father's.

"Then I think that's about enough," asserted Duncan, turning a challenging eye in my direction.

"What are you going to do?" I asked. My voice was shaking, in spite of myself.

"I'm going to whale that youngster within an inch of his life," said the master of the house, with a deadly sort of intentness.

"I don't want you to do that," I quavered, wondering why my words, even as I uttered them, should seem so inadequate.

"Of course you don't," mocked my husband. "But this is the limit. And what you want isn't going to count!"

"I don't want you to do that," I repeated. Something in my voice, I suppose, must have arrested him, for he stood there, staring at me, with a little knot coming and going on one side of his skull, just in front of his upper ear-tip.

"And why not?" he asked, still with that hateful rough ironic note in his voice.

"Because you don't know what you're punishing this child for," I told him with all the quietness I could command. "And because you're in no fit condition to do it."

"You needn't worry about my condition," he cried out—and I could see by the way he said it that he was still blind with rage. "Come here, you!" he called to Dinkie.

It was then that the fatal little bell clanged somewhere at the back of my head, the bell that rings down the curtain on all the slowly accumulated civilization the centuries may have brought to us. I not only faced my husband with a snort of scorn, but I tightened my grip on the child's hand. I tightened my grip on his hand and backed slowly and deliberately away until I came to the door of my sewing-room. Then, still facing my husband, I opened that door and said: "Go inside, Dinkie." I could not see the boy, but I knew that he had done as I told him. So I promptly slammed the door shut and stood there facing the gray-lipped man with the riding-quirt in his hand. He took two slow steps toward me. His chin was thrust out in a way that made me think of a fighting-cock's beak. He had not shaved that morning, and his squared jaw looked stubbled and blue and ugly.

"You can't pull that petticoat stuff this time," he said in a hard and throaty tone which I had never heard from him before. "Get out of my way!"

"You will not beat that child!" And I myself couldn't have made a very pretty picture as I flung that challenge up in his teeth.

"Get out of my way," he repeated. He did not shout it. He said it almost quietly. But I knew, even before he reached out a shaking hand to thrust me aside, that he was in deadly earnest, that nothing I could say would hold him back or turn him aside. And it was then that my eye fell on the big Colt in its stained leather holster, hanging up high over one corner of the book-cabinet, where it had been put beyond the reach of the children.

I have no memory of giving any thought to the matter. My reaction must have been both immediate and automatic. I don't think I even intended to bunt my husband in the short-ribs the way I did, for the impact of my body half twisted him about and sent him staggering back several steps. All I know is that holster and belt came tumbling down as I sprang and caught at the Colt handle. And I was back at the door before I had even shaken the revolver free. I was back just in time to hear my husband say, rather foolishly, for the third time: "Get out of my way!"

"You stay back there!" I called, quite as foolishly, for by this time I had the Colt balanced in my hand and was pointing it directly at his body.

He stopped short, with a vacuous look in his eyes.

"*You fool!*" he said, in a sort of strangled whisper. But it was my face, and not the weapon, that he was staring at all the while.

"Stay back!" I said again, with my eyes fixed on his.

He hesitated, for a moment, and made a sound that was like the short bark of a laugh. It was too hard and horrible, though, ever to be taken for laughter. And I knew that he was not going to do what I had said.

"Stay back!" I warned him still again. But he stepped forward, with a grim sort of deliberation, with his challenging gaze locked on mine. I could hear a thousand warning voices, somewhere at the back of my brain, and at the same time I could hear a thousand singing devils in my blood trying to drown out those voices. I could see my husband's narrowed eyes slowly widen, slowly open like the gills of a dying fish, for the hate that he must have seen on my face obviously arrested him. It arrested him, but it arrested him only for a moment. He dropped his eyes to the Colt in my hand. Then he moved deliberately forward until his body was almost against the barrel-end. I must have known what it meant, just as he must have known what it meant. It was his final challenge. And I must have met that challenge. For, without quite knowing it, I shut my eyes and pulled the trigger.

There had been something awful, I know, in that momentary silence. And there was something awful in the sound that came after it, though it was not the sound my subconscious mind was waiting for. It was distinct enough and significant enough, heaven knows. But instead of the explosion of a shell it was the sharp snap of steel against steel.

The revolver was empty. It was empty-had been empty for weeks. But the significant fact remained that I had deliberately pulled the trigger. I had stood ready, in my moment of madness, to kill the man that I lived with....

Had a ball of lead gone through that man's body, I don't think he could have staggered back with a more startled expression on his face. He looked more than bewildered; he looked vaguely humiliated, oddly and wordlessly affronted, as he stood leaning against the table-edge, breathing hard, his skin a mottled blue-white to the very lips. He made an effort to speak, but no sound came from him. For a moment the dreadful thought raced through me that I had indeed shot him, that in some mysterious way he was mortally hurt, without this particular bullet announcing itself as bullets usually do. I looked at the revolver, stupidly. It seemed to have grown heavy, as heavy as a cook-stove in my hand.

"You'd do that?" whispered my husband, very slowly, with a stricken light in his eyes which I couldn't quite understand. I intended to put the Colt on the table. But something must have been wrong with my vision, for the loathsome thing fell loathsomely to the floor. I felt sick and shaken and a horrible misty feeling of homelessness settled down about me, of a sudden, for I remembered how closely I had skirted the black gulf of murder.

"Oh, Dinky-Dunk!" I blubbered, weakly, as I groped toward him. He must have thought that I was going to fall, for he put out his arm and held me up. He held me up, but there wasn't an atom of warmth in his embrace. He held me up about the same as he'd hold up an open wheat-sack that threatened to tumble over on his granary floor. I don't know what reaction it was that took my strength away from me, but I clung to his shoulders and sobbed there. I felt as alone in the gray wastes of time as one of Gershom's lost stars. And I knew that my Dinky-Dunk would never bend down now and whisper into my ear any word of comfort, any word of forgiveness. For, however things may have been at the first, I was the one who was now so hopelessly in the wrong, *I* was the big offender. And that knowledge only added to my misery as I stood there clinging to my husband's shoulders and blubbering "Oh, Dinky-Dunk!"

It must have grown distasteful to him, my foolish hanging on to him as though he were a hitching-post, for he finally said in a remote voice: "I guess we've had about enough of this." He led me rather ceremoniously to a chair, and slowly let me down in it. Then he crossed over to the old leather holster and picked it up, and stooped for the revolver, and pushed it down in the holster and buckled the cover-flap and tossed the whole thing up to the top of the book-cabinet again. Then, without speaking to me, he walked slowly out of the room.

I was tempted to call him back, but I knew, on second thought, that it would be no use. I merely sat there, staring ahead of me. Then I shut my eyes and tried to think. I don't know why, but I was thinking about the bigness of Betelgeuse, which was twenty-seven million times as big as our sun and which was going on through its millions of miles of space without knowing anything about Chaddie McKail and what had happened to her that morning. I was wondering if there were worlds between me and Betelgeuse with women on them, with women as alone as I was, when I felt a pair of small arms tighten about my knees and an adoring small voice whispered "Mummsy!" And I forgot about Betelgeuse. For it was my Dinkie there, with his little rough hand reaching hungrily for mine....

Minty has been removed from Casa Grande. I took him over to the Teetzel ranch in the car, and young Dode Teetzel is to get a dollar a week for looking after him and feeding him. Only Elmer and I know of his whereabouts. And once a week the boy can canter over on Buntie and keep in touch with his pup.

We have a tacit understanding that the occurrences of yesterday morning are a closed chapter, are not to be referred to by word or deed. Duncan himself found it necessary to team in to Buckhorn and left word with Struthers that he would stay in town over night. The call for the Buckhorn trip was, of course, a polite fabrication, an expedient *pax in bello* to permit the dust of battle to settle a little about this troubled house of McKail. All day to-day I have felt rather languid. I suppose it's the lethargy which naturally follows after all violence. Any respectable woman, I used to think, could keep a dead-line in her soul, beyond which the impulses of evil dare not venture. But I must have been wrong.... All week I've been looking for a letter from Peter Ketley. But for once in his life he seems to have forgotten us.

Sunday the Twentieth

I've been wondering to-day just what I'd do if I had to earn my own living. I could run a ranch, I suppose, if I still had one, but two or three years of such work would see me a hatchet-faced old termagant with fallen arches and a prairie-squint. Or I could raise chickens and peddle dated eggs in a flivver-and fresco hen-coops with whitewash until the trap-nest of time swallowed me up in oblivion. Or I could take a rural school somewhere and teach the three R's to little Slovenes and Frisians and French-Canadians even more urgently in need of soap and water. Or perhaps I could be housekeeper for one of our new beef-kings in his new Queen-Anne Norman-Georgian Venetian palace of Alberta sandstone with tesselated towers and bungalow sleeping-porches. Or I might even peddle magazines, or start a little bakery in one of the little board-fronted shops of Buckhorn, or take in plain sewing and dispose of home-made preserves to the élite of the community.

But each and all of them would be mere gestures of defeat. I'm of no value to the world. There was a time when I regarded myself as quite a Somebody, and prided myself on having an idea or two. Didn't Percy even once denominate me as "a window-dresser"? There was a time when I didn't have to wait to see if the pearl-handled knife was the one intended for the fish-course, and I could walk across a waxed floor without breaking my neck and do a bit of shopping in the Rue de la Paix without being taken for a tourist. But that was a long, long time ago. And life during the last few years has both humbled me and taught me my limitations. I'm a house-wife, now, and nothing more—and not even a successful house-wife. I've let everything fall away except the thought of my home and my family. And now I find that the basket into which I so carefully packed all my eggs hasn't even a bottom to it.

But I've no intention of repining. Heaven knows I've never wanted to sit on the Mourner's Bench. I've never tried to pull a sour mug, as Dinky-Dunk once inelegantly expressed it. I love life and the joy of life, and I want all of it I can get. I believe in laughter, and I've a weakness for men and women who can sing as they work. But I've blundered into a black frost, and even though there was something to sing about, there's scarcely a blue-bird left to do the singing. But sometime, somewhere, there'll be an end to that silence. The blight will pass, and I'll break out again. I know it. I don't intend to be held down. I *can't* be held down. I haven't the remotest idea of how it's going to happen, but I'm going to love life again, and be happy, and carol out like a meadow-lark on a blue and breezy April morning. It may not come to-morrow, and it may not come the next day. But it's going to come. And knowing it's going to come, I can afford to sit tight, and abide my time....

I've just had a letter from Uncle Chandler, enclosing snap-shots of the place he's bought in New Jersey. It looks very palatial and settled and Old-Worldish, shaded and shadowed with trees and softened with herbage, dignified by the hand of time. It reminds me how many and many a long year will have to go by before our bald young prairie can be tamed and petted into a homeyness like that. Uncle Chandler has rather startled me by suggesting that we send Elmer through to him, to go to school in the East. He says the boy can attend Montclair Academy, that he can be taken there and called for every day by faithful old Fisher, in the cabriolet, and that on Sunday he can be toted regularly to St. Luke's Episcopal Church, and occasionally go into New York for some of the better concerts, and even have a governess of his own, if he'd care for it. And in case I should be worrying about his welfare Uncle Chandler would send me a weekly night-letter "describing the condition and the activities of the child," as the letter expresses it. It sounds very appealing, but every time I try to think it over my heart goes down like a dab-chick. My Dinkie is such a little fellow. And he's my first-born, my man-child, and he means so much in my life. Yet he and his father are not getting along very well together. It would be better, in many respects, if the boy could get away for a while, until the raw edges healed over again. It would be better for both of them. But there's one thing that would happen: he would grow away from his mother. He'd come back to me a stranger. He'd come back a little ashamed of his shabby prairie mater, with her ten-years-old style of hair-dressing and her moss-grown ideas of things and her bald-looking prairie home with no repose and no dignifying background and neither a private gym nor a butler to wheel in the cinnamon-toast. He'd be having all those things, under Uncle Chandler's roof: he'd get used to them and he'd expect them.

But there's one thing he wouldn't and couldn't have. He wouldn't have his mother. And no one can take a mother's place, with a boy like that. No one could understand him, and make allowances for him, and explain things to him, as his own mother could. I've been thinking about that, all afternoon as I ironed his waists and his blue flannellet pajamas with frogs on like his dad's. And I've been thinking of it all evening as I patched his brown corduroy knickers and darned his little stockings and balled them up in a neat little row. I tried to picture myself as packing them away in a trunk, and putting in beside them all the clothes he would need, and the books that he could never get along without, and the childish little treasures he'd have to carry away to his new home. But it was too much for me. There was one thing, I began to see, which could never, never happen. I could never willingly be parted from my Dinkie. I could think of nothing to pay me up for losing him. And he needed me as I needed him. For good or bad, we'd have to stick together. Mother and son, together in some way we'd have to sink or swim!

Wednesday the Thirtieth

The tension has been relieved by Dinky-Dunk going off to Calgary. Along with him he has taken a rather formidable amount of his personal belongings. But he explains this by stating that business will keep him in the city for at least six or seven weeks. He has been talking a good deal about the Barcona coal-mine of late, and the last night he was with us he talked to Gershom for an hour and more about the advantages of those newer mines over the Drumheller. The newer field has a solid slate roof which makes drifting safe and easy, a finer type of coal, and a chance for big money once the railway runs in its spur and the officials wake up to the importance of giving them the cars they need. The whole country, Dinky-Dunk claims, is underlaid with coal, and our province alone is estimated to contain almost seventeen per cent. of the world's known supply. And my lord and master expressed the intention of being in on the clean-up.

I don't know how much of this was intended for my ears. But it served to disquiet me, for reasons I couldn't quite discern. And the same vague depression crept over me when Dinky-Dunk took his departure. I kept up my air of blitheness, it is true, to the last moment, and was as casual as you please in helping Duncan to pack and reminding him to put his shaving-things in his bag and making sure the last button was on his pajamas. I kissed him good-by, as a dutiful wife ought, and held Pauline Augusta up in the doorway so that she might attempt a last-minute hand-waving at her daddy.

But I slumped, once it was all over. I felt mysteriously alone in an indifferent big world with the rime of winter creeping along its edges. Even Gershom, after the children had had their lesson, became conscious of my preoccupation and went so far as to ask if I wasn't feeling well.

I smilingly assured him that there was nothing much wrong with me.

"*Lerne zu leiden ohne zu klagen!*" as the dying Frederick said to a singularly foolish son.

"But you're upset?" persisted Gershom, with his valorous brand of timidity that so often reminds me of a robin defending her eggs.

"No, it's not that," I said with a shake of the head. "It's only that I'm—I'm a trifle too chilly to be comfortable."

And the foolish youth, at that, straightway fell to stoking the fire. I had to laugh a little. And that made him study me with solemn eyes.

"Just think, Gershom," I said as I gathered up my sewing, "my heart is perishing of cold in a province which is estimated to contain almost seventeen per cent. of the world's known coal supply!"

And that, apparently, left him with something to think about as I made my way off to bed ... It's hard to write coherently, I find, when you're not living coherently ...

Syd Woodward, of Buckhorn, having learned that I can drive a tractor, has asked me if I'll take part in the plowing-match to-morrow. And I've given my promise to show Mere Man what a woman can do in the matter of turning a mile-long furrow. I feel rather audacious over it all. And I'm glad to inject a little excitement into life ... I'm saving up for a new sewing-machine ... Tarzanette has got rather badly cut up in some of our barb-wire fencing.

Friday the Fifteenth

The plowing-match was good fun, and I enjoyed it even more than I had expected. The men "kidded" me a good deal, and gave me a cheer at the end (I don't quite know whether it was for my work or my costume) and I had to pose for photographs, and a moving-picture man even followed me about for a round, shooting me as I turned my prairie stubble upside down. But the excitement of the plowing-match has been eclipsed by a bit of news which has rather taken my breath away. *It is Peter Ketley who has bought the Harris Ranch.*

Saturday the Twenty-Third

The rains have brought mushrooms, slathers of mushrooms, and I joy in gathering them.

Yesterday afternoon I rode past the Harris Ranch. The old place brought back a confusion of memories. But I was most disturbed by the signs of building going on there. It seems to mean a new shack on Alabama Ranch. And a new shack of very considerable dimensions. I've been wondering what this implies. I don't know whether to be elated or depressed. And what business is it, after all, of mine?

My Dinkie—I have altogether given up trying to call my Dinkie anything but Dinkie—came home two evenings ago with a discolored eye and a distinct air of silence. Gershom, too, seemed equally reticent. So I set about discreetly third-degreeing Poppsy, who finally acknowledged, with awe in her voice, that Dinkie had been in a fight.

It was, according to my petticoated Herodotus, a truly terrible fight. Noses got bloodied, and no one could make the fighters stop. But Dinkie was unquestionably the conqueror. Yet, oddly enough, I am informed that he cried all through the combat. He was a crying fighter. And he had his fight with Climmie O'Lone—trust the Irish to look for trouble!—who seems to have been accepted as the ring-master of his younger clan. Their differences arose out of the accusation that Dinkie, my bashful little Dinkie, had been forcing his unwelcomed attention on one Doreen O'Lone, Climmie's younger sister. That's absurd, of course. And Dinkie must have realized it. He didn't want to fight, acknowledged Poppsy, from the first. He even cried over it. And Doreen also cried. And Poppsy herself joined in.

I fancy it was a truly Homeric struggle, for it seems to have lasted for round after round. It lasted, I have been able to gather, until Climmie was worsted and down on his back crying "Enough!" Which Poppsy reports Dinkie made him say three times, until Doreen nodded and said she'd heard. But my young son, apparently, is one of those crying fighters, who are reckoned, if I remember right, as the worst breed of belligerents!

I have decided not to tell Dinkie what I know. But I'm rather anxious to get a glimpse of this young Mistress Doreen, for whom lances are already being shattered in the lists of youth. The O'Lones regard themselves as the landed aristocracy of the Elk-trail District. And Doreen O'Lone impresses me as a very musical appellative. Yet I prefer to keep my kin free from all entangling alliances, even though they have to do with a cattle-king's offspring....

I had a short letter from Dinky-Dunk to-day, asking me to send on a package of papers which he had left in a pigeon-hole of his desk here. It was a depressingly non-committal little note, without a glimmer of warmth between the lines. I'm afraid there's a certain ugly truth which will have to be faced some day. But I intend to stick to the ship as long as the ship can keep afloat. I am so essentially a family woman that I can't conceive of life without its home circle. Home, however, is where the heart is. And it seems to take more than one heart to keep it going. I keep reminding myself that I have my children at the same time that I keep asking myself why my children are not enough, why they can't seem to fill my cup of contentment as they ought. Now that their father is so much away, a great deal of their training is falling on my shoulders. And I must, in some way, be a model to them. So I'll continue to show them what a Penelope I can be. Perhaps, after all, they will prove our salvation. For our offspring ought to be the snow-fences along the wind-harried rails of matrimony. They should prevent drifting along the line, and from terminal to lonely terminal should keep traffic open ... I have to-night induced Poppsy to write a long and affectionate letter to her *pater*, telling him all the news of Casa Grande. Perhaps it will awaken a little pang in the breast of her absent parent.

Monday the Twenty-Fifth

I have aroused the ire of the Dour Man. He has sent me a message strongly disapproving of my conduct. He even claims that I've humiliated him. I never dreamed, when that movie-man with the camera followed me about at the plowing-match, that my husband would wander into a Calgary picture-house and behold his wife in driving gauntlets and Stetson mounted on a tractor and twiddling her fingers at the camera-operator, just to show how much at home she felt! Dinky-Dunk must have experienced a distinctly new thrill when he saw his own wife come riding through that pictorial news weekly. He would have preferred not recognizing me, I suppose. But there I was, duly named and labeled—and hence the ponderous little note of disapproval.

But I'm not going to let Duncan start a quarrel over trivialities like this. I intend to sit tight. There'd be little use in argument, anyway, for Duncan would only ignore me as the predatory tom-cat ignores the foolishly scolding robin. I'm going to be a regular mallard, and stick to these home regions until the ice forms. And our most mountainous troubles, after all, can't quite survive being exteriorated through the ink-well. It relieves me to write about them. But I wish I had a woman of my own age to talk to. I get a bit lonely, now that winter is slipping down out of the North again. And I find that I'm not so companionable as I ought to be. It comes home to me, now and then, how far away from the world we are, how remote from everything that counts. The tragedy of life with Chaddie McKail, I suppose, is that she's let existence narrow down to just one thing, to her family. Other women seem to have substitutes. But I've about forgotten how to be a social animal. I seem to grow as segregative as the timber-wolf. There's nothing for me in the woman's club life one gets out here. I can't force myself into church work, and the rural reading-club is something beyond me. I simply couldn't endure those Women's Institute meetings which open with a hymn and end up with sponge-cake and green tea, after a platitudinous paper on the Beauty of Prairie Life. It has its beauties, God knows, or we'd all go mad. We women, in this brand-new land, try to bolster ourselves up with the belief that we have greatnesses which the rest of the world must get along without. But that is only the flaunting of *La Panache*, the feather of courage in our cap of discouragement. There is so much, so much, we are denied! So much we must do without! So much we must see go to others! So much we must never even hope for! Oh, pioneers, great you are and great you must be, to endure what you have endured! You must be strong in your hours of secret questioning and you must be strong in your quest for consolation. If nothing else, you must at least be strong. And these western men of ours should all be strong men, should all be great men, because they must have been the children of great mothers. A prairie mother *has* to be a great woman. She must be great to survive, to endure, to leave her progeny behind her. I've heard the Wise Men talk about nature looking after her own. I've heard sentimentalists sing about the strength that lies in the soil. But, oh, pioneers, you know what you know! In your secret heart of hearts you remember the lonely hours, the lonely years, the lonely graves! For in the matter of infant mortality alone, prairie life shows a record shocking to read. We are making that better, it is true, with our district nursing and our motherhood clubs and our rural phones and our organized letting in of light and passing on of knowledge. We are not so overburdened as those nobler women who went before us. But, oh, pioneers along these lonely northern trails, I salute you and honor you for your courage! Your greatness will never be known. It will be seen only in the great country which you gave up your lives to bring to birth!

Wednesday the Twenty-Seventh

What weather-cocks we are! My blue Monday is over and done with, this is a crystalline winter day with all the earth at peace with itself, and I've just had a letter from Peter asking if I could take care of his sister's girl, Susie Mumford, until after Christmas. The Mumfords, it seems, are going through the divorce-mill, and Susie's mother is anxious that her one and only child should be afar from the scene when the grist of liberty is a-grinding.

I know nothing of Susie except what Peter has told me, that she is not yet nineteen, that she is intelligent, but obstreperous, and much wiser than she pretends to be, that the machinery of life has always run much too smoothly about her for her own good, and that a couple of months of prairie life might be the means of introducing her to her own soul.

That's all I know of Susie, but I shall welcome her to Casa Grande. I'll be glad to see a city girl again, to talk over face-creams and the *Follies* and Tchaikowsky and brassieres and Strindberg with. And I'll be glad to do a little toward repaying big-hearted old Peter for all his kindnesses of the past. Susie may be both sophisticated and intractable, but I await her with joy. She seems almost the answer to my one big want.

But Casa Grande, I have been realizing, will have to be refurbished for its coming guest. We have grown a bit shoddy about the edges here. It's hard to keep a house spick and span, with two active-bodied children running about it. And my heart, I suppose, has not been in that work of late. But I've been on a tour of inspection, and I realize it's time to reform. So Struthers and I are about to doll up these dilapidated quarters of ours. And I intend to have my dolorously neglected Guest Room (for such I used to call it) done over before the arrival of Susie....

I rode over to the Teetzels' this afternoon, to explain about our cattle getting through on their land. It was the road-workers who broke down the Teetzel fence, to squat on a coulée-corner for their camp. And they hadn't the decency to restore what they had wrecked. So Bud Teetzel and I rode seven miles up the new turn-pike and overtook those road-workers and I harangued their foreman for a full fifteen minutes. But it made little impression on him. He merely grinned and stared at me with a sort of insolent admiration on his face. And when I had finished he audibly remarked to one of his teamsters that I made a fine figure of a woman on horseback.

Bud says they're thinking of selling out if they can get their price. The old folks want to move to Victoria, and Bud and his brother have a hankering to try their luck up in the Peace River District. I asked Bud if he wouldn't rather settle down in one of the big cities. He merely laughed at me. "No thank you, lady! This old prair-ee is comp'ny enough for me!" he said as he loped, brown as a nut, along the trail as tawny as a lion's mane, with a sky of steel-cold blue smiling down on his lopsided old sombrero. I studied him with a less impersonal eye. He was a handsome and husky young giant, with the joy of life still frankly imprinted on his face.

"Bud," I said as I loped along beside him, "why haven't you ever married?"

That made him laugh again. Then he turned russet as he showed me the white of an eye.

"All the peaches seemed picked, in this district," he found the courage to proclaim.

This made me trot out the old platitude about the fish in the sea being as good as any ever caught—and there really ought to be an excise tax on platitudes, for being addicted to them is quite as bad as being addicted to alcohol, and quite as benumbing to the brain.

But Bud, with his next speech, brought me up short.

"Say, lady, if *you* was still in the runnin' I'd give 'em a race that'd make a coyote look like a caterpillar on crutches!"

He said it solemnly, and his solemnity kept it respectful. But it was my turn to laugh. And ridiculous as it may sound, this doesn't impress me as such a dark world as I had imagined! A woman, after all, is a good deal like mother earth: each has to be cultivated a little to keep it mellow.

... Where the Female is, there also is the Unexpected. For when I got home I found that my decorous Poppsy, my irreproachable Poppsy, had succumbed before the temptation to investigate my new sewing-machine. And once having nibbled at the fruit of the tree of knowledge, she went rampaging through the whole garden. She made a stubborn effort to exhaust the possibilities of all the little hemmers, and tried the shirrer and the fire-stitch ruffler, and obviously had a fling at the binder and a turn at the tucker. What she did to the tension-spring heaven only knows. And my brand-new machine is on the blink. And my meek-eyed little Poppsy isn't as impeccable as the world about her imagined!

Wednesday the Third

Susie Mumford arrived yesterday. The weather, heaven be thanked, was perfect, an opal day with the earth as fresh-smelling as Poppsy just out of her bath. There was just enough chill in the air to make one's blood tingle and just enough warmth in the sunlight to make it feel like a benediction. Whinstane Sandy, in fact, avers that we're in for a spell of Indian Summer.

I motored in to Buckhorn and met Susie, who wasn't in the least what I expected. I was looking for a high-spirited and insolent-eyed young lady who'd probably be traveling with a French maid and a van-load of trunks, after the manner of Lady Alicia. But the Susie I met was a tired and listless and rather white-faced girl who reminds me just enough of her Uncle Peter to make me like her. The poor child knows next to nothing of the continent on which she was born, and the immensity of our West has rather appalled her. She told me, driving home, that she had never before been this side of the Adirondacks. Yet she has crossed the Atlantic eight times and knows western Europe about as well as she knows Long Island itself. There is a matter-of-factness about Susie which makes her easy to get along with. Poppsy took to her at once and was a garrulous and happy witness of Susie's unpacking. Dinkie, on the other hand, developed an altogether unlooked-for shyness and turned red when Susie kissed him. There was no melting of the ice until the strange lady produced a very wonderful toy air-ship, which you wind up and which soars right over the haystacks, if you start it right. This was a present which Peter sent out. Dinkie, in fact, spent most of his spare time last night writing a letter to his Uncle Peter, a letter which he intimated he had no wish for the rest of the family to read. He was willing to acknowledge, this morning, that since he and Susie both had the same Uncle Peter, they really ought to be cousins....

Susie has not been sleeping well, and for all her weariness last night had to take five grains of veronal before she could settle down. The result is that she looks whiter than ever this morning and ate very little of Struthers' really splendiferous breakfast. But she made a valorous enough effort to be blithe and has rambled about Casa Grande with the febrile, quick curiosity of a young setter, making friends with the animals and for the first time in her life picking an egg out of a nest. I was afraid, at first, that she was going to complain about the quietness of existence out here, for our pace must seem a slow one, after New York. But Susie says the one thing she wants is peace. It's not often a girl not yet out of her teens makes any such qualified demand on life. I can't help feeling that the break-up of her family must be depressing her more than she pretends. She speaks about it in a half-joking way, however, and said this morning: "Dad certainly deserves a little freedom!" We sat for an hour at the breakfast-table, pow-wowing about everything under the blessed sun.

In some ways Susie is a very mature woman, for nineteen and three-quarters. She is also an exceptionally companionable one. She has a sort of lapis-lazuli eye with paler streaks in the iris, like banded agate. It is a brooding eye, with a great deal of beauty in it. And she has a magnolia-white skin which one doesn't often see on the prairie. It's not the sort of skin, in fact, which could last very long on the open range. It's the sort that's had too much bevel plate between it and the buffeting winds of the world. But it's lovely to look upon, especially when it's touched with its almost imperceptible shell-pink of excitement as it was this afternoon when Susie climbed on Buntie and tried a canter or two about the corrals. Susie, I noticed, rode well. I couldn't quite make out why her riding made me at once think of Theobald Gustav. But she explained, later, that she had been taught by a German riding-master—and then I understood.

But I must not overlook Gershom, who duly donned his Sunday best in honor of Susie's arrival and who is already undertaking to educate the brooding-eyed young lady from the East. He explained to her that there were eight hundred and fifty thousand square miles of Canada still unexplored, and Susie said: "Then lead me into the most far-away part of it!" And when he told her, during their first meal together, that the human brain was estimated to contain half a billion cells and that the number of brain impressions collected by an average person during fifty years of life aggregated three billion, one hundred and fifty-five million, seven hundred and sixty thousand, Susie sighed and said it was no wonder women were so contradictory. Which impressed me as very like one of my own retorts to Gershom. I saw Susie studying him, studying him with a quiet and meditative eye. "I believe your Gershom is one of the few good men in the world," she afterward acknowledged to me. And I've been wondering why one so young should be saturated with cynicism.

A small incident occurred to-night which disturbed me more than I can explain to myself. Susie, who had been looking through one of Dinkie's school scribblers, guardedly passed the book over to me where I sat sewing in front of the fire. For, whatever may happen, a prairie mother can always find plenty of sewing to do. I looked at the bottom of the page which Susie pointed out to me. There I saw two names, one above the other, with certain of the letters stricken out, two names written like this:

Elmer McKail———love
Doreen O'Lone———friendship

And that set me off in a brown study which even Susie seemed to fathom. She smiled understandingly and turned and inspected Dinkie, bent over his arithmetic, with an entirely new curiosity.

"I suppose that's what every mother has to face, some day," she said as she sat down beside me in front of the fire.

But it seemed a fire without warmth. Life, apparently, had brought me to another of its Great Divides. My boy had a secret apart from his mother. My son was no longer all mine.

Friday the Fifth

This morning at breakfast, when Dinkie and I were alone at the table, I crossed over to him and sat down beside him.

"Dinkie," I said, with my hand on his tousled young head, "whom do you love best in all the world?"

"Mummy!" he said, looking me straight in the eye. And at that I drank in a deep breath.

"Are you sure?" I demanded.

"As sure as death and taxes," he said with his one-sided little smile. It was a phrase which his father used to use, on similar occasions, in the long, long ago. And it didn't quite drive the mists out of my heart.

"And who comes next?" I asked, with my hand still on his head.

"Buntie," he replied, with what I suspected to be a barricaded look on his face.

"No, no," I told him. "It has to be a human being."

"Then Poppsy," he admitted.

"And who next?" I persisted.

"Whinnie!" exclaimed my son.

But I had to shake my head at that.

"Aren't you forgetting somebody very important?" I hinted.

"Who?" he asked, deepening just a trifle in color.

"How about daddy?" I asked. "Isn't it about time for him there?"

"Yes, daddy," he dutifully repeated. But his face cleared, and my own heart clouded, as he went through the empty rite.

Dinkie was studying that clouded face of mine, by this time, and I began to feel embarrassed. But I was determined to see the thing through. It was hard, though, for me to say what I wanted to.

"Isn't there somebody, somebody else you are especially fond of?" I inquired, as artlessly as I could. And it hurt like cold steel to think that I had to fence with my own boy in such a fashion.

Dinkie looked at me and then he looked out of the window.

"I think I like Susie," he finally admitted.

"But in your own life, Dinkie, in your work and your play, in your school, isn't—isn't there *somebody*?" I found the courage to ask.

Dinkie's face grew thoughtful. For just a moment, I thought I caught a touch of the Holbein Astronomer in it.

"There's lots of boys and girls I like," he noncommittally asserted. And I began to see that it was hopeless. My boy had reservations from his own mother, reservations which I would be compelled to respect. He was no longer entirely and unequivocally mine. There was a wild-bird part of him which had escaped, which I could never recapture and cage again. The thing that his father had foretold was really coming about. My laddie would some day grow out of my reach. I would lose him. And my happiness, which had been trying its wings for the last few days, came down out of the sky like a shot duck. All day long, for Susie's sake, I've tried to be light-hearted. But my efforts make me think of a poor old worn-out movie-hall piano doing its pathetic level best to be magnificently blithe. It's a meaningless clatter in a meaningless world.

Thursday the Eleventh

It ought to be winter, according to the almanac, but our wonderful Indian Summer weather continues. Susie and I have been "blue-doming" to-day. We converted ourselves into a mounted escort for Gershom and the kiddies as far as the schoolhouse, and then rode on to Dead Horse Lake, in the hope of getting a few duck. But the weather was too fine, though I managed to bring down a couple of mallard, after one of which Susie, having removed her shoes and stockings, waded knee-deep in the slough. She enjoys that sort of thing: it's something so entirely new to the child of the city. And Susie, I might add, is already looking much better. She is sleeping soundly, at last, and has promised me there shall be no more night-caps of veronal. What is more, I am getting to know her better—and I have several revisions to make.

In the first place, it is not the family divorce cloud that has been darkening Susie's soul. She let the cat out of the bag, on the way home this afternoon. Susie has been in love with a man who didn't come up to expectations. She was very much in love, apparently, and disregarded what people said about him. Then, much to her surprise, her Uncle Peter took a hand in the game. It must have been rather a violent hand, for a person so habitually placid. But Peter, apparently, wasn't altogether ignorant of the club-talk about the young rake in question. At any rate, he decided it was about time to act. Susie declined to explain in just what way he acted. Yet she admits now that Peter was entirely in the right and she, for a time, was entirely in the wrong. But it is rather like having one's appendix cut out, she protests, without an anesthetic. It takes time to heal such wounds. Susie obviously was bowled over. She is still suffering from shock. But I like the spirit of the girl. She's not the kind that one disappointment is going to kill. And prairie life is already doing her good. For she announced this morning that her clothes were positively getting tight for her. And such clothes they are! Such delicate silks and cobwebs of lace and pale-pink contraptions of satin! Such neatly tailored skirts and short-vamped shoes and thing-a-ma-jigs of Irish linen and platinum and gold trinkets to deck out her contemptuous little body with. For Susie takes them all with a shrug of indifference. She loves to slip on my oil-stained old hunting-jacket and my weather-beaten old golf-boots and go meandering about the range.

Another revision which I am compelled to make is that while I expected to be the means of cheering Susie up, Susie has quite unconsciously been the means of rejuvenating *me*. I think I've been able to catch at least a hollow echo of her youth from her. I *know* I have. Two days ago, when we motored in to Buckhorn with my precious marketing of butter and eggs—and Susie never before quite realized how butter and eggs reached the ultimate consumer—a visiting Odd-Fellows' band was playing a two-step on the balcony of the Commercial Hotel. Susie and I stopped the car, and while Struthers stared at us aghast from the back seat, we two-stepped together on the main street of Buckhorn. We just let the music go to our heads and danced there until the crowd in front of the band began to right-about-face and a cowboy in chaps brazenly announced that he was Susie's next partner. So we danced to our running-board, stepped into our devil-wagon, and headed for home, in the icy aura of Struthers' sustained indignation.

I begin to get terribly tired of propriety. I don't know whether it's Struthers, or Struthers and Gershom combined, or having to watch one's step so when there are children about one. But I'm tired of being respectable. I'm tired of holding myself in. I warn the world that I'm about ready for anything, anything from horse-stealing to putting a dummy-lady in Whinstane Sandy's bed. I don't believe there's any wickedness that's beyond me. I'm a reckless and abandoned woman. And if that cold-blooded old Covenanter doesn't get home from Calgary pretty soon I'm going buckboard riding with Bud Teetzel!

I've been asking Susie if we measure up to her expectations. She said, in reply, that we fitted in to a T. For her Uncle Peter, she acknowledged, had already done us in oils on the canvas of her curiosity. She accused me, however, of reveling in that primitiveness which is the last resort of the sophisticated—like the log cabins the city folk fashion for themselves when they get up in the Adirondacks. And Casa Grande, she further amended, impressed her as being almost disappointingly comfortable.

After that Susie fell to talking about Peter. She is affectionately contemptuous toward her uncle, protesting that he's forever throwing away his chances and letting other people impose on his good nature. It was lucky, averred Susie, that he was born with a silver spoon in his mouth. For he was a hopeless espouser of Lost Causes. She inclined to the belief that he should have married young, should have married young and had a flock of children, for he was crazy about kiddies.

I asked Susie what sort of wife Peter should have chosen. And Susie said Peter should have hitched up with a good, capable, practical-minded woman who could manage him without letting him know he was being managed. There was a widow in the East, acknowledged his niece, who had been angling for poor Peter for years. And Peter was still free, Susie suspected, because in the presence of that widow he emulated Hamlet and always put an antic disposition on. Did the most absurd things, and appeared to be little more than half-witted. The widow in question had even spoken to Susie about her uncle's eccentricities and intimated that his segregative manner of life might in the end affect his intellect!

The thought of Peter marrying rather gave me a shock. It was like being told by some authority in astronomy that your earth was about to collide with Wernecke's Comet. And, vain peacock that I was, I rather liked to think of Peter going through life mourning for me, alone and melancholy and misogynistic for the rest of his days! Yet there must be dozens, there must be hundreds, of attractive girls along the paths which he travels. I found the courage to mention this fact to Susie, who merely laughed and said her Uncle Peter would probably be saved by his homeliness. But I can't say that I ever regarded Peter Ketley as homely. He may never carry off a blue ribbon from a beauty show, but he has the sort of face that a woman of sense can find tremendous appeal in. Your flapper type, I suppose, will always succumb to the curled Romeo, but it's the ruggeder and stronger man with the bright mind and the kindly heart who will always appeal to the clearer-eyed woman who has come to know life.... Susie has told me, by the way, that Josie Langdon and her husband quarreled on their honeymoon, quarreled the first week in Paris and right across the Continent for the momentous reason that Josie *insisted on putting sugar in her claret!*

I've been doing a good deal of thinking, the last few hours. I've been wondering if I'm a Lost Cause. And I've been wondering why women should want to put sugar in their claret. If it's made to be bitter, why not accept the bitterness, and let it go at that?

Friday the Twelfth

Dinky-Dunk has just sent word that he will be home to-morrow night and asks if I'll mind motoring in to Buckhorn for him.

It impresses me as a non-committal little message, yet it means more to me than I imagined. *My husband is coming home.*

Susie has been eying me all afternoon, with a pucker of perplexity about her lapis-lazuli eyes. We are busy, getting things to rights. And I've made an appallingly long list of what I must buy in Buckhorn to-morrow. Even Struthers has perked up a bit, and is making furtive preparations for a sage-tea wash in the morning.

Tuesday the Sixteenth

Why is life so tangled up? Why can't we be either completely happy or completely the other way? Why must wretchedness come sandwiched in between slices of hope and contentment, and why must happiness be haunted by some ghostly echo of pain? And why can't people be all good or all bad, so that the tares and the wheat never get mixed up together and make a dismal mess of our harvest of Expectation?

These are some of the questions I've been asking myself since Duncan went back to Calgary last night. He stayed only two days. And they were days of terribly complicated emotions. I went to the station for him, on Saturday, and in my impatience to be there on time found myself with an hour and a half of waiting, an hour and a half of wandering up and down that ugly open platform in the clear cool light of evening. There was a hint of winter in the air, an intimidating northern nip which made the thought of a warm home and an open fire a consolation to the chilled heart. And I felt depressed, in spite of everything I could do to bolster up my courage. In the first place, I couldn't keep from thinking of Alsina Teeswater. And in the second place, never, never on the prairie, have I watched a railway-train come in or a railway-train pass away without feeling lonesome. It reminds me how big is the outside world, how infinitesimal is Chaddie McKail and her unremembered existence up here a thousand miles from Nowhere! It humbles me. It reminds me that I have in some way failed to mesh in with the bigger machinery of life.

I had a lump in my throat, by the time Dinky-Dunk's train pulled in and I saw him swing down from the car-steps. I made for him through the crowd, in fact, with my all but forgotten Australian crawl-stroke, and accosted him with rather a briny kiss and so tight a hug that he stood back and studied my face. He wanted to ask, I know, if anything had happened. He was obviously startled, and just a trifle embarrassed. My lump, by this time, was bigger than ever, but I had to swallow it in secret. Dinky-Dunk, I found, was changed in many ways. He was tired, and he seemed older. But he was prosperous-looking, in brand-new raiment, and reported that luck was still with him and everything was flourishing. Give him one year, he protested, and he'd show them he wasn't a piker.

I waited for him to ask about the children, but his mind seemed full of his Barcona coal business. The railway was learning to treat them half decently and the coal was coming out better than they'd hoped for. They'd a franchise to light the town, developing their power from the mine screenings, and what they got from this would be so much velvet. And he had a chance to take over one of the finest houses in Mount Royal, if he had a family along with him to excuse such magnificence.

That final speech of his brought me up short. It was dark along the trail, and dark in my heart. And more things than one had happened that day to humble me. So I took one hand off the wheel and put it on his knee.

"Do you want me to go to Calgary?" I asked him.

"That's up to you," he said, without budging an inch. He said it, in fact, with a steel-cold finality which sent my soul cringing back into its kennel. And the trail ahead of me seemed blacker than ever.

"I'll have to have time to think it over," I said with a composure which was nine-tenths pretense.

"Some wives," he remarked, "are willing to help their husbands."

"I know it, Dinky-Dunk," I acknowledged, hoping against hope he'd give me the opening I was looking for. "And I want to help, if you'll only let me."

"I think I'm doing my part," he rather solemnly asserted. I couldn't see his face, in the dark, but there was little hope to be wrung from the tone of his voice. So I knew it would be best to hold my peace.

Casa Grande blazed a welcome to us, as we drove up to it, and the children, thank heaven, were relievingly boisterous over the adventure of their dad's return. He seemed genuinely amazed at their growth, seemed slightly irritated at Dinkie's long stares of appraisal, and feigned an interest in the paraded new possessions of Poppsy and her brother—until it came to Peter's toy air-ship, which was thrust almost bruskly aside.

And that reminds me of one thing which I am reluctant to acknowledge. Dinky-Dunk was anything but nice to Susie. He may have his perverse reasons for disliking everything in any way connected with Peter Ketley, but I at least expected my husband to be agreeable to the casual guest under his roof. Through it all, I must confess, Susie was wonderful. She made no effort to ignore Duncan, as his ignoring of her only too plainly merited. She remained, not only poised and imperturbable, but impersonal and impenetrable. She found herself, I think, driven just a tiny bit closer to Gershom, who still shows a placid exterior to Duncan's slightly contemptuous indifference.

My husband, I'm afraid, was not altogether happy in his own home. In one way, of course, I can not altogether blame him for that, since his bigger interests now are outside that home. But I begin to see how dangerous these long separations can be. Somewhere and at some time, before too much water runs under the bridges, there will have to be a readjustment.

I realized that, in fact, as I drove Duncan back to the station last night, after I'd duly signed the different papers he'd brought for that purpose. I had a feeling that every chug of the motor was carrying him further and further out of my life. Heaven knows, I was willing enough to eat crow. I was ready to bury the hatchet, and bury it in my own bosom, if need be, rather than see it swinging free to strike some deeper blow.

"Dinky-Dunk," I said after a particularly long silence between us, "what is it you want me to do?"

My heart was beating much faster than he could have imagined and I was grateful for the chance to pretend the road was taking up most of my attention.

"Do about what?" he none too encouragingly inquired.

"We don't seem to be hitting it off the way we should be," I went on, speaking as quietly as I was able. "And I want you to tell me where I'm failing to do my share."

That note of humility from me must have surprised him a little, for we rode quite a distance without a word.

"What makes you feel that way?" he finally asked.

I found it hard to answer that question. It would never be easy, at any rate, to answer it as I wanted to.

"Because things can't go on this way forever," I found the courage to tell him.

"Why not?" he asked. He seemed indifferent again.

"Because they're all wrong," I rather tremulously replied. "Can't you see they're all wrong?"

"But why do you want them changed?" he asked with a disheartening sort of impersonality.

"For the sake of the children," I told him. And I could feel the impatient movement of his body on the car seat beside me.

"The children!" he repeated with acid-drop deliberation. "The children, of course! It's always the children!"

"You're still their father," I reminded him.

"A sort of honorary president of the family," he amended.

Hope ebbed out of my heart, like air out of a punctured tire.

"Aren't you making it rather hard for me?" I demanded, trying to hold myself in, but feeling the bob-cat getting the better of the purring tabby.

"I've rather concluded that was the way you made it for *me*," countered Duncan, with a coolness of manner which I came more and more to resent.

"In what way?" I asked.

"In shutting up shop," he rather listlessly responded.

"I don't think I quite understand," I told him.

"Well, in crowbarring me out of your scheme of life, if you insist on knowing," were the words that came from the husband sitting so close beside me. "You had your other interests, of course. But you also seem to have had the idea that you could turn me loose like a range horse. I could paw for my fodder and eat snow when I got thirsty. You didn't even care to give me a wind-break to keep a forty-mile blizzard out of my bones. You didn't know where I was browsing, and didn't much care. It was up to me to rustle for myself and be rounded up when the winter was over and there was another spell of work on hand!"

We rode on in silence, for almost a mile, with the cold air beating against my body and a colder numbness creeping about the corner of my heart.

"Do you mean, Dinky-Dunk," I finally asked, "that you want your freedom?"

"I'm not saying that," he said, after another short silence.

"Then what is it you want?" I asked, wondering why the windshield should look so blurred in the half-light.

"I want to get something out of life," was his embittered retort.

It was a retort that I thought over, thought over with an oddly settling mind, like a stirred pool that has been left to clear itself. For that grown man sitting there beside me seemed ridiculously like a spoiled child, an indulged child forlornly alone in the fogs of his own arrogance. He made me think of a black bear which bites at the bullet wound in his own body. I felt suddenly sorry for him, in a maternal sort of way. I felt sorry for him at the same time that I remained a trifle afraid of him, for he still possessed, I knew, his black-bear power of inflicting unlooked-for and ursine blows. I simply ached to swing about on him and say: "Dinky-Dunk, what you need is a good spanking!" But I didn't have the courage. I had to keep my sense of humor under cover, just as you have to blanket garden-geraniums before the threat of a black frost. Yet, oddly enough, I felt fortified by that sense of pity. It seemed to bring with it the impression that Duncan was still a small boy who might some day grow out of his badness. It made me feel suddenly older and wiser than this overgrown child who was still crying for the moon. And with that feeling came a wave of tolerance, followed by a smaller wave of faith, of faith that everything might yet come out right, if only I could learn to be patient, as mothers are patient with children.

"And I, on my part, Dinky-Dunk, want to see you get the very best out of life," I found myself saying to him. My intentions were good, but I suppose I made my speech in a very superior and school-teachery sort of way.

"I guess I've got about all that's coming to me," he retorted, with the note of bitterness still in his voice.

And again I had the feeling of sitting mother-wise and mother-patient beside an unruly small boy.

"There's much more, Dinky-Dunk, if you only ask for it," I said as gently as I was able.

He turned, at that, and studied me in the failing light, studied me with a sharp look of interrogation on his face. I had the feeling, as he did so, of something epochal in the air, as though the drama of life were narrowing up to its climactic last moment. Yet I felt helpless to direct the course of that drama. I nursed the impression that we stood at the parting of the ways, that we stood hesitating at the fork of two long and lonely trails which struck off across an illimitable world, farther and farther apart. I vaguely regretted that we were already in the streets of Buckhorn, for I was half hoping that Duncan would tell me to stop the car. Then I vaguely regretted that I was busy driving that car, as otherwise I might have been free to get my arms about that granitic Dour Man of mine and strangle him into submitting to that momentary mood of softness which seems to come less and less to the male as he grows older.

But Duncan merely laughed, a bit uneasily, and just as suddenly grew silent again. I had a sense of asbestos curtains coming down between us, coming down before the climax was reached or the drama was ended. I couldn't help wondering, as we drove into the cindered station-yard where the lights were already twinkling, if Dinky-Dunk, like myself, sat waiting for something which failed to manifest itself, if he too had held back before the promise of some decisive word which I was without the power to utter. For we were only half-warm, the two of us, toying with the ghosts of the dead past and childishly afraid of the future. We were Laodiceans, neither hot nor cold, without the primal hunger to reach out and possess what we too timidly desired. We were more neutral even than Ferdinand and the Lady of the Bust, for we no longer cared sufficiently to let the other know we cared, but waited and waited in that twilight where all cats are gray.

There was, mercifully, very little time left for us before the train came in. We kept our masks on, and talked only of every-day things, about the receipt for the ranch taxes and what steers Whinnie should "finish" and the new granary roof and the fire-lines about the haystacks. Without quite knowing it, when the train pulled in, I put my arm through my husband's— and for the second time that evening he turned sharply and inspected my face. I felt as though I wanted to hold him back, to hold him back from something unescapable but tragically momentous. I think he felt sorry for me. At any rate, after he had swung his suit-case up on the car-platform, he turned and kissed me good-by. But it was the sort of kiss one gets at funerals. It left me standing there watching the tail-lights blink off down the track, as desolate as though I had been left alone on the deadest promontory of the deadest planet lost in space. I stood there until the lights were gone. I stood there until the platform was empty again and my car was the only car left along the hard-packed cinders. So I climbed into the driving-seat, and pulled on my gauntlets, and headed for home....

Back at Casa Grande I found Dinkie and Whinnie beside the bunk-house stove, struggling companionably through the opening chapters of *Treasure Island*. My boy smiled up at me, for a moment, but his mind, I could see, was intent on the page along which Whinnie's stubbled finger was crawling like a plowshare beside each furrow of text. He was in the South Pacific, a thousand miles away from me. In my own house Struthers was putting a petulant-voiced Poppsy to bed, and Gershom, up in his room, was making extraordinary smells at his chemistry experiments. Susie I found curled comfortably up in front of the fire, idling over my first volume of *Jean Christophe*.

She read three sentences aloud as I sat down beside her. "How happy he is! He is made to be happy!...Life will soon see to it that he is brought to reason."

She seemed to expect some comment from me, but I found myself with nothing to say. In fact, we both sat there for a long time, staring in silence at the fire.

"Why do you live with a man you don't love?" she suddenly asked out of the utter stillness.

It startled me, that question. It also embarrassed me, for I could feel my color mount as Susie's lapis-lazuli eyes rested on my face.

"What makes you think I don't love him?" I countered, reminding myself that Susie, after all, was still a girl in her teens.

"It's not a matter of thinking," was Susie's quiet retort. "I *know* you don't."

"Then I wish I could be equally certain," I said with a defensive stiffening of the lines of dignity.

But Susie smiled rather wearily at my forlorn little parade of *hauteur*. Then she looked at the fire.

"It's hell, isn't it, being a woman?" she finally observed, unconsciously paraphrasing a much older philosopher.

"Sometimes," I admitted.

"I don't see why you stand it," was her next meditative shaft in my direction.

"What would you do about it?" I guardedly inquired.

Susie's face took on one of its intent looks. She was only in her teens, but life, after all, hadn't dealt over-lightly with her. She impressed me, at the moment, as a secretly ardent young person whose hard-glazed little body might be a crucible of incandescent though invisible emotions.

"What would you do about it?" I repeated, wondering what gave some persons the royal right of doing the questionable and making it seem unquestionable.

"*Live!*" said Susie with quite unlooked-for emphasis. "*Live*—whatever it costs!"

"Wouldn't you regard this as living?" I asked, after a moment of thought.

"Not as you ought to be," averred Susie.

"Why not?" I parried.

Susie sighed. She began to see that it was beyond argument, I suppose. Then she too had her period of silence.

"But what are you getting out of it?" she finally demanded. "What is going to happen? What ever *has* happened?"

"To whom?" I asked, resenting the unconscious cruelty of her questioning.

"To you," was the reply of the hard-glazed young hedonist confronting me.

"Are you flattering me with the inference that I was cut out for better things?" I interrogated as my gaze met Susie's. It was her turn to color up a bit. Then she sighed again, and shook her head.

"I don't suppose it's doing either of us one earthly bit of good," she said with a listless small smile of atonement. "And I'm sorry."

So we let the skeletons stalk away from our pleasant fireside and secrete themselves in their customary closets of silence.

But I've been thinking a good deal about that question of Susie's. What *has* happened to me, out here on the prairie? What has indeed come into my life?...

I married young and put a stop to those romantic adventurings which enrich the lives of most girls and enlighten the days of many women. I married a man and lived with him in a prairie shack, and sewed and baked for him, and built a new home and lost it, and began over again. I had children, and saw one of them die, and felt my girlhood slip away, and sold butter and eggs, and loved the man of my choice and cleaved to him and planned for my children, until I saw the man of my choice love another woman. And still I clung to my sparless hulk of a home, hoping to hold close about me the children I had brought into the world and would some day lose again to the world. And that was all. That was everything. It is true, nothing much has ever happened to me....

But I stop, to think this over. If these are the small things, then what are the big things of life? What is it that other women get? I have sung and been happy; I have known great joy and walked big with Hope. I have loved and been loved. I have known sorrow, and I have known birth, and I have sat face to face with death. I have, after all, pretty well run the whole gamut, without perhaps realizing it. For these, after all, are the big things, the elemental things, of life. They are the basic things which leave scant room for the momentary fripperies and the hand-made ornaments of existence....

Heigho! I seem to grow into a melancholy Jacques with the advancing years. That's the way of life, I suppose. But I've no intention of throwing up the sponge. If I can no longer get as much fun out of the game as I want, I can at least watch my offspring taking their joy out of it. God be thanked for giving us our children! We can still rest our tired old eyes on them, just as the polisher of precious stones used to keep an emerald in front of him, to relieve his strained vision by gazing at its soft and soothing greenness.

I have just crept in to take a look at my precious Dinkie, fast asleep in the old cast-iron crib that is growing so small for him he has to lie catercornered on his mattress. He seemed so big, stretched out there, that he frightened me with the thought he couldn't be a child much longer. There are no babies left now in my home circle. And I still have a shamefaced sort of hankering to hold a baby in my arms again!

Wednesday the Thirty-First

Susie has promised to stay with us until after Christmas. And the holidays, I realize, are only a few weeks away. Struthers is knitting a sweater of flaming red and rather grimly acknowledged, when I pinned her down, that it was for Whinstane Sandy. There was a snow-flurry Sunday, and Gershom took Susie riding in the old cutter, scratching grittily along the half-covered trails but apparently enjoying it. My poor little Poppsy, who rather idolizes Gershom, is transparently jealous of his attentions to Susie. Yet Gershom, I know, is nice to Susie and nothing more. He is still my loyal but carefully restrained knight. It's a shame, I suppose, to bobweasel him the way I occasionally do. But I can't quite help it. His goody-goodiness is as provocative to my baser nature as a red flag to an Andulasian bull. And a woman who was once reckoned as a heart-breaker has to keep her hand in with *something*. I've got to convince myself that the last shot hasn't gone from the locker which Duncan   Argyll McKail once rifled. I spoiled Gershom's supper for him the other night by asking what it was made some people have such a mysterious influence over other people. And I caught him up short, last Sunday morning, when he tried to argue that I was a sort of paragon in petticoats.

"Don't you run away with the idea I'm that kind of an angel," I promptly assured him. "I'm an outlaw, from saddle to sougan, and I can buck like a bear fightin' bees. I'm a she-devil crow-hopping around in skirts. And I could bu'st every commandment slap-bang across my knee, once I got started, and leave a trail of crime across the fair face of nature that would make an old Bow-Gun vaquero's back-hair stand up. I'm just a woman, Gershom, a little lonely and a little loony, and there's so much backed-up bad in me that once the dam gives way there'll be a hell-roaring old whoop-up along these dusty old trails!"

Gershom turned white.

"But there's your little ones to think of," he quaveringly reminded me.

"Yes, there's my little ones to think of," I echoed, wondering where I'd heard that familiar old refrain before. My bark, after all, is much worse than my bite. About all I can do is take things out in talk. I'm only a faded beauty, brooding over my antique adventures as a heart-breaker. But I know of one heart I'd still like to break—if I had the power. No; not break; but bend up to the cracking point!

Monday the Nineteenth

How Time takes wing for the busy! It's only six days to Christmas and I've still my box to get off for Olga and her children. We've sent to Peter some really charming snap-shots of the children, which Susie took. The general effect of one, I must acknowledge, is seriously damaged by the presence of their Mummy.

Dinky-Dunk doubts if he'll be able to get home for the holidays. But I sent him a box, on Saturday, made up of those things which he likes best to eat and a set of the children's pictures, nicely mounted. I've also had Dinkie and Poppsy write a long letter to their dad, a task which they performed with more constraint than I had anticipated. I had my own difficulties, along the same line, for I had taken a photograph of poor little Pee-Wee's grave with a snow-drift across one end of it, and had written on the bottom of the mounting-card: *"We must remember."* But as I stood studying this, before putting it in next to Poppsy's huge Christmas-card gay with powdered mica I felt a foolish tear or two run down my cheek. And I realized it would never do to cloud my Dinky-Dunk's day with memories which might not be altogether happy. So I've kept the picture of the little white-fenced bed with the white snow-drift across its foot....

Susie is in bed with a bad cold, which she caught studying astronomy with Gershom. Poppsy was not in the least put out when she watched me preparing a mustard-plaster for the invalid. My daughter, I am persuaded, has a revived faith in the operation of retributive justice. But I hope Susie is better by the holiday. Whinnie has the Christmas Tree hidden away in the stable, and already a number of mysterious parcels have arrived at Casa Grande. Bud Teetzel very gallantly sent me over a huge turkey, an eighteen-pounder, and to-morrow I have to go into Buckhorn for my mail-order shipments. We have decorated the house with a whole box of holly from Victoria and I've hung a sprig of mistletoe in the living-room doorway. The children, of course, are on tiptoe with expectation. But I can't escape the impression that I'm merely acting a part, that I'm a Pagliacci in petticoats. Heaven knows I clown enough; no one can accuse me of not going through the gestures. But it seems like fox-trotting along the deck of a sinking ship.

I stood under the mistletoe, this morning, and dared Gershom to kiss me. He turned quite white and made for the door. But I caught him by the coat, like Potiphar's wife, and pulled him back to the authorizing berry-sprig and gave him a brazen big smack on the cheek-bone. He turned a sunset pink, at that, and marched out of the room without saying a word. But he was shaking his head as he went, at my shamelessness, I suppose. Poor old Gershom! I wish there were more men in the world like him. The other day Susie intimated that he was too homosexual and that it was the polygamous wretches who really kept the world going. But I refuse to subscribe to that sophomoric philosophy of hers which would divide the race into fools and knaves. "It's safer being sane than mad; it's better being good than bad!" as Robert remarked. And I know at least one strong man who is not bad; and one bad man who is not strong.

Tuesday the Twenty-Seventh

The great Day has come and gone. And I'm not sorry. There was a cloud over my heart that kept me from getting the happiness out of it I ought. I hoped we would hear from Peter, but for the first time in history he overlooked us.

Dinky-Dunk, as he had warned us, could not get home for the holidays. But he surprised me by sending a really wonderful box for the kiddies, and even a gorgeous silver-mounted collar for Scotty. Susie is up again, but she is still feeling a bit listless. I heard Gershom informing her to-night that her blood travels at the rate of seven miles per hour and that if all the energy of Niagara Falls were utilized it could supply the world with seven million horse-power. I do wish Gershom would get over trying to pat the world on the head, instead of shaking hands with it! I'm afraid I'm losing my lilt. I can't understand why I should keep feeling as blue as indigo. I am a well of acid and a little sister to the crab-apple. I think I'll make Susie come down so we can humanize ourselves with a little music. For I feel like a Marie Bashkirtseff with a bilious attack....

Whinstane Sandy has just come in with Peter's box, two days late. I felt sure that Peter would not utterly forget us. There is still a great deal of shouting down in the kitchen, where that most miraculous of boxes has been unpacked. As for myself, I've had a hankering to be alone, to think things over. But my meditations don't seem to get me anywhere.... Dinkie has just come up to show me his brand-new bridle for Buntie. It is a magnificent bridle, as shiny and jingly as any lad could desire. I tried to get him to put it down, so that I could draw him over close to me and talk to him. But Dinkie is too excited for any such demonstration. He's beginning, I'm afraid, to consider emotion a bit unmanly. He seems to be losing his craving to be petted and pampered. There are times, I can see, when he desires his fence-lines to be respected.

Sunday the Twenty-Ninth

Nearly six weeks, I notice, have slipped by. For a month and a half, apparently, the impulse to air my troubles went hibernating with the bears. Yet it has been a mild winter, so far, with very little snow and a great deal of sunshine—a great deal of sunshine which doesn't elate me as it ought. I can't remember who it was said a happy people has no history. But that's not true of a happy woman. It's when her heart is full that she makes herself heard, that she sings like a lark to the world. When she's wretched, she retires with her grief....

I haven't been altogether wretched, it's true, just as I haven't been altogether hilarious, but it disturbs me to find that for a month and a half I haven't written a line in this, the mottled old book of my life. It's not that the last month or two has been empty, for no months are really empty. They have to be filled with something. But there are times, I suppose, when lives lie fallow, the same as fields lie fallow, times when the days drag like harrow-teeth across the perplexed loam of our soul and nothing comes of it at all. Not, I repeat, that I have been momentously unhappy. It's more that a sort of sterilizing indifferency took possession of me and made the little ups and downs of existence as unworthy of record as the ups and downs of the waves on the deadest shores of the Dead Sea. It's not that I'm idle, and it's not that I'm old, and it's not that there's anything wrong with this disappointingly healthy body of mine. But I rather think I need a change of some kind. I even envy Susie, who has ambled on to the Coast and is staying with the Lougheeds in Victoria, playing golf and picking winter roses and writing back about her trips up Vancouver Island and her approaching journey down into California.

"What do we know of the New World," she parodied in her last letter that came to me, "who only the old East know?" Then she goes on to say: "I'm just back from a West Coast trip on the roly-poly *Maquinna* and if my thoughts go wobbly and my hand goes crooked it's because my head is so prodigiously full of

E A L S

A L M O N

U N S E T S

T A R S

U R F

O L A N D E R   I S L A N D

I W A S H E S

A G H A L I E   L A M O N T I S

K O O K U M   C H U C K

E A - L I O N S

and alas, also *Seasickness*, that I can't think straight!"

Susie's soul, apparently, has had the dry-shampoo it was in need of. But as for me, I'm like an old horse-shoe with its calks worn off. The Master-Blacksmith of Life should poke me deep into His fires and fling me on His anvil and make me over!

I've been worrying about my Dinkie. It's all so trivial, in a way, and yet I can't persuade myself it isn't also tragic. He told Susie, before she left, that he was quite willing to go to bed a little earlier one night, because then "he could dream about Doreen." And I noticed, not long ago, that instead of taking just *one* of our Newton Pippins to school with him, he had formed the habit of taking *two*. On making investigation, I discovered that this second apple ultimately and invariably found its way into the hands of Mistress Doreen O'Lone. And last week Dinkie autocratically commanded Whinstane Sandy to hitch Mudski up in the old cutter, to go sleigh-riding with the lady of his favor to the Teetzels' taffy-pull. Dinkie's mother was not consulted in the matter—and that is the disturbing feature of it all. I can't help remembering what Duncan once said about my boy growing out of my reach. If I ever lost my Dinkie I would indeed be alone, terribly and hopelessly alone.

Wednesday the Eighth

Dinkie, who has been disturbing me the last few days by going about with an air of suppressed excitement, brought my anxiety to a head yesterday by staring into my face and then saying:

"Mummy, I've got a secret!"

"What secret?" I asked, doing my best to appear indifferent.

But Dinkie was not to be trapped.

"It wouldn't be a secret, if I told you," he sagaciously explained.

I studied my child with what was supposed to be a reproving eye.

"You mean you can't even tell your own Mummy?" I demanded.

He shook his head, in solemn negation.

"But can you, some day?" I pursued.

He thought this over.

"Yes, some day," he acknowledged, squeezing my knee.

"How long will I have to wait?" I asked, wondering what could bring such a rhapsodic light into his hazel-specked eye. I thought, of course, of Doreen O'Lone. And I wished the O'Lones would follow in the footsteps of so many other successful ranchers and trek off to California. Then, as I sat studying Dinkie, I countermanded that wish. For its fulfillment would bring loneliness to the heart of my laddie—and loneliness is hell! So, instead, I struggled as best I could to banish all thought of the matter from my mind. But it was only half a success. I remembered that Gershom himself had been going about as abstracted as an ant-eater and as gloomy as a crow, during the last week; and I kept sniffing something unpropitious up-wind. I even hoped that Dinkie would return to the subject, as children with a secret have the habit of doing. But he has been as tight-lipped on the matter as his reticent old dad might have been.

Wednesday the Fifteenth

I got an altogether unlooked-for Valentine yesterday. It was a brief but a significant letter from Dinky-Dunk, telling me that he had "taken over" the Goodhue house in Mount Royal and asking me if I intended to be its mistress. He has bought the house, apparently, completely furnished and is getting ready to move into it the first week in March.

The whole thing has rather taken my breath away. I don't object to an ultimatum, but I do dislike to have it come like a bolt from the blue. I have arrived at my Rubicon, all right, and about everything that's left of my life, I suppose, will hang on my decision. I don't know whether to laugh or to cry, to be horrified or hilarious. At one moment I have a tendency to emulate Marguerite doing the Jewel-Song in *Faust*. "This isn't *me*! This isn't *me*!" I keep protesting to myself. But Marguerite, I know, would never be so ungrammatical. And then I begin to foresee difficulties. The mere thought of leaving Casa Grande tears my heart. When we go away, as that wise man of Paris once said, we die a little. This will always seem my home. I could never forsake it utterly. I dread to forsake it for even a portion of each year. I am a part of the prairie, now, and I could never be entirely happy away from it. And to accept that challenge—for however one may look at it, it remains a challenge—and go to the new home in Calgary would surely be another concession. And I have been conceding, conceding, for the sake of my children. How much more can I concede?

Yet, when all is said and done, I am one of a family. I am not a free agent. I am chained to the oar for life. When we link up with the race we have more than the little ring of our own Ego to remember. It is not, as Dinky-Dunk once pointed out to me, a good thing to get "Indianized." We have our community obligations and they must be faced. The children, undoubtedly, would have advantages in the city. And to find my family reunited would be *"le désir de paraître."* But I can't help remembering how much there is to remember. I'm humbler now, it's true, than I once was. I no longer say "One side, please!" to life, while life, like old Major Elmes on Murray Hill, declines to vary its course for one small and piping voice. Instead of getting gangway, I find, I'm apt to get an obliterating thump on the spine. Heaven knows, I want to do the right thing. But the issue seems so hopelessly tangled. I have brooded over it and I have even prayed over it. But it all seems to come to nothing. I sometimes nurse a ghostly sort of hope that it may be taken out of my hands, that some power outside myself may intervene to decide. For it impresses me as ominous that I should be able to hesitate at such a time, when a woman, for once in her life, should know her own mind, should see her own fixed goal and fight her way to it. I've been wondering if I haven't ebbed away into that half-warm impersonality which used to impress me as the last stage in moral decay.

But I'm not the fishy type of woman. I know I'm not. And I'm not a hardhead. I've always had a horror of being hard, for fear my hardness might in some way be passed on to my Dinkie. I want to keep my boy kindly and considerate of others, and loyal to the people who love him. But I balk at that word "loyal." For if I expect loyalty in my offspring I surely must have it myself. And I stood up before a minister of God, not so many years ago, and took an oath to prove loyal to my husband, to cleave to him in sickness and in health. I also took an oath to honor him. But he has made that part of the compact almost impossible. And my children, if I go back to him, will come under his influence. And I can't help questioning what that influence will be. I have only one life to live. And I have a human anxiety to get out of it all that is coming to me. I even feel that it owes me something, that there are certain arrears of happiness to be made up.... I wish I had a woman, older and wiser than myself, to talk things over with. I have had the impulse to write to Peter, and tell him everything, and ask him what I ought to do. But that doesn't impress me as being quite fair to Peter. And, oddly enough, it doesn't impress me as being quite fair to Dinky-Dunk. So I'm going to wait a week or two and let the cream of conviction rise on the pan of indecision. There's a tiny parliament of angels, in the inner chambers of our heart, who talk these things over and decide them while we sleep.

Friday the Seventeenth

We had to dig in, like bears, for two whole days while the first real snow-storm of the winter raged outside. But the skies have cleared, the wind has gone, and the weather is crystal-clear again. Dinkie and Poppsy, furred to the ears, are out on the drifts learning to use the snow-shoes which Percy and Olga sent down to them for Christmas. Dinkie has made himself a spear by lashing his broken-bladed jack-knife to the handle of my headless dutch-hoe and has converted himself into a stealthy Iluit stalking a polar bear in the form of poor old Scotty, who can't quite understand why he is being driven so relentlessly from crevice to Arctic crevice. They have also built an igloo, and indulged in what is apparently marriage by capture, with the reluctant bride making her repeated escape by floundering over drifts piled even higher than the fence-tops. It makes me hanker to get my own snow-shoes on my moccasined feet again and go trafficking over that undulating white world of snow, where barb-wire means no more than a line-fence in Noah's Flood. No one could remain morose, in weather like this. You must dress for it, of course, since that arching blue sky has sword-blades of cold sheathed in its velvety soft azure. But it goes to your head, like wine, and you wonder what makes you feel that life is so well worth living.

Tuesday, the Twenty-First

The armistice continues. And I continue to sit on my keg of powder and sing "*O Sole Mio*" to the northern moon.

I have had Whinstane Sandy build a toboggan-slide out of the old binder-shed, which has been pretty well blown to pieces by last summer's wind-storms. He picked out the soundest of the two-by-fours and made a framework which he boarded over with the best of the weather-bleached old siding. For when you haven't the luxury of a hill on your landscape, you can at least make an imitation one. Whinnie even planed the board-joints in the center of the runway and counter-sunk every nail-head—and cussed volubly when he pounded his heavily mittened thumb with the hammer. The finished structure could hardly be called a thing of beauty. We have only one of the stable-ladders to mount it from the rear, and instead of toboggans we have only Poppsy's home-made hand-sleigh and Dinkie's somewhat dilapidated "flexible coaster." But when water had been carried out to that smooth runway and the boards had been coated with ice, like brazil-nuts *glacé*, and the snow along the lower course had been well packed down, it at least gave you a run for your money.

The tip-top point of the slide couldn't have been much more than fourteen or fifteen feet above the prairie-floor, but it seemed perilous enough when I tried it out—much to the perturbation of Whinstane Sandy—by lying stomach-down on Dinkie's coaster and letting myself shoot along that well-iced incline. It was a kingly sensation, that of speed wedded to danger, and it took me back to Davos at a breath. Then I tried it with Dinkie, and then with Poppsy, and then with Poppsy and Dinkie together. We had some grand old tumbles, in the loose snow, and some unmentionable bruises, before we became sufficiently expert to tool our sleigh-runners along their proper trail. But it was good fun. The excitement of the thing, in fact, rather got into my blood. In half an hour the three of us were covered with snow, were shouting like Comanches, and were having an altogether wild time of it. There was climbing enough to keep us warm, for all the sub-zero weather, and I was finally allowed to escape to the house only on the promise that I risk my neck again on the morrow.

Friday the Twenty-Fourth

My Dinkie's secret is no longer a secret. It divulged itself to me to-day with the suddenness of a thunder-clap. *Peter Ketley has been back at Alabama Ranch for nearly three weeks.*

I was out with the kiddies this afternoon, having another wild time on the toboggan-slide, dressed in an old Mackinaw of Dinky-Dunk's buckled in close around my waist and a pair of Whinnie's heaviest woolen socks over my moccasins and a mangy old gray-squirrel cap on by head. The children looked like cherubs who'd been rolled in a flour-barrel, with their eyes shining and their cheeks glowing like Richmond roses, but I must have looked like something that had been put out to frighten the coyotes away. At any rate, there we were, all squealing like pigs and all powdered from tip to toe with the dry snow and all looking like Piutes on the war-path. And who should walk calmly about the corner of the buildings but Peter himself!

My heart stopped beating and I had to lean against the end of the toboggan-slide until I could catch my breath.

He called out, "Hello, youngsters!" as quietly as though he had seen us all the day before. I said "Peter!" in a strangled sort of whisper, and wondered what made my knees wabble as I stood staring at him as though he had been a ghost.

But Peter was no ghost. He was there before me, in the body, still smoking his foolish little pipe, wearing the familiar old coonskin cap and coat that looked as though the moths had made many a Roman holiday of their generously deforested pelt. He took the pipe out of his mouth as he stepped over to me, and pulled off his heavy old gauntlet before he shook hands.

"Peter!" I repeated in my ridiculous small whisper.

He didn't speak. But he smiled, a bit wistfully, as he stared down at me. And for just a moment, I think, an odd look of longing came into his searching honest eyes which studied my face as though he were counting every freckle and line and eyelash there. He continued to X-ray me with that hungry stare of his until I took my hand away and could feel the blood surging back to my face.

"It's a long time," he said as he puffed hard on his pipe, apparently to keep it from going out. The sound of his voice sent a little thrill through my body. I felt as rattle-headed as a rabbit, and was glad when Dinkie and Poppsy captured him by each knee and hung on like catamounts.

"Where did you come from?" I finally asked, trying in vain to be as collected as Peter himself.

Then he told me. He told me as nonchalantly as though he were giving me a piece of news of no particular interest. He had rather a difficult book to finish up, and he concluded the quietness of Alabama Ranch would suit him to a T. And when spring came he wanted to have a look about for a nest of the whooping crane. It has been rather a rarity, for some sixteen or seventeen years, this whooping crane, and the American Museum was offering a mighty handsome prize for a specimen. Then he was compelled to give his attention to Dinkie and Poppsy, and tried the slide a couple of times, and announced that our coaster was better than the chariot of Icarius. And by this time I had recovered my wits and my composure and got some of the snow off my Mackinaw.

"Have I changed?" I asked Peter as he turned to study my face for the second time.

"To me," he said as he brushed the snow from his gauntlets, "you are always adorable!"

"*Verboten!*" I retorted to that, wondering why anything so foolish could have the power to make my pulses sing.

"Why?" he asked, as his eyes met mine.

"For the same old reason," I told him.

"Reasons," he said, "are like shoes: Time has the trick of wearing them out."

"When that happens, we have to get new ones," I reminded him.

"Then what is the new one?" he asked, with an unexpectedly solemn look on his face.

"My husband has just asked me to join him in Calgary," I said, releasing my bolt.

"Are you going to?" he asked, with his face a mask.

"I think I am," I told him. For I could see, now, how Peter's return had simplified the situation by complicating it. Already he had made my course plainer to me. I could foresee what this new factor would imply. I could understand what Peter's presence at Alabama Ranch would come to mean. And I had to shut my eyes to the prospect. I was still the same old single-track woman with a clear-cut duty laid out before her. There were certain luxuries, for the sake of my own soul's peace, I could never afford.

"Why are you going back to your husband?" Peter was asking, with real perplexity on his face.

"Because he needs me," I said as I stood watching the children go racing down the slide.

"Why?" he asked, with what impressed me as his first touch of harshness.

"Must I explain?" I inquired with my own first movement in self-defense, for it had suddenly occurred to me that any such explaining would be much more difficult than I dreamed.

"Of course not," said Peter, changing color a little. "It's only that I'm so tremendously anxious to—to understand."

"To understand what?" I questioned, both hoping and dreading that he would go on to the bitter end.

"That *you* understand," was his cryptic retort. And for once in his life Peter disappointed me.

"I can't afford to," I said with an effort at lightness which seemed to hurt him more than it ought. Then I realized, as I stood looking up into his face, that I was doing little to merit that humble and magnificent loyalty of Peter's. *He* would play fair to the end. He was too big of heart to think first of himself. It was *me* he was thinking of; it was *me* he wanted to see happy. But I had my own road to go, and no outsider could guide me.

"It's no use, Peter," I said as I put my mittened hand on his gauntleted arm without quite knowing I was doing it. And I went on to warn him that he must not confront me with kindness, that I was a good deal like an Indian's dog which neither looks for kindness nor understands it. He laughed a trifle bitterly at that and reminded me, as he stood staring at me, of a Pribilof seal staring into an Arctic sun. Then he said an odd thing. "I wish I could make it a bit easier for you," he remarked as impersonally as though he were meditating aloud.

I asked him why he said that. He evasively explained that he thought it was because I had what the Romans called *constantia*. So I asked him to explain *constantia*. And he said, with a shrug, that we might regard it as firm consideration of a question before acting on it. I explained, at that, that it wasn't a matter of choice, but of character. He was willing to acknowledge that I was right. But before that altogether unsatisfactory little debate was over Peter made me promise him one thing. He has made me promise that before I leave we have a tramp over the prairie together. And we have agreed that Sunday would be as good a day as any.

Saturday the Twenty-Fifth

I have sent word to Duncan to expect me in Calgary as soon as I can get things ready. My decision is made. And it is final. Two ghostly hands have reached out and turned me toward my husband. One is the Past. The other is the Proprieties. If life out here were a little more like the diamond-dyed Westerns, Peter Ketley and Duncan McKail would fight with hammerless Colts, the victor would throw me over the horn of his saddle, and vanish in a cloud of dust, while Struthers was turning Casa Grande into a faro-hall and my two kiddies were busy holding up the Elk Crossing stage-coach.

But life, alas, isn't so dramatic as we dream it. It cross-hobbles us and hog-ties us and leaves us afraid of our own wilted impulses. I have a terror of failure. And it's plain enough I have only one mission on God's green footstool. I'm a home-maker, and nothing more. I'm a home-maker confronted by the last chance to make good at my one and only calling. And whatever it costs, I'm going to make my husband recognize me as a patient and long-suffering Penelope....

But enough of the rue! To-morrow I'm going snow-shoeing with Peter. I'm praying that the weather will be propitious. I want one of our sparkling-burgundy days with the sun shining bright and a nip in the air like a stiletto buried in rose leaves. For it may be the last time in all my life I shall walk on the prairie with my friend, Peter Ketley. The page is going to be turned over, the candle snuffed out, and the singing birds of my freedom silenced. I have met my Rubicon, and it must be crossed. But last night, for the first time in a month, I plastered enough cold cream on my nose to make me look like a buttered muffin, and rubbed enough almond-oil meal on my arms to make them look like a miller's. And I've been asking myself if I'm the sedate old lady life has been trying to make me. There are certain Pacific Islands, Gershom tells me, where the climate is so stable that the matter of weather is never even mentioned, where the people who bathe in that eternal calm are never conscious of the conditions surrounding them. That's the penalty, I suppose, that humanity pays for constancy. There are no lapses to record, no deviations to be accounted for, no tempests to send us tingling into the shelters of wonder. And I can't yet be quite sure whether this rebellious old heart of mine wants to be a Pacific Islander or not.

Monday the Twenty-Seventh

Peter and I have had our tramp in the snow. It wasn't a sunny day, as I had hoped. It was one of those intensely cold northern days without wind or sun, one of those misted days which Balzac somewhere describes as a beautiful woman born blind. It was fifty-three below zero when we left the house, with the smoke going up in the gray air as straight and undisturbed as a pine-tree and the drifts crunching like dry charcoal under our snow-shoes. We were wooled and mittened and capped and furred up to the eyes, however, and I was warmer than I've been many a time on Boston Common in March, even though we did look like a couple of deep-sea divers and steamed like fire-engines when we breathed.

We tramped until we were tired, swung back to Casa Grande, and Peter came in for a cup of tea and then trudged off to Alabama Ranch again. And that was the lee and the long of it, as the Irish say. What did we talk about? Heaven knows what we didn't talk about! Peter told me about a rancher named Bidwell, north of The Crossing, being found frozen to death in a snow-drift, frozen stiff, with the horse still standing and the rider still sitting upright in the saddle. He said there was a lot of rot talked about the great clean outdoors. The sentimentalists found that they naturally felt a bit niftier in fresh air, but the great outdoors, according to Peter, is an arena of endless murder and rapine and warfare, and the cleanest acre of forest or prairie under the sun somewhere has its stains of blood and its record of cruelty. We talked about Susie and the negative phrasing of the ten moral laws and the Horned Dinosaur from Sand Hill Creek (whose bones Peter reckoned to be at least three million years old) and the marriage customs of the Innuits. And we talked about Matzenauer and Kreisler and the best cure for chilblains and about Gershom and Poppsy and Dinkie—but most of all about Dinkie.

Peter asked me if I'd seen Dinkie's school essays on *The Flag* and *The Capture of Quebec*, and rather surprised me by handing over crumpled copies of the same, Dinkie having proudly despatched these masterpieces all the way to Philadelphia for his "Uncle Peter's" approval. It hurt me, for just one foolish fraction of a second, to think my boy had confidences with an outsider which he could not have with his own mother. And then I remembered that Peter wasn't an outsider. I realized how much he had brought into my laddie's life, how much, in a different way, he had brought into my own. I even tried to tell him about this. But he stopped me short by saying something in Latin which he later explained meant "by taking the middle course we shall not go amiss." So I came back to Casa Grande, not exactly with a feeling of frustration, but with a feeling of possibilities withheld and issues deferred. It was a companionable enough tramp, I suppose. But I'm afraid I was a disappointment to Peter. His gaiety impressed me as a bit forced. I am slightly mystified by his refusal, while taking serious things seriously, to take anything tragically. Even at tea, with all its air of the valedictory hanging over us, he was nice and gay, like the Christmas beeves the city butchers stick paper rosettes into, or the circus-band playing like mad while the tumbler who has had a fall is being carried out to the dressing-tent. Peter even offhandedly inquired, as he was going, if he might have Scotty to take care of, provided it was not expedient to take Dinkie's dog along to Calgary with us.... I'm not quite certain—I may be wrong, but there are moments, odd earthquakey moments, when I have a suspicion that Peter will be keeping more than Scotty after we've trekked off to Calgary!

Saturday the Fourth

This tearing up of roots is a much sorrier business than I had imagined. And more difficult. I find it hard to know what to take and what to leave behind. And there is so much to be thought of, so much to be arranged for, so much to be done. I have had to write Duncan and tell him I'll be a few days later than I intended. My biggest problem has been with Whinstane Sandy and Struthers. I called them in and had a talk with them and told them I wanted them to keep Casa Grande going the same as ever. Then I made myself into the god from the machine by calmly announcing the only way things could be arranged would be for the two of them to get married.

Struthers, at this suggestion, promptly became as coy as a partridge-hen. Whinnie, of course, remained Scottish and canny. He became more shrewdly magnanimous, however, after we'd had a bit of talk by ourselves. "Weel, I'll tak' the woman, rather than see her frettin' hersel' to death!" he finally conceded, knowing only too well he'd nest warm and live well for the rest of his days. He'd been hoping, he confessed to me, that some day he'd get back to that claim of his up in the Klondike. But he wasn't so young as he once was. And perhaps Dinkie, when he was grown to a man, could go up and look after his rights. 'Twould be a grand journey, he averred with a sigh, for a high-spirited lad turned twenty.

"I'll be stayin' with Pee-Wee and the old place here," concluded Whinstane Sandy, giving me his rough old hand as a pledge. And with tears in my eyes I lifted that faithful old hand up to my lips and kissed it. Whinnie, I knew, would die for me. But he would pass away before he'd be willing to put his loyalty and his courage and his kind-heartedness into pretty speeches. Struthers, on the other hand, has become too flighty to be of much use to me in my packing. She has plunged headlong into a riot of baking, has sent for a fresh supply of sage tea, and is secretly perusing a dog-eared volume which I have reason to know is *The Marriage Guide.*

Gershom, all things considered, is the most dolorous member of our home circle. He says little, but inspects me with the wounded eyes of a neglected spaniel. He will stay on at Casa Grande until the Easter holidays, and then migrate to the Teetzels'. As for Dinkie and Poppsy, they are too young to understand. The thought of change excites them, but they have no idea of what they are leaving behind.

Last night, when I was dog-tired after my long day's work, I remembered about Dinkie's school-essays and took them out to read. And having done so, I realized there was something sacred about them. They gave me a glimpse of a groping young soul reaching up toward the light.

"We have a Flag," I read, "to thrill our bones and be prod of and no man boy woman or girl" (and the not altogether artless *diminuendo* did not escape me!) "should never let it drag in the dust. It flotes at the bow of our ships and waves from the top of most post offices etc. And now we have a flag and a flag staf in front of our school and on holdays and when every grate man dies we put said flag up at haf mast.... It is the flag of the rich and the poor, the flag of our country which all of whose citizens have a right to fly, the hig" (obviously meant for *high*) "and the low, the rich and the poor. And we must not only keep our flag but blazen it still further with deeds nobely done. If ever you have to shed your blood for your country remeber its for the nobelest flag that flies the same being an emblen of our native land to which it represens and stands in high esteem by the whole people of a country." ... God bless his patriotic little bones! My bairn knew what he was trying to get at, but it's plain he didn't quite know how to get there.

But the drama of the Capture of Quebec plainly put him on easier ground. For here was a story worth the telling. And what could be more glorious than the death of Wolfe as I see it through my little Dinkie's eyes?

For I read: "The french said Wolfe" (*can* has first been written and then scratched out and *would* substituted) "never get up that rivver but Wolfe fooled them with a trick by running the french flag up on his shipps so the french pilots without fear padled out and come abord when Wolfe took them prissoners and made them pilot the english ships safe to the iland of Orlens. He wanted to capsture the city of Quebec without distroiting it. But the clifs were to high and the brave Montcalm dified Wolfe who lost 400 men and got word Amherst could not come and so himself took sick and went to bed. But a desserter from the french gave Wolfe the pass word and when his ships crept further up the rivver in the dark a french senntry called out qui vive and one of Wolfe's men who spoke french well ansered la france and the senntry said to himself they was french ships and let them go on. Next day Wolfe was better and saw a goat clime up the clifs near the plains of Abraham and said where a goat could go he could go to. So he forgot being sick and desided to clime up Wolfe's cove which was not then called that until later. It was a dark night and they went in row boats with all the oars mufled. It was a formadible sight that would have made even bolder men shrink with fear. But it was the brave Higlanders who lead with their muskits straped to their sholdiers climing up the steep rock by grabbing at roots of trees and shrubs and not a word was wispered but the french senntrys saw the tree moving and asked qui vive again. The same sholdier who once studdied hard and lernt french said la france as he had done before and they got safe to the top and faced the city. At brake of day they stood face to face, french and english. But Montcalm marched out to cut them off there and Wolfe lined his men up in a line and said hold your fire until they are within forty paces away from us. The french caused many causilties but the english never wavered. Montcalm still on horse back reseaved a mortal wound, he would of fell off if two of his tall granadeers hadn't held him up and Wolfe too was shot on the wirst but went right on. Again he was shot this time more fataly and as they were laying him down one of the men exclaimed See how they run. Who run murmurred the dieing Wolfe. The enemy sir replied the man. Then I die happy said Generral Wolfe and with a great sigh rolled over on his side and died.... And when the doctor told Montcalm he could only live a few hours he said God be prased I shall not live to see Quebec fall. Brave words like those should not be forgoten and what Wolfe said was just as brave. No more fiting words could be said by anybody than those he said in the boats with the mufled oars that night that the paths of glory leed but to the grave." ...

I have folded up the carefully written pages, reverently, remembering my promise to return them to Peter. But for a while at least I shall keep them with me. They have set me thinking, reminding me how time flies. Here is my little boy, grown into an historian, sagely philosophizing over the tragedies of life. My wee laddie, expressing himself through the recorded word.... It seems such a short time ago that he was taking his first stumbling steps along the dim hallways of language. I have been turning back to the journal I began shortly after his birth and kept up for so long, the naïve journal of a young mother registering her wonder at the unfolding mysteries of life. It became less minute and less meticulous, I notice, as the years slipped past, and after the advent of Poppsy and Pee-Wee the entries seem a bit hurried and often incoherent. But I have dutifully noted how my Dinkie first said "Ah goom" for "All gone," just as I have fondly remarked his persistent use of the reiterative intensive, with careful citations of his "da-da" and his "choo-choo car," and a "bow-wow" as applied to any living animal, and "wa-wa" for water, and "me-me" for milk, and "din-din" for dinner, and going "bye-bye" for going to sleep on his little "tum-tum." I even solemnly ask, forgetting my Max Müller, what lies at the root of this strange reduplicative process. Then I come to where I have set down for future generations the momentous fact that my Dinkie first said "let's playtend" for "let's pretend," and spoke of "nasturtiums" as "excursions," and announced that he could bark loud enough to make Baby Poppsy's eyes "bug out" instead of "bulge out." And I come again to where I have affectionately registered the fact that my son says "set-sun" for "sunset" and speaks of his "rumpers" instead of his "rompers," and coins the very appropriate word "downer" to go with its sister word of "upper" and describes his Mummy as "*wearing* Daddy's coffee-cup" when he really meant *using* Daddy's coffee-cup.

It all seems very fond and foolish now, just as at one time it all seemed very big and wonderful. And I remember schooling my Poppsy to say "Daddy's all sweet" and how her little tongue, stumbling over the sibilant, converted it into the non-complimentary "Daddy's all feet," which my Dinky-Dunk so scowlingly resented. And I have even compiled a list of Dinkie's earliest "howlers," from the time he was first interested in Adam and Eve and asked to be told about "The Garden of Sweden" until he later explained one of Poppsy's crying-spells by announcing she had dug a hole out by the corral and wanted to bring it into the house. I used to smile a bit skeptically over these tongue-twists of children, but now I know they are re-born with each new generation, the same old turns of thought and the same old kinks of utterance. I don't know why, but there is even a touch of sadness about the old jokes now. The patina of time gathers upon them and mellows them and makes me realize they belong to the past—the past with its pain and its joy, that can never come back to mortal mothers again.

Monday the Thirtieth

"We die a little, when we go away." How true it is! By to-morrow we will be gone. My heart is heavy as lead. I go about, doing things for the last time, looking at things for the last time, and pretending to be as matter-of-fact as a tripper breaking camp. But there's a laryngitis lump in my throat and there are times when I'm glad I'm almost too busy to think.

I was hoping that the weather would be bad, as it ought to at this time of the year, so that I might leave my prairie with some lessened pang of regret. But the last two days have been miraculously mild. A Chinook has been blowing, the sky has been a palpitating soft dome of azure, and a winey smell of spring has crept over the earth.... To-night, knowing it was the last night, I crept out to say good-by to my little Pee-Wee asleep in his lonely little bed. It was a perfect night. The Lights were playing low in the north, weaving together in a tangle of green and ruby and amethyst. The prairie was very still. The moonlight lay on everything, thick and golden and soft with mystery. I knelt beside Pee-Wee's grave, not in bitterness, but bathed in peace. I knelt there and prayed.

It frightened me a little, when I looked up, to see Peter standing beside the little white fence. I thought, at first, that he was a ghost, he stood so still and he seemed so tall in the moonlight.

"I'll watch your boy," he said very quietly, "until you come back."

He made me think of the Old Priest in *The Sorrowful Inheritance*. He seemed so calmly benignant, so dependable, so safe in his simple other-worldliness.

"Oh, Peter!" was all I could say as I moved toward him in the moonlight. He nodded, as much to himself as to me, as he took my hand in his. I felt a great ache, which was not really an ache, and a new kind of longing which never before, in all my life, I had nursed or known. I must have moved closer to Peter, though I could feel his hand pull itself away from mine. It made me feel terribly alone in the world.

"Aren't you going to kiss me good-by?" I cried out, with my hand on his shoulder.

Peter shook his head from side to side, very slowly.

"*Verboten!*" he said as he put his hand over the hand which I had put on his shoulder.

"But I may never come back. Peter!" I whispered, feeling the tears go slowly down my wet cheek.

Peter took my unsteady fingers and placed them on the white pickets of the little rectangular fence.

"You'll come back," he said very quietly. And when I looked up he had turned away.

I could see him walking off in the yellow moonlight with his shoulders back and his head up. He walked slowly, with an odd wading movement, like a man walking through water. I was tempted, for a moment, to call after him. But some power that was not of me or any part of me prompted me to silence. I stood watching him until he seemed a moving shadow along the level floor of the world flooded with primrose-yellow, until he became a shifting stroke of umber on a background of misty gold. I stood looking after him as he passed away, out of my sight, and far, far off to the north a coyote howled and over Casa Grande I could see a thin pennon of chimney-smoke going up toward Arcturus.... Good-by, Peter, and God bless you....

Unlimited, indeed, is the power of Eros. For when I went to slip quietly into the house, I found Whinnie and Struthers seated together beside the kitchen range. And Struthers was reading *Tam O'Shanter* aloud to her laird.

"Read slow, noo, lassie, an' tak' it a' in," said the placidly triumphant voice of Whinstane Sandy, "for it'll be lang before ye ken its like!"

Thursday the Seventeenth

The migration has been effected ... I am alone in my room, I have two and three-quarters trunks unpacked, and I feel like a President's wife the night after Inauguration. It is well past midnight, but I am too tired and too unsettled to sleep. Things turn out so differently to what one expects! And all change, to the home-staying heart, can be so abysmally upsetting!...

We were a somewhat disheveled and intimidated flock when we emerged from our train and found Duncan awaiting us with an amazingly big touring-car which, as he explained with a short laugh at my gape of wonder, the Barcona Mines would pay for in a week.

"It's no piker you're pulling with now," he exclaimed as we climbed stiff and awkward into that deep-upholstered grandeur on wheels. He said that the children had grown but would have to be togged out with some new duds—little knowing how I had stayed up until long past midnight mending and pressing and doing my best to make my bucolic offspring presentable. And he told me it was *some* city I had come to, as I'd very soon see for myself. And it was *some* shack he'd corralled for his family, he added with a chuckle of pride.

I tried to be interested in the skyscrapers he showed me along Eighth Avenue, and the Palliser, and the concreted subway, and the Rockies, in the distance, with the wine-glow on their snow-clad peaks. And while I did my best to shake off the Maud-Muller feeling which was creeping over me, by studying the tranquillizingly remote mountain-tops, Duncan confided to me that he had first said: "Fifty thousand or bu'st!" But two months ago he had amended that to "A hundred thousand or bu'st!" and now he had his reasons for saying, with his jaw set: "Just a cool quarter of a million, before I quit this game!"

It was for us, I told myself as I looked down at my kiddies, that the Dour Man behind the big mahogany wheel was fighting. This, I felt, should bring me happiness, and a new sense of security. And it was only because my stomach was empty, I tried to assure myself, that my poor old prairie heart felt that way. I should have been happy, for I was going to a brand-new home—and it was one of those foot-hill late afternoons that make you think of the same old razor-blade muffled up in the same old panne-velvet, an evening of softness shot through with a steely sharpness. There was a Chinook arch of Irish point-lace still in the sky, very much like the one I had left behind me, and the sky itself was a canopy of robin-egg blue *crêpe de chine* hemmed with salmon pink.

But as we whirled up out of the city into the higher ground of some boulevarded and terraced residential district the evening air seemed colder and the solemn old Rockies toward the west took on an air of lonesomeness. It made the thought of home and open fires and quiet rooms very welcome. The lights came out along the asphalted streets, spangling the slopes of that sedate new suburb with rectangular lines of brilliants. Duncan, in answer to the questions of the children, explained that he was taking the longer way round, so as to give us the best view of the house as we drove in.

"Here we are!" he exulted as we slowed down and turned into a crescent lined with baby poplar and Manitoba maple.

I leaned out and saw a big new house of tapestry brick, looking oddly palatial on its imposing slope of rising ground. My husband stopped, in fact, midway in a foolishly pillared gate that bisected a long array of cobble-stone walls, so that we might get a look at the gardens. They seemed very new gardens, but much of their newness was lost in that mercifully subduing light in which I saw trim-painted trellises and sepulchral white flower-urns and pergolas not yet softened with creepers. There was also a large iron fountain, painted white, which Duncan apparently liked very much, from the way he looked at it. From two of the chimneys I could see smoke going up in the quiet air. In the windows I could see lights, rose-shaded and warm, and beyond the shrubbery somewhere back in the garden a workman was driving nails. His hammer fell and echoed like a series of rifle-shots. From the garage chimney, too, came smoke, and it was plain from the sounds that somebody inside was busy tuning up a car-engine.

I sat staring at the grounds, at the cobble-stone walls, at the tapestry-brick house with the high-shouldered French cornices. It began to creep over me how it meant service, how it meant protection, how it meant guarded lives for me and mine, how it stood an amazingly complicated piece of machinery which took much thought to organize and much money to maintain. And the mainspring behind it all, I remembered, was the man sitting at the mahogany wheel so close to me. Light and warmth and comfort and safety—they were all to come from the conceiting and the struggling of my Dour Man, fighting for an empty-headed family who were scarcely worth it. He was, after all, the stoker down in the hole, and without him everything would stop. So when I saw that he was studying my face with that intent sidelong glance of his, I reached over and put my hand on his knee, as I had done so often, in the old days.

He looked down, at that, with what was almost an appearance of embarrassment.

"I want to play my part," I said with all the earnestness of my earnest old heart, as he let in his clutch and we started up the winding drive.

"It ought to be a considerable part," he said as we drew up under a bone-white porte-cochère where a small-bodied Jap stood respectfully impassive and waiting to open the door for us.

My husband got down out of the car. I sat wondering why I should feel so much like a Lady Jane Grey approaching the headsman's *makura*.

"Come on, kids!" Duncan called out with a parade of joviality, like a cheer-leader who realized that things weren't going just right. For Dinkie, I could see, was shrinking back in the padded seat. His underlip was trembling a trifle as he sat staring at the strange new house. But Poppsy, true little woman that she was, smiled appreciatively about at the material grandeurs which confronted her. If she'd had a tail, I'm sure, she'd have been wagging it. And this so tickled her dad that he lifted her out of the car and carried her bodily and triumphantly up the steps.

I waited for Dinkie, whose eye met mine. I did my best to show my teeth, that he might understand how everything was eventually to be for the best. But his face was still clouded as we climbed the steps and passed under the yoke.

The little Jap, whose name, I have since found out, is Tokudo, bowed a jack-knife bow and said *"Irashai"* as I passed him. And *"Irashai"* I have also discovered, is perfectly good Japanese for "Welcome."

We had dinner at seven. It was a well-ordered meal, but it went off rather dismally. I was depressed, for reasons I couldn't quite fathom, and the children were tired, and Duncan, I'm afraid, was a bit disappointed in us all. Tokudo had brought cocktails for us, and Duncan, seeing I wasn't drinking mine, stowed both away in his honorable stomach. He ate heartily, I noticed, and gave scant appearance of a man pining away with a broken heart. After dinner he sat back and bit off the end of a cigar.

"This is my idea of living," he proclaimed as he sent a blue cloud up toward the rather awful dome-light above the big table. "There's stir and movement here, all day long. Something more than sunsets to look at! You'll see—something to fill up your day! Why, night seems to come before I even know it. And before I'm out of bed I'm brooding over what's ahead of me for that particular date and day—Say, that girl of ours is falling asleep in her chair there!"

So I escaped and put the children to bed. And while thus engaged I discovered that some of Duncan's new friends were dropping in on him. I wanted to stay up-stairs, for my head was aching a lot and my heart just a little, but Duncan called to me from the bottom of the stairs. So down I went, like a dutiful wife, to the room full of smoke and talk, where two big men and one very thin woman in a baby-bear motor coat were drinking Scotch highballs with my lord and master. They were genial and jolly enough, but I couldn't understand their allusions and I couldn't see the points to their jokes. And they seemed to stay an interminable length of time. I was secretly uncomfortable, until they went, but I became still more uncomfortable after they had gone.

For as we sat there together, in that oppressive big room, I made rather an awful discovery. I found that my husband and I had scarcely anything we could talk about together. So I sat there, like an alligator in a bayou, wondering why his rather flushed face should be turned toward me every now and then.

My heart beat a little faster as I saw him take out his watch and wind it up.

"Let's go to bed," he said as he pushed it back in his waistcoat pocket. My heart stopped beating altogether, for a moment or two. I felt like a slave-girl in a sheik's tent, like a desert-woman just sold into bondage.

It was the smoky air and the highballs, I suppose, which left his eyes a little bloodshot as he turned slowly about and studied my face. Then he repeated what he had said before.

"*I can't!*" I told him, with a foolish surge of terror.

He sat quite a long time without speaking. I could see the corners of the Holbein-Astronomer mouth go down.

"As you say," he finally remarked, with a grim sort of quietness. But every bit of color had gone from his face. I was glad when Tokudo came in to take away the glasses.

Duncan stood up, after the servant had gone again, and bowed to me very solemnly.

"*Oyasumi nasi,*" he said with a stabilizing ironic smile.

"What does that mean?" I asked, doing my best to smile back at him.

"That means 'sleep well,'" explained my husband. "But Tokudo would probably translate it into 'Condescend to enjoy honorable tranquillity.'"

Instead of enjoying honorable tranquillity, however, I am sitting up into the wee sma' hours of the night, patrolling the gloomy ramparts of my soul's unrest.

Wednesday the Twenty-Third

This change to the city means a new life to my children. But I can also see it means new dangers and new influences. The simplicity of ranch life has vanished. And Dinkie and Poppsy are already getting acquainted with their neighbors. A Ford truck came within an inch of running over Poppsy this morning. She has announced a curiosity to investigate ice-cream sodas, and Dinkie has proclaimed his intention of going to the movies Saturday afternoon with Benny McArthur, the banker's son in the next block. On Monday I'm to take my children to school. "One of the finest school-buildings in all the West," Duncan has proudly explained. I can't help thinking of Gershom and his little cubby-hole of a wooden building where he is even now so solemnly and yet so kind-heartedly teaching the three R's to a gathering of little prairie outlaws.

I shall have time on my hands, I see, for Hilton and his wife, our English gardener-chauffeur and our portly maid-of-all-work, pretty well cover what the wonderful Tokudo overlooks. And Tokudo *is* a wonder. That cat-footed little Jap does the ordering and cooking and serving; he answers the door and the telephone; he attends to the rugs and the hardwood floors; he rules over the butler's pantry and polishes the silver and inspects the linen, and even keeps the keys to Duncan's carefully guarded wine-cellar, which the mistress of the house herself has not yet dared to invade.

My husband seems to be very busy with his coal-mines and his other interests. He said last night that his idea of happiness is to be so immersed in his work as to be unconscious of time and undisturbed by its passing. And he *has* been happy, in that way. But Time, that patient remodeler of all things mortal, can still work while we sleep. And something has been happening, without Duncan quite knowing it. He has changed. He is older, for one thing. I don't mean that my husband is an old man. But I can see a number of early-autumnal alterations in him. He's a trifle heavier and stiffer. He's lost a bit of his springiness. And he seems to know it, in his secret heart of hearts, for he tries to make up for that loss with a sort of coerced blitheness which doesn't always carry. He affects a sort of creaking jauntiness which sometimes falls short of its aim. When he can't clear the hurdle, I notice, he has the habit of whipping up his tired spirits with a cocktail or a highball or a silver-fizz. But he is preoccupied, at times. And at other times he is disturbingly short-tempered. He announced this morning, almost gruffly, that we'd had about enough of this "Dinkie and Poppsy business," and the children might as well be called by their real names. So I shall make another effort to get back to "Elmer" and "Pauline Augusta."

But I feel, in my bones, that those pompous appellatives will not be always remembered. It has just occurred to me that my old habit of calling my husband "Dinky-Dunk" has slipped away from me. Endearing diminutives, I suppose, are not elicited by polar bears.

Thursday the Thirty-First

I don't quite know what's the matter with me. I'm like a cat in a strange garret. I don't seem to be fitting in. I sat at the piano last night playing "What's this dull town to me, Robin Adair?" And Duncan, with the fit and natural spirit of the home-booster, actively resented that oblique disparagement of his new business-center. He believes implicitly in Calgary and its future.

As for myself, I am rigidly suspending all judgments. I'm at least trying to play my part, even though my spirit isn't in it. There are times when I'm tempted to feel that a foot-hill city of this size is neither fish nor fowl. It impresses me as a frontier cow-town grown out of its knickers and still ungainly in its first long trousers. But I can't help being struck by people's incorruptible pride in their own community. It's a sort of religious faith, a fixed belief in the future, a stubborn optimism that is surely something more than self-interest. It's the Dutch courage that makes deprivation and long waiting endurable.

It's the women, and the women alone, who seem left out of the procession. They impress me as having no big interests of their own, so they are compelled to *playtend* with make-believe interests. They race like mad in the social squirrel-cage, or drug themselves with bridge and golf and the country club, or take to culture with a capital C and read papers culled from the Encyclopedias; or spend their husbands' money on year-old Paris gowns and make love to other women's mates. The altitude, I imagine, has quite a little to do with the febrile pace of things here. Or perhaps it's merely because I'm an old frump from a back-township ranch!

But I have no intention of trying to keep up with them, for I have a constitutional liking for quietness in my old age. And I can't engross myself in their social aspirations, for I've seen a bit too much of the world to be greatly taken with the internecine jealousies of a twenty-year-old foot-hill town. My "day" in this aristocratic section is Thursday, and Tokudo this afternoon admitted callers from seven closed cars, two landaulets, three Detroit electrics and one hired taxi. I know, because I counted 'em. The children and I posed like a Raeburn group and did our best to be respectable, for Duncan's sake. But he seems to have taken up with some queer people here, people who drop in at any time of the evening and smoke and drink and solemnly discuss how a shandygaff should be mixed and tell stories I wouldn't care to have the children hear.

There's one couple Duncan asked me to be especially nice to, a Mr. and Mrs. Murchison. The latter, I find, is usually addressed as "Slinkie" by her friends, and the former is known as "Cattalo Charley" because he once formed a joint-stock company which was to make a fortune interbreeding buffalo and range-cattle, the product of that happy union being known, I believe, as "cattalo." Duncan calls him a "promoter," but my earlier impression of him as a born gambler has been confirmed by the report that he's interested in a lignite briquetting company, that he's fathering a scheme, not only to raise stock-yard reindeer in the sub-Arctics but also to grow karakule sheep in the valleylands of the Coast, that he once sold mummy wheat at forty dollars a bushel, and that in the old boom days he promoted no less than three oil companies. And the time will come, Duncan avers, when that man will be a millionaire.

As for "Slinkie," his wife, I can't be quite sure whether I like her or not. I at least admire her audacity and her steel-trap quickness of mind. She has a dead white skin, green eyes, and most wonderful hair, hair the color of a well-polished copper samovar. She is an extremely thin woman who affects sheathe skirts and rather reminds me of a boa-constrictor. She always reeks of *Apres londre* and uses a lip-stick as freely before the world as an orchestra conductor uses a baton or a street-sweeper a broom. She is nervous and sharp-tongued and fearless and I thought, at first, that she was making a dead set at my Duncan. But I can now see how she confronts all men with that same dangerous note of intimacy. Her real name is Lois. She talks about her convent days in Belgium, sings *risque* songs in very bad French, and smokes and drinks a great deal more than is good for her. In Vancouver, when informed that she was waiting for a street-car on a non-stop corner, she sat down between the tracks, with her back to the approaching car. The motorman, of course, had to come to a stop— whereupon she arose with dignity and stepped aboard. Duncan has told me this story twice, and tends to consider Lois a really wonderful character. I am a little afraid of her. She asked me the other day how I liked Calgary. I responded, according to Hoyle, that I liked the clear air and the clean streets and the Rockies looking so companionably down over one's shoulder. Lois hooted as she tapped a cigarette end against her hennaed thumb-nail.

"Just wait until the sand-storms, my dear!" she said as she struck a match on her slipper-heel.

Saturday the Second

My old friend Gershom has very slyly written a *rondeau* to me. I have just found it enclosed in my *Golden Treasury*, which he handed back to me that last night at Casa Grande. It's the first actual *rondeau* I ever had indited to my humble self, and while I'm a bit set up about it, I can't quite detach from Gershom's lines a vaguely obituarial atmosphere which tends to depress me.

I can see that it may not be the best *rondeau* in the world, but I'm going to keep it until my bones are dust, for good old Gershom's sake. And some day, when he marries the nice girl he deserves to marry, and has a kiddy or two of his own, I'll shame his gray hairs by parading it before his offspring! I have just been re-reading the lines, in Gershom's copperplate script. They are as follows:

To C. McK.

On Returning Her Copy of the Golden Treasury

This golden book, dear friend, wherein each line
Holds close a charm for knowing eyes to meet,
Holds doubly mystical and doubly sweet
An inner charm no language may define:

For o'er each page a woman's soul divine
Bent low a space for kindred souls to greet,
And here her eyes were lit with gladness fleet
Because of songs that graced with rare design
This book of thine!

And now I give back into Beauty's hand
Her borrowed songs, but I shall hold always
Secret and safe from every care's demand,
A flame of light to fill my emptier days,
That quieter fellowship, which made a shrine
This book of thine!

G. B.

Tuesday the Fifth

The weather is balmier, and just a tinge of green is creeping into the tan of the foot-hill slopes. Spring is coming again.

I went shopping in the Hudson Bay Store yesterday and found it much more metropolitan than I had expected. And I find I am three whole laps behind in that steeplechase known as Style. But I got a raft of things for Pauline Augusta, and a Boy Scout outfit for my laddie.

One of the few women I like in Calgary is Dinkie's—I mean Elmer's—new school-teacher. Her name is Lossie Brown and she is an earnest-eyed girl who's saving up to go to Europe some day and study art. She's a trifle shy, and unmistakably moody, but her mind is as bright as a new pin. And some bright morning, when the rose of womanhood has really opened, she's going to wake up a howling beauty. I love her, too, for the interest she has taken in my boy, whom she reports as getting along much better than she had expected. So I have asked her to write a little note to Gershom Binks, advising him of his ex-pupil's advance. For Lossie is a girl I'd like Gershom to know. And she has done this for me. I ask her over to the house as often as I can and yesterday I had Dinkie slip a little platinum-banded fountain-pen, with a card, into the pocket of her rather threadbare ulster. Duncan, however, is not in the least interested in Lossie. He despises what he calls insignificant people.

On my way home from shopping I had Hilton drive me about some of the less-known parts of the city. And I have been compelled to recast some of my earlier impressions of Calgary. It is wonderful, in many ways, and some day, I can see, it will be beautiful, just as Lossie Brown will some day be beautiful.

In the first place, it is so happily situated, lying as it does half-way between the mountains and the plain. And the blue Bow comes dancing so joyously down from the Rockies and the older city sleeps so happily in the sunny crook of its valley-arm, while the newer suburbs seem to boil up and run over the surrounding hills like champagne bubbling over the rim of a glass. There are raw edges, of course, but time will eventually attend to these. Now and then, between the motor-cars, you will see a creaking Red River cart. Next to an office-building of gray sandstone you're likely to spot what looks like a squatter's wickyup of rusty galvanized iron. Yesterday, on our main street where the electric-cars were clanging and the limousines were throwing their exhaust incense to the gods of the future, I caught sight of a lonely and motionless figure, isolated in the midst of a newer world. It was the figure of a Cree squaw, blanketed and many-wrinkled and unmistakably dirty, blinking at the devil-wagons and the ceaseless hurry of the white man. And being somewhat Indianized, as my husband once assured me I was, I could sympathize with that stolid old lady in the blanket.

I'm even beginning to find that one can get tired of optimism, especially when it is being so plainly converted from a psychic abstraction into a municipal asset. There's a sort of communal Christian Science in this place which ordains that thought shall not dwell on such transient evils as drought or black rust or early frost or hail-storms or money stringencies. And there's a sort of youthful greediness in people's longing to live all there is of life to live and to know all there is of life to know. For there is a limit to the sensations we can digest, just as there is a limit to the meat we can digest. And out here we have a tendency to bolt more than is good for us, to bolt it without pausing to get the true taste of it. The women of this town remind me more and more of mice in an oxygen bell; they race round and round, drunk with an excitement they can't quite understand, until they burn up their little lives the same as the mice burn up their little lungs.

... I've had a letter from Whinstane Sandy to-day, writing about seed-wheat and the repairs for the tractor. It seems like a message from another world. He reports that poor old Scotty is eating again and no longer mourns day in and day out for his lost master. And Mr. Ketley has very kindly brought over the liniment for Mudski's shoulder. ... Whatever I may be, or whatever I may have done, I feel that I can still cleanse my heart by sacrifice.

Friday the Ninth

One can get out of the habit, apparently, of having children about. My kiddies, I begin to see, occasionally grate on Duncan. He brought tears to the eyes of Pauline Augusta yesterday by the way he scolded her for using a lead-pencil on the living-room woodwork. And the night before he shouted much strong language at Elmer for breaking a window-pane in the garage with Benny McArthur's new air-gun.

Elmer and his father, I'm afraid, have rather grown away from each other. More than once I've caught Duncan staring at his son and heir in a puzzled and a slightly frustrated sort of way. And Elmer's soul promptly becomes *incommunicado* when his iron-browed pater is in the neighborhood.

Duncan is very proud of his grand new house. He is anxious to build a conservatory out along the southwest wing. But he has asked how long a conservatory would last with two young mountain-goats gamboling along its leads.... Lossie, little suspecting the pang she was giving me, laughingly showed me a manuscript which she found by accident in my Dinkie's reader. It was a poem, dedicated to "D. O'L." And written in a stiff little hand I read:

"Your lips are lined with roses,
Your eyes they shinne like gold
If you call me from the sunlight,
I'll answer from the cold.
But I wonder why, Oh, why,
You stay so far from me?
If you whisper from the prarrie,
I'll call from Calgary."

"Won't it be wonderful," said Lossie as I sat pondering over those foolish little lines, "won't it be wonderful, if Dinkie grows up to be a great poet?"

Monday the Eleventh

Elmer, *alias* Dinkie, after many days' mourning for his lost Scotty, is consoling himself, as other men do, with a substitute. Last Friday he Brought home a flop-eared pup with a drooping tail and an indefinite ancestry, explaining that he had come into possession of the aforementioned animal by the duly delivered purchase-price of thirty-seven cents.

Remembering Minty and certain matters of the past, I was troubled in spirit. But I couldn't see why my son shouldn't have an animal to love. And I have had Hilton fix a little box in one corner of the garage for Dinkie's new pet, which he has christened Rowdy.

Rowdy, I now see, is a canine of limited spirit and is not likely to repeat the offenses of Minty. But Dinkie really loves his new pup, despite the latter's indubitably democratic ancestry. And I begin to suspect that my laddie's weakness for mongrels may arise from his earlier experience with Duncan's blooded bulldog, which he struggled with for three whole days, fondly and foolishly trying to teach that stolid animal the art of "pointing."

On Saturday Dinkie smuggled the verminous Rowdy to the upper bathroom and gave him a thorough but quite unrelished soaping ... Dinkie, by the way, is now a "cub" in the Boy Scouts and after adorning himself in khaki goes off on hikes and takes lessons in woodcraft. Saturday the Scouts of his school marched behind a real band and Lossie and I sat in the car waiting for my laddie to appear. He wiggled one hand, and smiled sheepishly, as he caught sight of us. But he kept "eyes front" and refused to give any further sign as he marched bravely on behind that brave music. He is learning the law of the pack. For some first frail ideas of service are beginning to incubate in that egoistic little bean of his. And he's suffering, I suppose, the old contest between the ancestral lust to kill and the new-born inclination to succor and preserve. That means he may some day be "a gentleman." And I've a weakness for that old Newman definition of a gentleman as one who never inflicts pain—"tender towards the bashful, gentle towards the distant, and merciful towards the absurd"—conducting himself toward his enemy as if he were some day to be his friend. And I also wish there were a few more of them in this hard old world of ours!

Speaking of gentlemen, there's a Captain Goodhue here whom I rather like. Lois Murchison brought us together in the tea-room of the Palliser. In more ways than one he reminds me of Peter. But Captain Goodhue is a much older man, and is English, coming from a very excellent family in

Sussex. He's one of those iron-gray ex-Army men who still believe in a monocle and can be loyal to a queen even though she wears a basque with darts in it. And he doesn't talk to a woman with that ragging air of condescension which seems to be peculiar to western American civilization. He is courteous and thoughtful and sincere, though I noticed that he winced a trifle when I suddenly remembered, as he was taking his departure, that the McKails were living in what must have once been his house. He blinked, like a well-groomed old eagle, when I reminded him of this. I never dreamed, of course, that the subject would be painful to him. But it was an honor, he acknowledged with a bow, to pass his household gods on to a lady to whom so much had already been given.

When I asked Lois about it, later on, she rather indifferently acknowledged that the old gentleman had been making a mess of his different business ventures. He was much better at golf than getting in on the ground-floor of a land deal. He was too old fogy, said Slinkie, to make good in the West. He still kept his head up, but they'd pretty well picked him to the bones.... Lois, by the way, describes me as something new in her menagerie and drops in to see me at the most unexpected moments. Then her tongue goes like a mower-knife. She is persuaded that I should permanent-wave my hair, lower my waist-line, and go in for amethysts. "And interest yourself, my dear, in an outside man or two," she has sagely advised me. "For husbands, you'll find, always accept you at the other mutt's valuation!"

I was tempted to make her open her jade-green eyes, for a moment, by telling her I was already interested in an outside man or two and that my lord and master hadn't been much influenced by the extraneous appreciations. But I'm a little afraid of Slinkie and her serpent's tongue. And I'm a little afraid of this new circle into which my Duncan has so laboriously engineered himself. They more and more impress on my simple old prairie soul that the single-track woman is the woman who gets most out of life, that there's nothing really great and nothing really enduring that is not built on loyalty and truth. Character is Fate, as I once before inscribed in this book of my life. And I've been sitting up to-night, while the eternal bridge game is going on below, asking myself if all is well with Chaddie McKail. Have I, or have I not, conceded too much? Am I turning into nothing more than a mush of concession? Haven't I been bribed by comfort, and blinded to a situation which I am now almost afraid to face? Haven't I been selfishly scheming for the welfare of my children and endangering all their future and my own by the price I am paying? Haven't I been crazily manning a rickety old pump, trying to keep afloat a family hulk whose seams are wide open and whose timbers are water-logged? And how long can this sort of thing go on? And what will be the end of it?

I try to warn myself not to smash my goods to kill a rat, as the Chinese say. I try to flatter myself that I am not letting circumstances stampede me into any hasty decision. There's many a woman, I suppose, with a husband whose legal promise has outlived his loyalty. But all is not well here about my heart. I know that, by the way it keeps sending up little trial-balloons, to see which way the wind is really blowing.

... And Sunday night Cattalo Charlie went home quite drunk. And our local member, emboldened by his seventh highball, offhandedly invited me to accompany him on a little run up to Banff, stabbing me with a hurt look when I told him I'd see when Duncan could get away from his work....

I wonder if spring is coming to Casa Grande? And at Alabama Ranch? And are the pussy-willows showing in the slough-ends? And why doesn't Peter Ketley ever write to me?

Saturday the Sixteenth

Lossie and Gershom, I find, have drifted into the habit of writing to each other. It is, of course, all purely platonic and pedagogic, arising out of a common interest in my Dinkie's academic advancement. But Lossie borrowed Dinkie this morning to have a photograph taken with him, one copy of which she has very generously promised to send on to Gershom.... Struthers has sent me a very satisfactory report from Casa Grande, which I dreamed last night had burned to the ground, compelling me and my kiddies to live in the old prairie-schooner, laboriously pulled about the prairie by Tithonus and Calamity Kate. And when I applied at Peter's door for a handful of meal for my starving children, he called me worse than a fallen woman and drove me off into the wilderness.

Duncan asked me to-day if I'd motor up to the mines with him for the week-end. I had to tell him that I'd promised to take Elmer and Pauline Augusta to hear Kathleen Parlow and that it wouldn't seem quite fair to break my word. Duncan said that I was the best judge of that. Then he slammed a drawer shut and asked me, in his newer manner, how long I intended to pull this iceberg stuff. "For I can't see," he concluded after calling out for Tokudo to bring his hat and coat, "that I'm getting such a hell of a lot out of this arrangement!"

I asked him, as quietly as I could, what he expected of me. But I could feel my heart pounding quick against my ribs. I am not, and never pretended to be, any stained-glass saint. And there were a few things I felt it was about time to unload. But Tokudo cat-footed back with the coat, and I could hear Lossie's clear laugh as she came in through the front door with the returning Dinkie, and some inner voice warned me to hold my peace. So Duncan and I merely stood there staring at each other, for a moment or two, across an abysmal and unbridgeable gulf of silence. Then he strode out to his car without as much as a howdy-do to the startled and slightly mystified Lossie.

Monday the Eighteenth

I have just learned that we were blackballed from the Country Club. My husband, at least, has met with that experience.

It was Lois who let the cat out of the bag. She wasn't clear on all the details, but it was that old has-been of a Goodhue who was at the bottom of it all, according to the lady known as Slinkie. Duncan and he had clashed, from the first. Then Duncan had bought up his paper, and compelled him to mortgage his home. It was because of something to do with the Barcona Mines directorate, Lois thought, that Captain Goodhue had had Duncan blackballed when he applied for membership in the Country Club, the Captain being vice-president of the original holding company. Lois laughed none too pleasantly when she added that her Charley and my Duncan had joined hands to go after the old man's scalp. And they had got it. They turned him inside out, before they got through with him. They took his fore-lock and his teepee and his last string of wampum. And the old snob, of course, would never forgive them.

... They took his fore-lock, and his teepee ... And it was Chaddie McKail and her bairns who were now housing warm in that captured teepee! And all this toiling and moiling, on the part of my husband, all this scheming and intriguing and juggling with figures, had been a campaign for power, a plotting and working to get even with this haughty old enemy who could carry his defeat so lightly! To be blackballed like that, I remembered, was to be proclaimed not a gentleman. And it must have cut deep. At one time, I suppose, Duncan would have called his monocled captain out. But men seem to fight differently nowadays. They fight differently, but no less grimly. And Duncan, whether it is a virtue or a vice in his make-up, would always be a fighter.... Yet I have no sense of gratitude to Lois Murchison for depositing her painful truths in my lap. She warned me, in her artless soprano, that there wasn't much good in sentimentalizing the situation. But she has thrown a shadow across the house which I was trying to make into a home. Without quite knowing it, she has cheapened her life-mate in my eyes. Without quite intending it, she has left my own husband more ignominious than he once stood. I was trying hard to school myself into a respect for his material successes. I was struggling to excuse a great many things by the engrossing nature of his work. But the motive behind all his efforts seemed suddenly a sordid one, in many ways a mean one.

I keep remembering what Lois said about not sentimentalizing a situation. But I'm not yet such a mush of concession that I can't tell black from white. And there's some part of us, some vague but unescapable part of us, which we must respect, otherwise we have no right to walk God's good earth....

I want to get away, for a day or two, to think things out. I think, before Duncan gets back to-morrow, I shall take Poppsy and run up to Banff. I may get my view-point back. And the mountain quietness may do me good....

I keep having that same dull ache of disappointment which came to me as a girl, after I'd idolized a great man called Meredith and after I'd almost prayed to a great poet called Browning, on finding that one was so imperfectly monogamous and that the other philandered and talked foolishly to women. I had thrust my girlish faith in their hands, as so often befalls with the young, and they had betrayed it.... But for the second time since I married, I have been reading *Modern Love*. And I can almost forgive the Apollo of Box Hill for that betrayal which he knew nothing about.

Thursday the Twenty-Eighth

This is Thursday the twenty-eighth of April. I want to be sure of that. For there are very few things I can be sure of now.

The bottom has fallen out of my world. I sit here, telling myself to be calm. But it's not easy to sit quiet when you face the very worst that all life could confront you with. *My Dinkie has run away.*

My boy has left me, has left his home, has vanished like smoke into the Unknown. He is gone and I have no trace of him.

I find it hard to write. Yet I *must* write, for the mere expression of what I feel tends to ease the ache. It helps to keep me sane. And already I realize I was wrong when I wrote "the very worst that all life could confront you with." For my laddie, after all, is not dead. He must still be alive. And while there's life, there's hope.

I got back from Banff yesterday morning about nine, and Hilton was there with the car to meet me, as I had told him to be. I was anxious to know at once if everything was all right, but I found it hard to put a question so personal before that impersonal-eyed Englishman. So I strove to give my interrogation an air of the casual by offhandedly inquiring: "How's Rowdy, Hilton?"

"Dead, ma'am," was his prompt reply.

This rather took my breath away.

"Do you mean to say that Rowdy is *dead?*" I insisted, noticing Poppsy's color change as she listened.

"Killed, ma'am," said the laconic Hilton.

"By whom?" I demanded.

"Mr. Murchison, ma'am," was the answer.

"How?" I asked, feeling my vague dislike for that particular name sharpen up to something dangerously like hatred.

"He always comes up the drive a bit fast-like, ma'am. He hit the pup, and that was the end of him!"

"Does Dinkie know?" was my first question, after that.

"He *saw* it, ma'am," admitted my car-driver.

"Saw what?"

- 167 -

"Saw Mr. Murchison throw the dog over the wall into the brush!"

"What did he say?"

"He swore a bit, ma'am, and then laughed," admitted Hilton, after a pause.

"Dinkie laughed?" I cried, incredulous.

"No; Mr. Murchison, ma'am," explained Hilton.

"What did Dinkie say?" I insisted. And again the man on the driving-seat remained silent a moment or two.

"It was what he *did*, ma'am," he finally remarked.

"What did he do?" I demanded.

"Ran into the house, ma'am, and snatched the icepick off the kitchen table. Then he went to the big car like a mad 'un, he did. Pounded holes in every blessed tire with his pick!"

"And then what?" I asked, with my heart up in my throat.

Hilton waited until he had taken a crowded corner before answering.

"Then he found the dead dog, ma'am, and bathed it, and borrowed the garden spade from me. Then he took it somewheres back in the ravine and buried it. I gave him the tool-box off the old roadster, to put what was left of the pup in."

"And then?" I prompted, with a quaver in my voice I couldn't control.

"He met Mr. Murchison coming out and he called him w'at I'd not like to repeat, ma'am, until Mr. McKail stepped out to see what was wrong, and interfered."

"*How* did he interfere?" was my next question.

"By taking the lad into the house, ma'am," was my witness's retarded reply.

"Then what happened?" I exacted.

I waited, knowing what was coming, but I dreaded to hear it.

"He gave him a threshing, ma'am," I heard Hilton's voice saying, far away, as though it came to me over a long-distance telephone on a wet night.

I sat rigid as we mounted American Hill. I sat rigid as we swerved in through the ridiculous manor-like gate and up the winding drive and in under the ugly new porte-cochère. I didn't even wait for Poppsy as I got out of the car. I didn't even speak to Tokudo as he ran mincingly to take my things. I walked straight to the breakfast-room where I saw my husband sitting at the end of the oblong white table, stirring a cup of coffee with a spoon.

"Where's Dinkie?" I asked, trying to keep my voice low but not quite succeeding.

Duncan looked up at me with a coldly meditative eye.

"Where he usually is at this time of day," he finally answered.

"Where?" I repeated.

"At school, of course," admitted my husband as he reached out for a piece of buttered toast. He was making a pretense at being very tranquil-minded. But his hand, I noticed, wasn't so steady as it might have been.

"Is he all right?" I demanded, with my voice rising in spite of myself.

"Considerably better, I imagine, than he has been for some time," was the deliberate answer from the man with the bloodshot eyes at the end of the table.

"What do you mean by that?" I asked. And any one of intelligence, I suppose, could see I was making that question a challenge.

"I mean that since you saw him last he's had a damned good whaling," said Duncan, with his jaw squared, so that he reminded me of a King-Lud bulldog.

I paid no attention to Tokudo, who came into the room to repeat that his master was wanted at the telephone.

"Do you mean you struck that child?" I demanded, leaning on the table and looking straight into his eyes, which met mine quite unabashed, and with an air of mockery about them.

My husband nodded as he pushed back his chair.

"He got a good one," he asserted as he rose to his feet and rather leisurely brushed a crumb or two from his vest-front. He could even afford to smile as he said it. My expression, I suppose, would have made any man smile. But there was something maddening in his mockery, at such a moment. There was something gratuitously cruel in his parade of unconcern. Yet, oddly enough, as I looked at his slightly blotched face I couldn't help remembering that that was the face I had once kissed and held close against my cheek, had *wanted* to hold against my cheek. And now I hated it.

I had to wait and cast about for words of hatred strong enough to carry the arrows of enmity which nothing could stop me from delivering. But while I waited Tokudo announced for the third time that my husband was wanted at the telephone. And a very simple thing happened. My husband answered his call.

I saw Duncan turn and walk out of the room. I could hear his steps in the hallway, loud on the waxed hardwood and low on the rugs. I could hear his deliberated chest-tones as he talked over the wire, talked quietly and earnestly, talked me and my hatred out of his head and out of his world. And I realized, as I sat there at the table-end with my gloves twisted up under my hands and my heart even more twisted up under my ribs, that it was all useless, that it was all futile. He was beyond the reach of my resentment. We were in different worlds, forevermore.

I was still sitting there when he looked in at the door, with his hat and coat on, on his way out. I could feel him there, without directly seeing him. And I could feel, too, that he wanted to say something. But I declined to lift my head, and I could hear the door close as he went out to the waiting car.

I sat there for a long time, thinking about my Dinkie. Twice I almost surrendered to the impulse to telephone to Lossie Brown. But I knew it would be no easy matter to get in touch with her. And in two hours it would be twelve, and any minute after that my boy would be home again. I tried to cross-examine Tokudo, but I could get nothing out of that tight-lipped Jap. I watched the clock. I noticed Hilton, when he got back, raking blood-stains off the gravel of the driveway. I wandered about, like a lost turkey-hen, trying to dramatize my meeting with Dinkie, doing my best to cooper together some incident which might keep our first minute or two together from being too hard on my poor kiddie. I heard the twelve o'clock whistles, at last, and then the Westminster-chimes of the over-ornate clock in the library announce that noon had come. And still the minutes dragged on.

And when the tension was becoming almost unbearable I heard a step on the gravel and my heart started to pound.

But instead of Dinkie, it was Lossie, Lossie with smiling lips and inquiring brown eyes and splashes of rose in her cheeks from rapid walking.

"Where's Dinkie?" I asked.

She stopped short, still smiling.

"That's exactly what I was going to ask?" I heard her saying. Then her smile faded as she searched my face. "There's—there's nothing happened, has there?"

I groped my way to a pillar of the porte-cochère and leaned against it.

"Didn't Dinkie come to school this morning?" I asked as the earth wavered under my feet.

"No," acknowledged Lossie, still searching my face. And a frown of perplexity came into her own.

I knew then what had happened. I knew it even before I went up to Dinkie's room and started my frantic search through his things. I could see that a number of his more treasured small possessions were gone. I delved forlornly about, hoping that he might have left some hidden message for me. But I could find nothing. I sat looking at his books and broken toys, at the still open copy of *The Count of Monte Cristo* which he must have been poring over only the night before, at his neatly folded underclothes and the little row of gravel-worn shoes. They took on an air of pathos, an atmosphere of the memorial. Yet, oddly enough, it was Lossie, and Lossie alone, who broke into tears. The more she cried, in fact, the calmer I found myself becoming, though all the while that dead weight of misery was hanging like lead from my heart.

I went at once to the telephone and called up Duncan's office. He was still there, though I had to wait several minutes before I could get in touch with him.

I had thought, at first, that he would be offhandedly skeptical at the message which I was sending him over the wire, the message that my boy had run away. He might even be flippantly indifferent, and remind me that much worse things could have happened.

But I knew at once that he was genuinely alarmed at the news which I'd given him. It apparently staggered him for a moment. Then he said in his curt telephonic chest-tones, "I'll be up at the house, at once."

He came, before I'd even completed a second and more careful search. His face was cold and non-committal enough, but his color was gone and there was a look that was almost one of contrition in his troubled eyes, which seemed unwilling to meet mine. He questioned Lossie and cross-examined Hilton and Tokudo, and then called up the Chief of Police. Then he telephoned to the different railway stations, and carried Lossie off in the car to the McArthurs', to interview Benny, and came back an hour later with that vague look of frustration still on his face.

He sat down to luncheon, but he ate very little. He was silent for quite a long time.

"Your boy's all right," he said in a much softer voice than I had expected from him. "He's big enough to look after himself. And we'll be on his trail before nightfall. He can't go far."

"No; he can't go far," I echoed, trying to fortify myself with the knowledge that he must have taken little more than a dollar from the gilded cast-iron elephant which he used as a bank.

"I don't want this to get in the papers," explained my husband. "It's—it's all so ridiculous. I've put Kearney and two of his men on the job. He's a private detective, and he'll keep busy until he gets the boy back."

Duncan got up from the table, rather heavily. He stood hesitating a moment and then stepped closer to my chair.

"I know it's hard," he said as he put a hand on my shoulder. "But it'll be all right. We'll get your boy back for you."

I didn't speak, because I knew that if I spoke I'd break down and make an idiot of myself. My husband waited, apparently expecting me to say something. Then he took his hand away.

"I'll get busy with the car," he said with a forced matter-of-factness, "and let you know when there's any news. I've wired Buckhorn and sent word to Casa Grande—and we ought to get some news from there."

But there was no news. The afternoon dragged away and the house seemed like a tomb. And at five o'clock I did what I had wanted to do for six long hours. I sent off a forty-seven word telegram to Peter Ketley, telling him what had happened....

Duncan came back, at seven o'clock, to get one of the new photographs of Dinkie and Lossie for identification purposes. They had rounded up a small boy at Morley and Kearney was motoring out to investigate. We'd know by midnight....

It is well after midnight, and Duncan has just had a phone-message from Morley. The little chap they had rounded up was a Barnado boy fired with a sudden ambition to join his uncle in the gold-fields of Australia. Somewhere, in the blackness of this big night, my homeless Dinkie is wandering unguarded and alone.

Friday the Twenty-Ninth

I have had no word from Peter.... I've had no news to end the ache that pins me like a spear-head to the wall of hopelessness. Duncan, I know, is doing all he can. But there is so little to do. And this world of ours, after all, is such a terrifyingly big one.

Saturday the Thirtieth

I was called to the phone before breakfast this morning and it was the blessed voice of Peter I heard from the other end of the wire. My telegram had got out to him from Buckhorn a day late. But he had no definite news for me. He was quite fixed in his belief, however, that Dinkie would be bobbing up at his old home in a day or two.

"The boy will travel this way," he assured me. "He's bound to do that. It's as natural as water running down-hill!"

Duncan asked me whom I'd been talking to, and I had to tell him. His face clouded and the familiar quick look of resentment came into his eyes.

"I can't see what that Quaker's got to do with this question," he barked out. But I held my peace.

Sunday the First

I have found a message from my Dinkie. I came across it this morning, by accident. It was in my sewing-basket, the basket made of birch-bark and stained porcupine quills and lined with doe-skin, which I'd once bought from a Reservation squaw in Buckhorn with a tiny papoose on her back. Duncan had upbraided me for passing out my last five-dollar bill to that hungry Nitchie, but the poor woman needed it.

My fingers were shaking as I unfolded the note. And written there in the script I knew so well I read:

"Darligest Mummsey:

I am going away. But dont worry about me for I will be alright. I couldn't stay Mummsey after what hapened. Some day I will come back to you. But I'm not as bad as all that. I'll love you always as much as ever. I can take care for myself so don't worry, please. And please feed my two rabits reglar and tell Benny I'll save his jacknife and rember every day I'm rembering you. X X X X X X X

Your aff'cte son,

DINKIE."

It seemed like a voice from the dead, it was bittersweet consolation, and, in a way, it stood redemption of Dinkie himself. I'd been upbraiding him, in my secret heart of hearts, for his silence to his mother. That's a streak of his father in him, had been my first thought, that unthinking cruelty which didn't take count of the anguish of others. But he hadn't forgotten me. Whatever happens, I have at least this assuaging secret message from my son. And some day he'll come back to me. "Ye winna leave me for a', laddie?" I keep saying, in the language of old Whinstane Sandy. And my mind goes back, almost six years at a bound, to the time he was lost on the prairie. That time, I tell myself, God was good to me. And surely He will be good to me again!

Tuesday the Third

We still have no single word of our laddie.... They all tell me not to worry. But how can a mother keep from worrying? I had rather an awful nightmare last night, dreaming that Dinkie was trying to climb the stone wall about our place. He kept falling back with bleeding fingers, and he kept calling and calling for his mother. Without being quite awake I went down to the door in my night-gown, and opened it, and called out into the darkness: "Is anybody there? Is it you, Dinkie?"

My husband came down and led me back to bed, with rather a frightened look on his face.

They tell me not to worry, but I've been up in Dinkie's room turning over his things and wondering if he's dead, or if he's fallen into the hands of cruel people who would ill-use a child. Or perhaps he has been stolen by Indians, and will come back to me with a morose and sullen mind, and with scars on his body....

Thursday the Fifth

What a terrible thing is loneliness. The floors of Hell, I'm sure, are paved with lonesome hearts. Day by day I wait and long for my laddie. Always, at the back of my brain, is that big want. Day by day I brood about him and night by night I dream of him. I turn over his old playthings and his books, and my throat gets tight. I stare at the faded old snap-shots of him, and my heart turns to lead. I imagine I hear his voice, just outside the door, or just beyond a bend in the road, and a two-bladed sword of pain pushes slowly through my breast-bone. Dear old Lossie comes twice a day, and does her best to cheer me up. And Gershom has offered to give up his school and join in the search. Peter Ketley, he tells me, has been on the road for a week, in a car covered with mud and clothes that have never come off.

Friday the Sixth

There is no news of my Dinkie. And *that*, I remind myself, is the only matter that counts.

Lois Murchison drove up to-day in her hateful big car. She did not find me a very agreeable hostess, I'm afraid, but curled up like a nonchalant green snake in one of my armchairs and started to smoke and talk. She asked where Duncan was and I had to explain that he'd been called out to the mines on imperative business. And that started her going on the mines. Duncan, she said, should clean up half a million before he was through with that deal. He had been very successful.

"But don't you feel, my dear," she went on with quiet venom in her voice, "that a great deal of his success has depended on that bandy-legged little she-secretary of his?"

"Is she that wonderful?" I asked, trying to seem less at sea than I was.

"She's certainly wonderful to him!" announced the woman known as Slinkie. And having driven that poisoned dart well into the flesh, she was content to drop her cigarette-end into the ash-receiver, reach for her blue-fox furs, and announce that she'd have to be toddling on to the hair-dresser's.

Lois Murchison's implication, at that moment, didn't bother me much, for I had bigger troubles to occupy my thoughts. But the more I dwell on it, the more I find myself disturbed in spirit. I resent the idea of being upset by a wicked-tongued woman. She has, however, raised a ghost which will have to be laid. To-morrow I intend to go down to my husband's office and see his secretary, "to inspect the whaup," as Whinnie would express it, for I find myself becoming more and more interested in her wonderfulness.... Peter sent me a hurried line or two to-day, telling me to sit tight as he thought he'd have news for me before the week was out.

I suspect him of trying to trick me into some forlorn new lease of hope. But I have pinned my faith to Peter—and I know he would not trifle with anything so sacred as mother-love.

Saturday the Seventh

There is no news of my Dinkie.... But there is news of another nature.

Between ten and eleven this morning I had Hilton motor me down to Duncan's office in Eighth Avenue. It struck me as odd, at first, that I had never been there before. But Duncan, I remembered, had never asked me, the domestic fly, to step into his spider's parlor of commerce. And I found a ridiculous timidity creeping over me as I went up in the elevator, and found the door-number, and saw myself confronted by a cadaverous urchin in horn-rimmed specs, who thrust a paper-covered novel behind his chair-back and asked me what I wanted. So I asked him if this was Mr. McKail's office.

"Sure," he said in the established vernacular of the West.

"What is your name, little boy?" I inquired, with the sternest brand of condescension I could command.

The young monkey drew himself up at that and flushed angrily. "Oh, I don't know as I'm so little," he observed, regarding me with a narrowing eye as I stepped unbidden beyond the sacred portals.

"Where will I find Mr. McKail's secretary?" I asked, noticing the door in the stained-wood partition with "Private" on its frosted glass. The youth nodded his head toward the door in question and crossed to a desk where he proceeded languidly to affix postage-stamps to a small pile of envelopes.

I hesitated for a moment, as though there was something epochal in the air, as though I was making a step which might mean a great deal to me. And then I stepped over to the door and opened it.

I saw a young woman seated at a flat-topped desk, with a gold-banded fountain-pen in her fingers, checking over a column of figures. She checked carefully on to the end of her column, and then she raised her head and looked at me.

Her face stood out with singular distinctness, in the strong side-light from the office-window. And the woman seated at the flat-topped desk was Alsina Teeswater.

I don't know how long I stood there without speaking. But I could see the color slowly mount and recede on Alsina Teeswater's face. She put down her fountain-pen, with much deliberation, and sat upright in her chair, with her barricaded eyes every moment of the time on my face.

"So this has started again?" I finally said, in little more than a whisper.

I could see the girl's lips harden. I could see her fortifying herself behind an entrenchment of quietly marshaled belligerency.

"It has never stopped, Mrs. McKail," she said in an equally low voice, but with the courage of utter desperation.

It took some time, apparently, for that declaration to filter through to my brain. Everything seemed suddenly out of focus; and it was hard to readjust vision to the newer order of things. But I was calmer, under the circumstances, than I expected to be.

"I'm glad I understand," I finally admitted.

The woman at the desk seemed puzzled. Then she looked from me to her column of figures and from her column of figures to the huddled roofs and walls of the city and the greening foot-hills and the solemn white crowns of the Rockies behind them.

"Are you quite sure, Mrs. McKail, that you do understand?" she asked at last, with just a touch of challenge in the question.

"Isn't it quite simple now?" I demanded.

She found the courage to face me again.

"I don't think this sort of thing is ever simple," she replied, with much more emotion than I had expected of her.

"But it's at least clear how it must end," I found the courage to point out to her.

"Is that clear to *you*?" demanded the woman who was stepping into my shoes. It seemed odd, at the moment, that I should feel vaguely sorry for her.

"Perhaps you might make it clearer," I prompted.

"I'd rather Duncan did that," she replied, using my husband's first name, obviously, without knowing she had done so.

"Wouldn't it be fairer—for the two of us—now? Wouldn't it be cleaner?" I rather tremulously asked of her.

She nodded and stared down at the sheet covered with small columns of figures.

"I don't know whether you know it or not," she said with a studied sort of quietness, "but last week Mr. McKail began making arrangements to establish a residence in Nevada. He will have to live there, of course, for at least six months, perhaps even longer."

I could feel this sinking in, like water going through blotting-paper. The woman at the desk must have misinterpreted my silence, for she was moved to say, in a heavier effort at self-defense, "He *knew*, of course, that you cared for some one else."

I looked at her, as though she were a thousand miles away. I stood there impressed by the utter inadequacy of speech. And the thing that puzzled me was that there was an air of honesty about the woman. She still so desperately clung to her self-respect that she wanted me to understand both her predicament and her motives. I could hear her explaining that my husband had no intention of going to Reno, but would live in Virginia City, where he was taking up some actual mining interests. Such things were not pleasant, of course. But this one could be put through without difficulty. Mr. McKail had been assured of that.

I tried to pull myself together, wondering why I should so suddenly feel like a marked woman, a pariah of the prairies, as friendless and alone as a leper. Then I thought of my children. And that cleared my head, like a wind sweeping clean a smoky room.

"But a case has to be made out," I began. "It would have to be proved that I—"

"There will be no difficulty on that point, Mrs. McKail," went on the other woman as I came to a stop. "Provided the suit is not opposed."

The significance of that quietly uttered phrase did not escape me. Our glances met and locked.

"There are the children," I reminded her. And she looked a very commercialized young lady as she sat confronting me across her many columns of figures.

"There should be no difficulty there—*provided* the suit is not opposed," she repeated with the air of a physician confronted by a hypochondriacal patient.

"The children are mine," I rather foolishly proclaimed, with my first touch of passion.

"The children are yours," she admitted. And about her hung an air of authority, of cool reserve, which I couldn't help resenting.

"That is very generous of you," I admitted, not without ironic intent.

She smiled rather sadly as she sat looking at me.

"It's something that doesn't rest with either of us," she said with the suspicion of a quaver in her voice. And *she*, I suddenly remembered, might some day sit eating her pot of honey on a grave. I realized, too, that very little was to be gained by prolonging that strangest of interviews. I wanted quietude in which to think things over. I wanted to go back to my cell like a prisoner and brood over my sentence....

And I have thought things over. I at last see the light. From this day forward there shall be no vacillating. I am going back to Casa Grande.

I have always hated this house; I have always hated everything about the place, without having the courage to admit it. I have done my part, I have made my effort, and it was a wasted effort. I wasn't even given a chance. And now I shall gather my things together and go back to my home, to the only home that remains to me. I shall still have my kiddies. I shall have my Poppsy and—But sharp as an arrow-head the memory of my lost boy strikes into my heart. My Dinkie is gone. I no longer have him to make what is left of my life endurable....

It is raining to-night, I notice, steadily and dismally. It is a dark night, outside, for lost children....

Duncan has just come home, wet and muddy, and gone up to his room. The gray-faced solemnity with which he strode past me makes me feel sure that he has been conversing with his lady-love. But what difference does it make? What difference does *anything* make? In the matter of women, I have just remembered, what may be one man's meat is another man's poison. But I can't understand these reversible people, like house-rugs, who can pretend to love two ways at once.... I only know one man, in all the wide world, who has not shattered my faith in his kind. He is one of those neck-or-nothing men who never change.

There are many ranchers, out in this country, who keep what they call a blizzard-line. It's a rope that stretches in winter from their house-door to their shed or their stable, a rope that keeps them from getting lost when a blizzard is raging. Peter, I know, has been my blizzard-line. And in some way, please God, he will yet lead me back to warmth. He is himself out there in the cold, accepting it, all the time, with the same quiet fortitude that a Polar bear might. But he will thole through, in the end. For with all his roughness he can be unexpectedly adroit. Whinstane Sandy once told me something he had learned about Polar bears in his old Yukon days: with all their heaviness, they can go where a dog daren't venture. If need be, they can flatten out and slide over a sheet of ice too thin to support a running dog. And the drift-ice may be widening, but I refuse to give up my hope of hope. "Let the mother go," as the Good Book says, "that it may be well with thee!" ...

I have just remembered that I tried to shoot my husband once. He may make use of *that*, when he gets down to Virginia City. It might, in fact, help things along very materially. And Susie's eyes will probably pop out, when she reads it in a San Francisco paper....

I've thought of so many clever things I should have said to Alsina Teeswater. As I look back, I find it was the other lady who did about all the talking. There were old ulcerations to be cleared away, of course, and I let her talk about the same as you let a dentist work with his fingers in your mouth.... But now I must go up and make sure my Poppsy is safely tucked in. I have just opened the door and looked out. It is storming wretchedly. God pity any little boys who are abroad on such a night!

Two Hours Later

It is well past midnight. But there is no sleep this night for Chaddie McKail. I am too happy to sleep. I am too happy to act sane. For my boy is safe. *Peter has found my Dinkie!*

I was called to the telephone, a little after eleven, but couldn't hear well on the up-stairs extension, so I went to the instrument down-stairs, where the operator told me it was long-distance, from Buckhorn. So I listened, with my heart in my mouth. But all I could get was a buzz and crackle and an occasional ghostly word. It was the storm, I suppose. Then I heard Peter's voice, thin and faint and far away, but most unmistakably Peter's voice.

"Can you hear me now?" he said, like a man speaking from the bottom of the sea.

"Yes," I called back. "What is it?"

"Get ready for good news," said that thin but valorous voice that seemed to be speaking from the tip-top mountains of Mars. But the crackling and burring cut us off again. Then something must have happened to the line, or we must have been switched to a better circuit. For, the next moment, Peter's voice seemed almost in the next room. It seemed to come closer at a bound, like a shore-line when you look at it through a telescope.

"Is that any better?" he asked through his miles and miles of rain-swept blackness.

"Yes, I can hear you plainly now," I told him.

"Ah, yes, that *is* better," he acknowledged. "And everything else is, too, my dear. For I've found your Dinkie and—"

"You've found Dinkie?" I gasped.

"I have, thank God. And he's safe and sound!"

"Where?" I demanded.

"Fast asleep at Alabama Ranch."

"Is he all right?"

"As fit as a fiddle—all he wants is sleep."

"*Oh, Peter!*" It was foolish. But it was all I could say for a full minute. For my boy was alive, and safe. My laddie had been found by Peter—by good old Peter, who never, in the time of need, was known to fail me.

"Where are you now?" I asked, when reason was once more on her throne.

"At Buckhorn," answered Peter.

"And you went all that way through the mud and rain, just to tell me?" I said.

"I had to, or I'd blow up!" acknowledged Peter. "And now I'd like to know what you want me to do."

"I want you to come and get me, Peter," I said slowly and distinctly over the wire.

There was a silence of several seconds.

"Do you understand what that means?" he finally demanded. His voice, I noticed, had become suddenly solemn.

"Yes, Peter, I understand," I told him. "Please come and get me!" And again the silence was so prolonged that I had to cut in and ask: "Are you there?"

And Peter's voice answered "Yes."

"Then you'll come?" I exacted, determined to burn all my bridges behind me.

"I'll be there on Monday," said Peter, with quiet decision. "I'll be there with Tithonus and Tumble-Weed and the old prairie-schooner. And we'll all trek home together!"

"*Skookum!*" I said with altogether unbecoming levity.

I patted the telephone instrument as I hung up the receiver. Then I sat staring at it in a brown study.

Then I went careening up-stairs and woke Poppsy out of a sound sleep and hugged her until her bones were ready to crack and told her that our Dinkie had been found again. And Poppsy, not being quite able to get it through her sleepy little head, promptly began to bawl. But there was little to bawl over, once she was thoroughly awake. And then I went careening down to the telephone again, and called up Lossie's boarding-house, and had her landlady root the poor girl out of bed, and heard *her* break down and have a little cry when I told her our Dinkie had been found. And the first thing she asked me, when she was able to talk again, was if Gershom Binks had been told of the good news. And I had to acknowledge that I hadn't even *thought* of poor old Gershom, but that Peter Ketley would surely have passed the good word on to Casa Grande, for Peter always seemed to think of the right thing.

And then I remembered about Duncan. For Duncan, whatever he may have been, was still the boy's father. And he must be told. It was my duty to tell him. So once more I climbed the stairs, but this time more slowly. I had to wait a full minute before I found the courage, I don't know why, to knock on Duncan's bedroom door.

I knocked twice before any answer came.

"What is it?" asked the familiar sleepy *bass*—and I realized what gulfs yawned between us when my husband on one side of that closed door could be lying lost in slumber and I on the other side of it could find life doing such unparalleled things to me. I felt for him as a girl home, tired from her first dance, feels for a young brother asleep beside a Noah's Ark.

"What is it?" I heard Duncan's voice repeating from the bed.

"It's me," I rather weakly proclaimed.

"What has happened?" was the question that came after a moment's silence.

I leaned with my face against the painted door-panel. It was smooth and cool and pleasant to press one's skin against.

"They've found Dinkie," I said. I could hear the squeak of springs as my husband sat up in bed.

"Is he all right?"

"Yes, he's all right," I said with a great sigh. And I listened for an answering sigh from the other side of the door.

But instead of that Duncan's voice asked: "Where is he?"

"At Alabama Ranch," I said, without realizing what that acknowledgment meant. And again a brief period of silence intervened.

"Who found him?" asked my husband, in a hardened voice.

"Peter Ketley," I said, in as collected a voice as I could manage. And this time the significance of the silence did not escape me.

"Then your cup of happiness ought to be full," I heard the voice on the other side of the door remark with heavy deliberateness. I stood there with my face leaning against the cool panel.

"It is," I said with a quiet audacity which surprised me almost as much as it must have surprised the man on the bed a million miles away from me.

Sunday the Eighth

How different is life from what the fictioneers would paint it! How hopelessly mixed-up and macaronic, how undignified in what ought to be its big moments and how pompous in so many of its pettinesses!

I told my husband to-day that Poppsy and I were going back to Casa Grande. And that, surely, ought to have been the Big Moment in the career of an unloved invertebrate. But the situation declined to take off, as the airmen say.

"I guess that means it's about time we got unscrambled," the man I had once married and lived with quietly remarked.

"Wasn't that your intention?" I just as quietly inquired.

"It's what I've had forced on me," he retorted, with a protective hardening of the Holbein-Astronomer jaw-line.

"I'm sorry," was all I could find to say.

He turned to the window and stared out at his big white iron fountain set in his terraced lawn behind his endless cobble-stone walls. I couldn't tell, of course, what he was thinking about. But I myself was thinking of the past, the irrecoverable past, the irredeemable past, the singing years of my womanly youth that seemed to be sealed in a lowered coffin on which the sheltering earth would soon be heaped, on which the first clods were already dropping with hollow sounds. We each seemed afraid to look the other full in the eyes. So we armored ourselves, as poor mortals must do, in the helmets of pretended diffidence and the breast-plates of impersonality.

"How are you going back?" my husband finally inquired. Whatever ghosts it had been necessary to lay, I could see, he had by this time laid. He no longer needed to stare out at the white iron fountain of which he was so proud.

"I've sent for the prairie-schooner," I told him.

His flush of anger rather startled me.

"Doesn't that impress you as rather cheaply theatrical?" he demanded.

"I fancy it will be very comfortable," I told him, without looking up. I'd apparently been attributing to him feelings which, after all, were not so desolating as I might have wished.

"Every one to his own taste," he observed as he called rather sharply to Tokudo to bring him his humidor. Then he took out a cigar and lighted it and ordered the car. And that was the lee and the long of it. That was the way we faced our Great Divide, our forked trail that veered off East and West into infinity!

Thursday the Eleventh

The trek is over. And it was not one of triumph. For we find ourselves, sometimes, in deeper water than we imagine. Then we have to choke and gasp for a while before we can get our breath back.

Peter, in the first place, didn't appear with the prairie-schooner. He left that to come later in the day, with Whinnie and Struthers. He appeared quite early Monday morning, with fire in his eye, and with a demand to see the master of the house. Heaven knows what he had heard, or how he had heard it. But the two men were having it hot and heavy when I felt it was about time for me to step into the room. To be quite frank, I had not expected any such outburst from Duncan. I knew his feelings were not involved, and where you have a vacuum it is impossible, of course, to have an explosion. I interpreted his resentment as a show of opposition to save his face. But I was wrong. And I was wrong about Peter. That mild-eyed man is no plaster saint. He can fight, if he's goaded into it, and fight like a bulldog. He was saying a few plain truths to Duncan, when I stepped into the room, a few plain truths which took the color out of the Dour Man's face and made him shake with anger.

"For two cents," Duncan was rather childishly shouting at him, "I'd fill you full of lead!"

"Try it!" said Peter, who wasn't any too steady himself. "Try it, and you'd at least end up with doing something in the open!"

Duncan studied him, like a prize-fighter studying his waiting opponent.

"You're a cheap actor," he finally announced. "This sort of thing isn't settled that way, and you know it."

"And it's not going to be settled the way you intended," announced Peter Ketley.

"What do you know about my intentions?" demanded Duncan.

"Much more than you imagine," retorted Peter. "I've got your record, McKail, and I've had it for three years. I've stood by, until now; but the time has come when I'm going to have a hand in this thing. And you're not going to get your freedom by dragging this woman's name through a divorce-court. If there's any dragging to be done, it's your carcass that's going to be tied to the tail-board!"

Duncan stood studying him with a face cheese-colored with hate.

"Aren't you rather double-crossing yourself?" he mocked.

"I'm not thinking about myself," said Peter.

"Then what's prompting all the heroics?" demanded Duncan.

"For two years and more, McKail," Peter cried out as he stepped closer to the other man, "you've given this woman a pretty good working idea of hell. And I've seen enough of it. It's going to end. It's got to end. But it's not going to end the way you've so neatly figured out!"

"Then how do you propose to end it?" Duncan demanded, with a sort of second-wind of composure. But his face was still colorless.

"You'll see when the time comes," retorted Peter.

"You may have rather a long wait," taunted Duncan.

"I have waited a number of years," answered the other man, with a dignity which sent a small thrill up and down my spine. "And I can wait a number of years more if I have to."

"We all knew, of course, that you were waiting," sneered my husband.

Peter turned to fling back an answer to that, but I stepped between them. I was tired of being haggled over, like marked-down goods on a bargain-counter. I was tired of being a passive agent before forces that seemed stripping me of my last shred of dignity. I was tired of the shoddiness of the entire shoddy situation.

And I told them so. I told them I'd no intention of being bargained over, and that I'd had rather enough of men for the rest of my natural life, and if Duncan wanted his freedom he was at liberty to take it without the slightest opposition from me. And I said a number of other things, which I have no wish either to remember or record. But it resulted in Duncan staring at me in a resurrection-plant sort of way, and in Peter rather dolorously taking his departure. I wanted to call him back, but I couldn't carpenter together any satisfactory excuse for his coming back, and I couldn't see any use in it.

So instead of journeying happily homeward in the cavernous old prairie-schooner, I felt a bit ridiculous as Tokudo impassively carried our belongings out to the canvas-covered wagon and Poppsy and I climbed aboard. The good citizens of American Hill stared after us as we rumbled down through the neatly boulevarded streets, and I felt suspiciously like a gypsy-queen who'd been politely requested by the local constabulary to move on.

It wasn't until we reached the open country that my spirits revived. Then the prairie seemed to reach out its hand to me and give me peace. We camped, that first night, in the sheltering arm of a little coulée threaded by a tiny stream. We cooked bacon and eggs and coffee while Whinnie out-spanned his team and put up his tent.

I sat on an oat-sack, after supper, with Poppsy between my knees, watching the evening stars come out. They were worlds, I remembered, some of them worlds perhaps with sorrowing men and women on them. And they seemed very lonely and far-away worlds, until I heard the drowsy voice of my Poppsy say up through the dusk: "In two days more, Mummy, we'll be back to Dinkie, won't we?"

And there was much, I remembered, for which a mother should be thankful.

Sunday the Fourteenth

Dark, and true, and tender is the North. Heaven bless the rhymster who first penned those words. Spring is stealing hack to the prairie, and our world is a world of beauty. The sky to-day is windrowed with flat-bottomed cumulus-clouds, tier beyond tier above a level plane of light, marking off the infinite distance like receding mile-stones on a world turned over on its back. Occasionally the outstretched head of a wild duck, pumping north with a black throb of wings, melts away to a speck in the opaline air. Back among the muskeg reeds the waders are courting and chattering, and early this morning I heard the plaintive winnowing call-note of the Wilson snipe, and later the *punk-e-lunk* love-cry of a bittern to his mate. There's an eagle planing in lazy circles high in the air, even now, putting a soft-pedal on the noise of the coots and grebes as he circles over their rush-lined cabarets. And somewhere out on the range a bull is lowing. It is the season of love and the season of happiness. Dinkie and Poppsy and I are going out to gather prairie-crocuses. They are thick now in the prairie-sod, soft blue and lavender and sometimes mauve. We must dance to the vernal saraband while we can: Spring is so short in this norland country of ours. It comes late. But as Peter says, A late spring never deceives....

I thought I had offended Peter for life. But when he appeared late this afternoon and I asked him why he had kept away from me, he said these first few days naturally belonged to Dinkie and he'd been busy studying marsh-birds. He looked rather rumpled and muddy, and impressed me as a man sadly in need of a woman to look after his things.

"Let's ride," said Peter. "I want to talk to you."

I was afraid of that talk, but I was more afraid something might happen to interfere with it. So I changed into my old riding-duds and put on my weather-stained old sombrero and we saddled Buntie and Laughing-Gas and went loping off over the sun-washed prairie with our shadows behind us.

We rode a long way before Peter said anything. I wanted to be happy, but I wasn't quite able to be. I tried to think of neither the past nor the future, but there were too many ghosts of other days loping along the trail beside us.

"What are you going to do?" Peter finally inquired.

"About what?" I temporized as he pulled up beside me.

"About everything," he ungenerously responded.

"I don't know what to do, Peter," I had to acknowledge. "I'm like a barrel without hoops. I want to stick together, but one more thump will surely send me to pieces!"

"Then why not get the hoops around?" suggested Peter.

"But where will I get the hoops?" I asked.

"Here," he said. He was, I noticed, holding out his arms. And I laughed, even though my heart was heavy.

"Men have been a great disappointment to me, Peter," I said with a shake of my sombrero.

"Try me," suggested Peter.

But still again I had to shake my head.

"That wouldn't be fair, Peter," I told him. "I can't spoil your life to see what's left of my own patched up."

"Then you're going to spoil two of 'em!" he promptly asserted.

"But I don't believe in that sort of thing," I did my best to explain to him. "I've had my innings, and *I'm out*. I've a one-way heart, the same as a one-way street. I don't think there's anything in the world more odious than promiscuity. That's a big word, but it stands for an even bigger offense against God. I've always said I intended to be a single-track woman."

"But your track's blown up," contended Peter.

"Then I'll have to lay me a new one," I said with a fine show of assurance.

"And do you know where it will lead?" he demanded,

"Where?" I asked.

"Straight to me," he said as he studied me with eyes that were so quiet and kind I could feel a flutter of my heart-wings.

But still again I shook my head.

"That would be bringing you nothing but a withered up old has-been," I said with a mock-wail of misery.

And Peter actually laughed at that.

"It'll be a good ten years before you've even grown up," he retorted. "And another twenty years before you've really settled down!"

"You're saying I'll never have sense," I objected. "And I know you're right."

"That's what I love about you," averred Peter.

"What you love about me?" I demanded.

"Yes," he said with his patient old smile, "your imperishable youthfulness, your eternal never-ending eternity-defying golden-tinted girlishness!"

A flute began to play in my heart. And I knew that like Ulysses's men I would have to close my ears to it. But it's easier to row past an island than to run away from your own heart.

"I know it's a lie, Peter, but I love you for saying it. It makes me want to hug you, and it makes me want to pirouette, if I wasn't on horseback. It makes my heart sing. But it's only the singing of one lonely little chickadee in the middle of a terribly big pile of ruins. For that's all my life can be now, just a hopeless smash-up. And you're cut out for something better than a wrecking-car for the rest of your days."

"No, no," protested Peter. "It's *you* who've got to save *me*."

"Save you?" I echoed.

"You've got to give me something to live for, or I'll just rust away in the ditch and never get back to the rails again."

"Peter!" I cried.

"What?" he asked.

"You're not playing fair. You're trying to make me pity you."

"Well, don't you?" demanded Peter.

"I would if I saw you sacrificing your life for a woman with a crazy-quilt past."

"I'm not thinking of the past," asserted Peter, "I'm thinking of the future."

"That's just it," I tried to explain. "I'll have to face that future with a clouded name. I'll be a divorced woman. Ugh! I always thought of divorced women as something you wouldn't quite care to sit next to at table. I hate divorce."

"I'm a Quaker myself," acknowledged Peter. "But I occasionally think of what Cobbett once said: 'I don't much like weasels. Yet I hate rats. Therefore I say success to the weasels!'"

"I don't see what weasels have to do with it," I complained.

"Putting one's house in order again may sometimes be as beneficent as surgery," contended Peter.

"And sometimes as painful," I added.

"Yet there's no mistake like not cleaning up old mistakes."

"But I hate it," I told him. "It all seems so—so cheap."

"On the contrary," corrected Peter, "it's rather costly." He pulled up across my path and made me come to a stop. "My dear," he said, very solemn again, "I know the stuff you're made of. I know you've got to climb to the light by a path of your own choosing. And you have to see the light with your own eyes. But I'm willing to wait. I *have* waited, a very long time. But there's one fact you've got to face: I love you too much ever to dream of giving you up."

I don't think either of us moved for a full moment. The flute was singing so loud in my heart that I was afraid of myself. And, woman-like, I backed away from the thing I wanted.

"It's not *me*, Peter, I must remember now. It's my bairns. I've two bairns to bring up."

"I've got the three of you to bring up," maintained Peter. And that made us both sit silent for another moment or two.

"It's not that simple," I finally said, though Peter smiled guardedly at my ghost of a smile.

"It would be if you cared for me as much as Dinkie does," he said with quite unnecessary solemnity.

"Oh, Peter, I do, I do," I cried out as the memory of all I owed him surged mistily through my mind. "But a gray hair is something you can't joke away. And I've got five of them, right here over my left ear. I found them, months ago. And they're there to stay!"

"How about my bald spot?" demanded my oppressor and my deliverer rolled into one.

"What's a bald spot compared to a bob-cat of a temper like mine?" I challenged, remembering how I'd once heard a revolver-hammer snap in my husband's face.

"But it's your spirit I like," maintained the unruffled Peter.

"You wouldn't always," I reminded him.

Yet he merely looked at me with his trust-me-and-test-me expression.

"I'll chance it!" he said, after a quite contented moment or two of meditative silence.

"But don't you see," I went forlornly arguing on, "it mustn't be a chance. That's something people of our age can never afford to take."

And Peter, at that, for some reason I couldn't fathom, began to wag his head. He did it slowly and lugubriously, like a man who inspects a road he has no liking for. But at the same time, apparently, he was finding it hard to tuck away a small smile of triumph.

"Then we must never see each other again," he solemnly asserted.

"Peter!" I cried.

"I must go away, at once," he meditatively observed.

"*Peter!*" I said again, with the flute turning into a pair of ice-tongs that clamped into the corners of my heart.

"Far, far away," he continued as he studiously avoided my eye. "For there will be safety now only in flight."

"Safety from what?" I demanded.

"From you," retorted Peter.

"But what will happen to *me*, if you do that?" I heard my own voice asking as Buntie started to paw the prairie-floor and I did my level best to fight down the black waves of desolation that were half-drowning me. "What'll there be to hold me up, when you're the only man in all this world who can keep my barrel of happiness from going slap-bang to pieces? What—?"

"*Verboten!*" interrupted Peter. But that solemn-soft smile of his gathered me in and covered me, very much as the rumpled feathers of a mother-bird cover her young, her crazily twittering and crazily wandering young who never know their own mind.

"What'll happen to me," I went desperately on, "when you're the only man alive who understands this crazy old heart of mine, when you've taught me to hitch the last of my hope on the one unselfish man I've ever known?"

This seemed to trouble Peter. But only remotely, as the lack of grammar in the Lord's Prayer might affect a Holy Roller. He insisted, above all things, on being judicial.

"Then I'll have to come back, I suppose," he finally admitted, "for Dinkie's sake."

"Why for Dinkie's sake?" I asked.

"Because some day, my dear, our Dinkie is going to be a great man. And I want to have a hand in fashioning that greatness."

I sat looking at the red ball of the sun slipping down behind the shoulder of the world. A wind came out of the North, cool and sweet and balsamic with hope. I heard a loon cry. And then the earth was still again.

"*We'll be waiting*," I said, with a tear of happiness tickling the bridge of my nose. And then, so that Peter might not see still another loon crying, I swung Buntie sharply about on the trail. And we rode home, side by side, through the twilight.

THE END